The Saboteur

By Susan Page Davis

Chapter 1

Debra Griffin turned her face into the breeze as she pumped gas into the tank of her forest green Sentra. Pale green leaves were just unfurling on the big maple tree at the edge of the parking lot. Another fleeting Maine summer was on the way. The sun warmed her skin, and she wrinkled her nose as the gas fumes rose around her.

Behind her, the door to the convenience store closed, and she turned her head slightly. A young man hurried toward the Jeep Cherokee parked on the other side of the pumps. He pulled off a knit cap, and she thought he was overdressed for the warm spring day. His tousled brown hair eclipsed the goatee he was growing. He glanced toward her, and their eyes met for an instant. Debra turned away, not liking his sharp expression.

The Jeep started, and he pulled out of the lot onto the main road through town, driving swiftly away to the south. Massachusetts license plate, Debra noted. That figured. An early tourist. They always thought it was chilly.

She replaced the hose in its niche on the pump. Every week when she was at home, she bought gas at Farnham's. The small general store had somehow survived on the edge of the city of Rushton, catering to people who had lived in the area for many years. Debra entered the little emporium, which sold everything from stovepipe to cappuccino, and was surprised that Belinda was not behind the counter.

She stood for a moment uncertainly, perusing the displays of small items on the counter. Lollipops, fudge, "penny candy" that sold for a dime, Maine key rings, Slim Jims, and bookmarks. Behind the counter was a lottery ticket dispenser and a rack of cigarette cartons. No other customers were in the store.

Debra turned around and called heartily, "Hey, B'linda! Where are you?"

"Back here!" came her friend's voice, from the office at the back corner of the store. Debra walked swiftly through the aisles of Band-aids and tube socks.

"It was a guy in a black Jeep," Belinda said as Debra entered the tiny office.

Belinda put her hand over the telephone receiver. "Sorry, Deb, we've been robbed."

Debra stood, incredulous, as Belinda returned to her conversation.

"Yes, he left here about thirty seconds ago. I don't know which way he went."

"South," said Debra.

"What?" Belinda looked up at her.

"The guy in the black Jeep went south."

Belinda said into the phone, "A customer saw the man leave and head south. All right. Sure. Thanks."

Debra heard the bell on the front door clang, and looked over her shoulder into the store.

"Customer," she said.

"Can I hang up now?" Belinda asked the person on the other end of the line. "Well, someone else came into the store. Can I put my friend on, so I can go wait on the customer? Thanks."

She thrust the phone into Debra's hand. "Here, talk to this woman until the cops get here, okay?" She hurried past Debra toward the checkout.

"Hello?" Debra said tentatively.

"Hello, who's this?"

"My name is Debra Griffin. I was pumping gas when the robber left the store."

"You saw him?"

"Yes."

"One of our detectives should be there soon, ma'am. He was in the area when Mrs. Farnham called, and we've sent him over. When he gets there, be sure to tell him."

"I will," Debra said.

"Can you describe his vehicle?"

"It was a black Jeep Cherokee."

"What year?"

"I have no idea, but it had a Massachusetts license plate, and he headed south."

A couple of minutes elapsed before Debra heard the bell ring again. She leaned out the office doorway and saw a tall, dark-haired man in a gray suit walking toward the counter.

"Is your officer in uniform?" she asked the dispatcher.

"No, plain clothes, unmarked car."

"I'd say he's here, then. Thanks for your help." Debra hung up and went out into the store, walking briskly toward Belinda, who was giving change to her customer, but hung back near the newspaper rack as her friend addressed the newcomer.

"I'm so glad you're here," Belinda said to the man, as the customer went out the door. "I'm Belinda Farnham, and my husband and I own the store." She hesitated. "You *are* a police officer, aren't you?"

He smiled at her. "Yes, ma'am. Detective Van Sant. Can you describe the robber?"

"He just left here. Aren't you going to chase him?" Belinda asked.

"We have a description of the vehicle, and the dispatcher sent out two of our units and notified the state police. They'll be watching for him on the interstate. Black Jeep Cherokee with a Massachusetts plate?"

"That's right," Debra said, and he turned toward her.

"And you are?"

Debra swallowed as the deep brown eyes riveted on her. Talking to strangers always brought out a latent panic that she knew was unreasonable. "Debra Griffin. I-I was pumping gas when the man came out of the store. Of course, I didn't know he'd robbed Belinda."

"You didn't happen to get the license number?"

"Something B-C," Debra said, feeling foolish. "Those were the last two letters, and there was a 7 in it."

"Good," said Van Sant, taking a pen and pad from his breast pocket. "I'll call it in. What else can you tell me?"

"He had on a ski mask, just a plain blue knit one," Belinda said. "He was a little taller than me, and he had a pistol."

"What kind of a pistol?"

"A big one."

Van Sant smiled again, and jotted in his notebook.

"I didn't see the gun," Debra said. "He was taking the hat off when he came out, and carrying a six pack in the other hand. I didn't realize—well, if I'd known the hat was a mask, I'd have come in sooner. He had brown hair and a goatee. Black jacket, I think." She hesitated, not sure she was helping with her uncertain recollections, but the detective seemed to be taking down every word.

The bell rang, and a man and a boy entered and went toward the milk cooler.

"How old?" asked the detective.

"Twenty-five or younger," Debra said with a little shrug. "I didn't like his—the way he looked at me."

"But you'd know him again."

"I think so. I'd know his vehicle. It had a bumper sticker that said, *Back off*. Attitude, you know?" She met his eyes for a moment, then looked down quickly.

"That's helpful," said Van Sant.

Belinda was examining the end of the cord that dangled from the telephone behind the counter, next to the lottery ticket rack.

"Are you all right, Mrs. Farnham?" the detective asked.

"Yes, I'm fine. Scared me a little. Mack and I have talked about what to do if this happened, but I still wasn't ready."

"The telephone is out of commission?"

"This one is. He reached over and pulled the cord out of the wall. I think he broke the end off. Cell reception isn't very good here, so I went back to the office and called 911 after he went out the door. He said not to do anything for five minutes, but I didn't care."

"Good for you," the detective said.

"I'd have run out and gotten his plate number, but I could see Debbie at the gas pump, and I didn't want him to do anything." She flashed Debra an apologetic look.

"I'm going to call in the information you've given me. I'll be right back," Van Sant said. He stepped outside.

"Where's Mack?" Debra asked Belinda.

"He had to go downtown. Can you believe it? The middle of the day." Belinda pushed her short brown hair back from her forehead in exasperation. "I always figured if we got held up, it would be at night, just before closing, and I'm never here alone after dark."

Debra had known Belinda since grade school. They had formed a close friendship early, although they often disagreed on abstract issues. When they had graduated from high school, Debra had gone off to college outside New England, and Belinda had stayed behind to marry the boy whose father owned the general store with the gas pumps on the edge of town. Three years later, Mack's father had retired, turning the store over to Mack and Belinda.

"Hey, I haven't paid you for the gas yet," Debra said. She opened her purse.

"Thanks. I'm just glad you didn't come in while he had the gun out."

"Me too," Debra admitted.

The customer with the little boy came to the counter with a gallon of milk and a bag of potato chips. Debra stepped back while he paid for them and left.

"Stay with me 'til Mack comes back?" Belinda wheedled.

"Sure." Debra thought her friend trembled a little as she closed the cash register, and she stepped around the counter and gave her a hug. Belinda returned the embrace, then swiped a tear from her cheek with the back of her hand.

"He's good looking," Belinda said with a little laugh.

"Who?"

"The cop. He looks familiar."

5

"I've never seen him before."

Belinda snapped her fingers. "His picture was in the paper a week or so ago."

"I didn't see it."

"It was probably right before you came home. Do you think he's good looking?"

Debra shrugged. "Nice hair," she said grudgingly. She and Belinda had always talked about boys in high school, but since Debra had been away to college, their relationship had taken on a new dignity, or so Debra had thought.

Belinda chuckled. "It was one of those profiles of a new city employee. Can't remember if it said he was married."

"Belinda," Debra protested. She had always been the quiet half of the duo, and Belinda was the bubbly, outgoing one who made friends as easily as she made change.

"He has a Samoyed, though. I remember that, because Mack's brother had one. It was a reject sled dog. I think the P.D. hired this guy from down on the coast somewhere."

Debra shook her head. Belinda was always interested in the minutia. She wished she hadn't noticed that the detective's left hand holding his notebook was ringless. If Belinda asked her, she'd have to admit it, and it was the kind of thing Belinda would ask her. He wore a heavy gold class ring with a dark stone on his right hand. It had reflected the light as he wrote swiftly. Not a cheap plastic pen—a silver, retractable one. Belinda was watching her, and Debra felt her face heat.

*****

Michael Van Sant stood with one arm on top of his unmarked car as he called in the partial license plate, the bumper sticker information, and the description of the robber. Could be worse. The customer was observant and coherent. Better than a lot of witnesses.

"So, what was stolen?" he asked briskly as he re-entered the store. Mrs. Farnham was straightening the items on the counter.

The other young woman turned away quickly and studied the headlines of the Waterville, Bangor, and Boston newspapers in the rack.

"He had me give him a roll of lottery tickets and the cash from the register," Belinda Farnham said.

"How much?"

"About seven hundred dollars, I think."

Mike whistled softly. It was more than he had expected.

"If it had been Thursday, it would have been three times that," Belinda said. "That's the day Stark Paper pays its employees, and we cash checks for people."

"Anything else?"

"He grabbed a six-pack of beer." Belinda quoted the price.

Debra Griffin walked toward the large front window and looked outside. A red pickup had pulled in on the side of the gas pumps opposite the Sentra that Mike assumed was her car. He gave his attention to Mrs. Farnham, taking down her address and telephone number.

"And you said he went south," he said in Debra's direction. She nodded without looking directly into his eyes. "I think we have a pretty good chance of catching him. I'll get back to you if we do."

"So, if you catch him, we'll get the money back, right?" Belinda asked.

"Certainly. If we recover the property, it's yours."

"Thanks."

Mike continued writing for a moment, then looked toward Debra. "Could I get your address, ma'am? We need to be able to contact all our witnesses."

"Sure." She turned came toward him.

A middle-aged man in dirty jeans came into the store and walked toward the checkout.

"Hi, Josh," Belinda said.

Mike drew Debra aside, away from the counter, with an apologetic smile. They stood in the aisle between nails and jigsaw puzzles. Debra looked decidedly nervous as she faced him, but she swallowed hard and looked directly into his eyes. She was a few years younger than he was, but definitely over twenty, he judged. She pushed her windblown, shoulder-length dark blonde hair behind her left ear.

"I'm Debra Griffin, and I live at 315 Hudson Road."

"Phone number?"

She looked away as she recited her cell number and her parents' landline, staring at the bins of shingle nails.

"Do you know Mrs. Farnham well?" Mike glanced toward the counter.

"Yes, most of my life. We went to school together, and we're close friends."

"Would you say she's handling this well, or should I call some help for her?"

"I think she's all right." Debra looked toward her friend. "It was a shock, but she's tough."

He nodded, evaluating her. "How about yourself. Are you okay?"

"Yes. I … well, when I realized it was a robbery, I got a little shaky. Of course, if I'd known what he'd done when I saw him—"

"You kept your cool when you needed to," he assured her. "Well, I'll get going, but I'll probably be back later. Are you going be here for a while with her?"

"I told her I'd stay."

"So, you're not on the way to work or anything?" His brief glance took in her olive drab skirt and ivory and green striped sweater, suitable for a job in an office or an upscale store.

"No. I can stay here until her husband—" She hesitated and looked down again. Obviously strangers made her nervous. Or maybe it was his badge. That intimidated some people.

He nodded, trying to project sympathy. "Good, it's best not to leave a crime victim alone immediately after the incident." He smiled, and she took a step backward, blushing furiously. "Thank you," she managed.

One more thing about Miss Griffin, but he wouldn't write it down: She was very attractive.

*****

Debra poked around the stationery aisle reading greeting cards while Belinda waited on more customers. When the store was empty again she joined her friend at the counter. Her pulse had returned to normal by then, but she was glad the policeman was gone. Even though he'd been cordial, talking to him gave her the jitters.

"You okay?" she asked.

"Yeah, I'm fine." Belinda looked mournfully into the cash drawer. "Mack is gonna be mad. I'd better call the Lottery Commission and tell them we lost a roll of tickets."

"The robber can't collect on those, can he?"

"Not if I report it right away. He's probably parked somewhere right now, scratching tickets." Belinda headed for the office.

Debra meandered into the video corner and began rearranging the cases. She put the family movies at a child's eye level and moved the thrillers with more lurid cover art to the top shelf. She wished Mack and Belinda would stop carrying R-rated movies, but she had told them how she felt years earlier and figured it was a lost battle.

Mack's father had always carried cigarettes, beer, lottery tickets and racy movies, and the mill workers came in expecting to find them. Debra had hoped Mack and Belinda would drop those items when they took over the store a year before, but they hadn't.

"It's a lot of our profit," Belinda had explained. "We don't make much on gas and soda pop."

Debra had let it go. When she visited the Farnhams during her college breaks, she stopped mentioning it and remained a loyal customer. Mack and Belinda seemed to be making a living.

"So, no job yet?" Belinda called, when she returned.

"No. I had an interview this morning at a doctor's office. They need a receptionist, but I don't think they'll hire me."

"You'd be a good receptionist."

"Well, they'd like someone with a little experience."

"That's silly. How can an inexperienced person get experience?"

Debra shrugged. "I'm not very good at interviews."

"Oh, come on. I know you used to panic every time the teacher called on you in class. But we're not kids anymore."

Debra smiled ruefully. "Tell that to the dragon lady who just grilled me on my lack of work experience."

"I take it your spanking new degree didn't impress her?"

"No, they're not looking for a receptionist with a pre-law degree."

Belinda shook her head. "You should have switched to something else."

"By the time I figured out I didn't want to go to law school, I was nearly done. If I'd switched majors, I'd have had to stay another year and, well, to be frank, Mom and Dad couldn't afford that. Julie started college last fall, and this year was a real strain on the family financially. If I want more schooling, I've got to pay for it myself."

"Hence you're home and scrounging for a job." Belinda nodded at a neighbor who entered the store with her two children and headed for the cooler. "Mack and I could give you a few hours while you're looking."

"Thanks. I may take you up on it."

"Well, here." Belinda reached over the counter and picked up a newspaper. "See if there are any new ads today."

Debra went behind the kitchenette counter, where Belinda made sandwiches and pizzas, and sat on a stool with the newspaper while her friend tended to her customers.

Most of the ads were repeats of the ones she'd combed all week, things she wasn't qualified for. Nurses, office administrators, truck drivers, special education teachers.

"Find anything?" Belinda asked a few minutes later.

10

"Not really. The grocery store is taking applications for stock clerks, and the police department wants a typist."

"There you go," said Belinda. "You could always type faster than I could in school."

"I haven't typed anything for four years except a few term papers," Debra said.

"Come on, you have a computer."

"Yeah, but I don't do a lot of actual typing, you know?"

"Get one of those typing programs and brush up. Here's Mack." Belinda hurried out the door to meet her husband in the parking lot. Debra watched out the window as Belinda put her hands on his arms and looked up at him, talking earnestly. Mack's blue eyes clouded, and his expression turned to one of dismay.

"You're kidding," he was saying as they came in together. He nodded toward Debra. "Hi, Deb. You were here when this happened?"

"Well, I was pumping gas."

"She came in right after the jerk left," said Belinda. "She gave the cops a good description of him. They sent out a handsome new detective." She winked at Debra.

"Well, listen, you guys can sort it out. I'm going home," Debra said. "Mom will be wondering about me. I'll call you tonight, B'linda, and see how it's going."

"Okay, thanks for everything," Belinda said, but her eyes were on Mack.

"Thanks, Deb." Mack pulled Belinda into his arms as Debra left the store.

Chapter 2

The locks were stiff from disuse and grime. It was years since he or anyone else had been in here, which made it a good option to keep open. A little WD-40 would loosen up the keyhole.

The door creaked as he swung it open. He would leave the dust and spiders and cobwebs. It was best if he disturbed the place as little as possible.

He closed the barred door and walked quietly to the big room's outer entrance. He flipped the light off. The single bulb overhead went out. He listened. As he'd anticipated, all was still. Very few people moved about this side of the building at night. And no one ever came near this door anymore. Few people remembered it existed. Even fewer had keys.

He opened the door and looked out into the space beneath the stairs, holding his breath. Nothing. He went out and shut the door quietly. After locking it, he pocketed the shiny new keys and peeled off his latex gloves. He might not ever need this place, but it was good to know it was here, handy but practically hidden. Out of sight, out of mind, unless he needed it.

*****

"What are you doing?" Debra's younger brother Grant asked that evening.

Debra sat frowning before the computer monitor, willing her fingers to find the right keys without her looking at the keyboard.

"Trying to see how fast I can type. I'm not very good. Have you seen that typing program Mom got you a couple of years ago?"

"You mean *Squidman Teaches Typing*?"

"Whatever."

"I think it was a download," Grant said. "Just do a search for it. It's on there someplace. How come you're suddenly so interested in improving your typing?"

"I need a job."

It didn't seem fair. Debra, the college graduate, was having trouble landing the most mundane position. Grant, who was finishing his junior year of high school, was paid minimum wage on weekends to collect shopping carts at a big box store. Julie had decided to stay in her college town in Rhode Island for the summer to work at an elderly care home for a wage Debra envied. Their older brother, Rick, had stepped into an editing job in Portland when he'd graduated from college two years earlier. All of them had jobs, but then, all of her siblings radiated self-confidence.

"You spent four years in college to become a typist?" Grant asked.

"It's worse than that," Debra moaned, typing the name of the program she wanted. "I spent four years and eighty thousand dollars to be competing without much hope for a typist's job."

"So, you have this totally useless degree?"

Debra winced. The memory of her speech class, when she'd frozen in senseless panic and had to leave the room, was still fresh after three years, and her senior forensics class, when she'd had to argue her first mock trial, was a disaster she preferred to keep buried in the recesses of her subconscious.

"That doesn't mean you shouldn't go to college, Grant. Just make sure you know what you want to do before you lock in your major."

"I'm going to take engineering."

"Well, in that case, I wish you the best, and if I don't have a job by the time you graduate, will you support me?"

She found Grant's program on the hard drive and opened it. She keyed her way through the game's opening to the first level of typing the letters on the home row. "Can't I skip past this to the next level?"

"Nope. If Squidman doesn't get all the turtles, you can't advance."

"Oh, great. Why didn't Mom buy you a program that just plain teaches you to type fast?" She glanced up. Grant was eyeing her sheepishly. "Don't answer that. Just leave me alone for an hour."

Fifteen minutes later Grant was back, leaning on the door jamb.

"Did I hear screaming?"

"Probably. I got through the underwater level and into the dungeon, but I can't seem to crack forty words a minute, and they won't let me out."

"You're pitiful."

"Thanks. I really needed that."

Grant smiled. "So, where's the job? Have you got an interview?"

"No, I haven't dared to call them yet. It's at the police station, and if I lie and tell them I can type, they'll probably arrest me."

"Well, I'll tell you a secret." Grant nodded toward the computer screen. "Typing those stupid things they give you isn't like typing real stuff. You probably type faster in real life than you do in Squidman World."

Debra sighed. "Thanks. They probably have a million applicants. Guess I'd better go down to the grocery tomorrow and apply as a stock clerk."

"They wouldn't hire you."

"How do you know?"

"Jason Fuller works there. He says they don't hire college graduates because they know they won't be happy, and they'll leave soon."

"Great."

"For what it's worth."

"Sure."

"So, are you done with the computer now?" Grant asked.

"You can use it."

She closed the program and walked slowly up the stairs toward her bedroom. Her mother was coming down the hall carrying a basket of dirty laundry.

"Don't be discouraged, dear. You've only been home from school a week."

"I know, but I need something soon. I'm just mooching off you and Dad."

"We're thrilled to have you home for the summer."

"Well, you won't stay thrilled if I can't land a job soon."

"The interview at the doctor's office didn't go well?"

"I don't think so. I get so nervous, Mom."

"Well, call the police station. At least you'll have something else to think about if you set up another interview."

Debra followed her mother into the bathroom, where she began stuffing the clothes down the laundry chute. "I could work for Mack and Belinda part time. Maybe I should, just to pay for my share of the groceries."

"Then you'd have less time to look for a real job."

"Nobody wants a pre-law grad with no legal future," Debra said.

"So you'll be starting something new. Have you thought about what you *do* want to do?"

"Not really." She hated admitting that. At twenty-two, she had no idea what she wanted to do with the rest of her life. She had concentrated on law for so long, nothing else had drawn her interest. "I just know I don't want to get up in front of people and talk."

Her mother put her hand on Debra's shoulder. "Don't some lawyers do legal research for the ones who try the cases?"

"Paralegals, maybe."

"Maybe you could look into that. Something where you could use the legal training you have without being in the spotlight."

"I'll think about it."

Debra went to her bedroom and sat on the crazy quilt that covered her maple bed. She didn't like to feel helpless, and she

16

certainly didn't want other people to see her as incompetent. She had a good education, and she could do lots of useful jobs, but her confidence deserted her at the worst possible times.

She lay back on the quilt and prayed silently for a moment. *You must have a job out there for me, Lord. Please help me to stay calm long enough to prove I can do it.* Funny how the thought of a job interview terrified her more than the knowledge that she'd witnessed a robbery. That was not logical, and Debra's mind insisted on logic. She took out her cell phone and hit the number for Farnham's.

"Hey, B'linda? Would you consider interviewing me tonight? About twenty times, I mean, for practice?"

Chapter 3

At one o'clock the next afternoon, Debra sat utterly still on a wooden bench in the hallway at the local police station. She tried not to draw attention to herself. The green paint of the bench was peeling, showing that it had once been black, and before that, yellow. She could hear muffled voices from the duty room behind her, and from the communications room, where the dispatchers were at work. Uniformed men walked past her occasionally, throwing curious glances her way. She grew increasingly self-conscious as the hands of her watch crept onward.

Could she be comfortable working in such a male-oriented environment? The city had two female patrol officers and several civilian secretaries and dispatchers, but the stares she got from the parade of patrolmen unnerved her.

"Well, hello."

She jerked her head around. Detective Van Sant was gazing down at her.

Debra stood hastily, her heart accelerating with a senseless rush of adrenaline. "Hello. Nice to—" She had forgotten how tall he was. His charcoal gray suit was flawless, and the shirt and striped tie complemented it perfectly. His dark hair stayed meticulously in place without looking combed, and his badge gleamed on his belt.

"You're not here about the robbery at Farnham's, are you?" he asked uncertainly.

"No." She gulped. "But since you mention it, is there any news? Belinda told me last night you'd caught the man."

"Yes, the state police picked him up on I-95. With your testimony, we have a good chance at a conviction."

Debra made herself breathe evenly, although she wanted to run out the door. "Great. I'm glad. And Belinda said they got their property back."

"Yes, he'd spent twenty dollars and drank most of the beer, but other than that, I think we recovered everything. You'll be on the witness list, if he goes to trial."

She nodded, glad to find herself carrying on a coherent conversation. She refused to think about being a trial witness. Plenty of time for that later.

"So ... if I may ask, what are you here for?"

"Uh... " Debra felt a flush creeping up her neck to her cheeks.

"You can't be under arrest," he said with a smile. "No handcuffs."

The laugh that came out betrayed her nerves. "Nothing like that. They advertised for a typist."

"Oh, right. The deputy chief is tearing out his hair. Can't find anybody who fits the bill. Say, you mean you're applying?" His apparent approval surprised her.

"Well, I thought I would, but I've been sitting here half an hour, and I'm wondering if it's a test. You know, to see how I'll react when they keep me waiting. Are there ... hidden cameras in here?" She looked up toward the ceiling.

He laughed, as if he thought her very witty. "I think Pete is probably just late getting back from lunch. Let me check on it for you."

He took a few steps to the door of the com room, opened it, and called, "Hey, Trina, is Pete back from lunch yet?"

The reply was muffled, but distinct. "I just saw him go into his office, but he's got an appointment. Another would-be typist."

Debra's blush deepened and she wished she hadn't come. She thought she had concealed her trepidation, but it would be much more humiliating to be rejected for the job, now that Van Sant knew she was applying.

She picked up her purse as he came back to her.

"Sounds like he's back. He ought to see you soon."

"Thank you, but I think it was a mistake for me to come here. I'm not—not sure the job is right for me, or that I'm right for the job."

"Well, you're here," Van Sant said. "You might as well give it a shot."

The door from the outer hallway opened, admitting a gray-haired woman in a navy skirt and lavender print blouse. She had a grandmotherly air, incongruous in the stark atmosphere of the police station.

"Miss Griffin?"

"Yes," Debra replied, trying to look and sound cool, but knowing her face was scarlet.

"The deputy chief will see you now."

Debra glanced at Van Sant, and he smiled and gave her an encouraging nod. "Good luck."

"Thanks." As she followed the woman into the next hallway and waited for her to open the security door that led into another wing of the police station, Debra thought of all the things she might have said to Van Sant in that moment. That she would never have come to the police station if she'd known she would encounter him again. That she couldn't even type her way out of Squidman's dungeon. That she didn't believe in luck. Or the bottom line, that she was terrified and would rather be anywhere but here.

His direct gaze had unnerved her, and the thought of working in the same building with him kept the flush from leaving her cheeks. No, she definitely could not work in the same office with a man like that. He was too good looking and too polite, the kind of man who made her tongue-tied, when he was only being courteous.

Seconds later she forgot Van Sant and focused all her energy on the 45-year-old deputy chief, Peter Nye, who faced her across his cluttered desk. His light brown hair had a hint of gray, and he was a little heavy. Debra thought perhaps he had let his physical training go a bit since winning the desk job. He appraised her with cool gray eyes that had seen many applicants and were tired of looking.

"So, Miss Griffin, you understand the job is for a secretary in the detectives' unit?"

"I—no, the ad just said typist."

"Well, we do need a regular typist, too, in the records room, but the detectives' secretary has announced she's taking maternity leave, and I need to fill that position right away."

"So, it's a temporary job?"

"I have my doubts that Gretchen will come back after the baby is born."

"Oh?" Debra thought it was a bit unprofessional of him to share that information with her.

"She's my wife," Nye said with a grin.

"Oh, I see." Debra smiled with him. Maybe he wasn't so intimidating, after all.

"It's our third child, and probably the last. She really wants to stay home," he said. "The other two are in school and—well, we just think it's time for Gretchen to retire."

"When does she begin her leave?"

"As soon as I can find a replacement. See, she's thirty-seven, and her doctor thinks she ought to take it easy. She's healthy, but, you know, I want to pamper her while I have the chance."

Debra was beginning to like Pete Nye.

"Would she be willing to train someone who's not exactly a whiz?"

"Hey, Miss Griffin, if you can type and take orders, I'll take you right in to meet her. I've interviewed six candidates already this week, and all I can say is, if we can't find someone better, we're in trouble. I think we're not paying enough, that's what I think. Truly qualified people don't want to work here for what the city pays." He stopped and looked piercingly into her eyes. "You do know the pay is twelve-fifty an hour?"

"I—yes."

"And you can type?"

"A—a little."

"Ever use a computer?"

"Yes."

He stood up. "Would you mind giving me a sample? The last woman who was here was scared to death of the computer. Didn't have a clue where to put the flash drive."

He turned to a computer station at the side of his desk and brought up a word processing program.

"Could you just type this in for me, please, Miss Griffin?"

Debra took the swivel chair. Nye stood back, watching over her shoulder. Her hands shook as she positioned the sheet of paper he had laid beside the keyboard. It was an officer's report.

"Just type it in?"

"Yes, if you will."

She began typing, deciding to opt for accuracy rather than speed. At least she didn't have to look at him while she typed, and she knew that, slow as her typing was, it was better than her speaking ability. When she was halfway down the page, Nye held out a flash drive.

"That's fine, Miss Griffin. Now, if you could just save your work on this, please."

She glanced up at him, but his face gave her no clues as to his thoughts. She opened the drive and stuck the end into a USB slot and moved the mouse to select File, then Save As. She directed the computer to save into the F drive as "Report," then extracted the flash drive and handed it to him.

Nye was smiling when he took it. "I see you've had some legal courses."

"Yes, I thought I'd go to law school, but I changed my mind."

"But you're familiar with legal terminology."

"Yes."

"And you've never been arrested. We'll do a complete background check if we decide to hire you."

"I don't have a problem with that."

"You're making me happy. I assume you can pass a drug test?"

23

"I'm sure I can."

"Come this way, please."

He headed out the door and down the hallway, deeper into the building. Debra followed, feeling she had passed the initial part of the inquisition.

"This is the detectives' area." Nye entered a narrower hallway, from which several doors opened. That's their break room—" Debra glanced in and saw a table, several comfortable chairs, a coffee maker and a vending machine. "This is their interview room." He walked past it so fast, she only got an impression of a bare, windowless room with an oak table and several straight chairs.

"The secretary's desk is in here." He stepped into a small office, and Debra stayed on his heels. A pretty, auburn-haired woman rose from behind the desk, her smile enveloping the deputy chief.

"Pete!" she cried, and advanced toward him. She wore a pink maternity top over a brown print skirt.

Nye turned slightly and said, "Honey, I've got a possible replacement for you. This is Miss Griffin."

Gretchen stopped, her hand on her husband's arm, and smiled at Debra.

"You have no idea how happy I am to meet you. Pete was despairing of finding anyone."

"Could you spend a few minutes with Miss Griffin and give me your impressions?" Nye asked her.

"Certainly."

"Good. She can type and use the computer. You ladies know where to find me." He planted a kiss on Gretchen's cheek and left the room.

Debra, blushing once more, faced Mrs. Nye.

"You'll be doing some typing for all the detectives, but mostly for the detective sergeant," Gretchen began.

She didn't qualify her remarks with *if you're hired*, Debra noted. "I'm not sure I'd be very good at it," she put in. "I don't

24

type very fast, and I'm probably not familiar with your computer programs."

"Are you willing to learn?"

"Of course."

"I'm willing to stay a week or two to train you," Gretchen said. "Pete wants me to quit right away, but I'm feeling fine, and I wouldn't mind staying a bit longer."

"When is the baby due?"

"In July. We're so pleased. Our other two are ten and twelve years old, and we weren't expecting to have another baby, but we're delighted. But the doctor has been giving me all this depressing drivel about my being over thirty-five. Pete thinks I need to take it easy. And guess what?" She smiled conspiratorially at Debra. "I won't mind a bit. But I wouldn't want to just drop you in here without showing you the ropes."

"How is it, working here?" Debra asked.

"It's great. The detectives are a good bunch of guys. The sergeant's office is right here." She nodded toward a door that opened beyond her desk.

"He has to go through here to get to his office?" Debra asked.

"Yes, unless he starts climbing in the window."

Debra swung around and looked at her, and Gretchen laughed. "He doesn't bite. He's actually an easy person to work for. You'll like him. And the other detectives will bring in the things they need you to type and file for them. Like this morning, Johnny Young brought me a file from El Paso, Texas, on a guy they arrested here a couple of days ago. He's wanted in Texas, and we have to extradite him, so Johnny asked me to put the information from El Paso into our system, so we'd have everything in one place."

"So, I wouldn't have to type up all their reports?"

"No, they do that themselves. A lot of what you'll do is for the sergeant, stuff that pertains to the unit. Management stuff. Evaluations, transfers, requisitions, things like that. You'll answer the phone here for the unit, and transfer the calls to the appropriate extension."

"Is that hard?"

"No, an idiot could do it. A lot of what I do is screening the calls and deciding just what I really need to bother Mike with."

"Mike?"

"The detective sergeant. And you have to type up witness statements if they write them by hand. That can be tricky, especially if the handwriting is poor, and you have to be really careful to get it right. When they bring witnesses and family in, you might need to help with them. Serve coffee in the interview room, or look up records. Lawyers are always calling for data, and the D.A.'s office works pretty closely with our detectives. Look, sit down here with me, and I'll show you some things."

Debra sat beside Gretchen and watched her work for twenty minutes, asking questions occasionally, and finally consenting to typing one short document herself.

"You're doing great," Gretchen assured her.

The telephone rang intermittently, and Debra's respect for Gretchen climbed as she observed.

"Don't all the calls to the police station go through the dispatcher?" she asked, when Gretchen had transferred a call to Detective Beaulieu.

"No, not if the caller has the direct number. They can call each detective in his office, or they can call here, for the unit. We don't give out Mike's number for his desk phone. We want people to call here first, so they don't bother him with trivial things. You won't exactly be his private secretary, but it's the next best thing."

Debra nodded, finally feeling that she was actually going to be working in the police station, and that she might survive the trauma of the new job.

"All the new cases are in the computer, and we keep paperwork on open cases in the file cabinets in here, but for anything over two years old, you'll have to run down to Records."

"And how many detectives are there?"

"Four, besides Mike. Leon Beaulieu, John Young, Jared Dore, and Brian Estes. They're mostly great guys. Leon and Brian don't always get along so well. You just have to defuse things once in a while."

"How do you do that?" Debra didn't like the sound of it.

"Well, if you're working on something for Leon, and Brian brings something in, you have to stop what you're doing and do Brian's job, or he goes through the roof."

"Why?"

Gretchen looked at her sympathetically. "It's an old feud. Brian has seniority, because he made detective six months before Leon did, but a lot of people thought Leon should have gotten the promotion at that time. So, since he did make it, Brian is always trying to make sure Leon isn't nipping at his heels and trying to show him up. It's just office politics, but you have to be sure Brian doesn't think you're favoring Leon—" Gretchen dropped her voice and whispered, "even though Leon's a lot nicer and smarter."

Debra nodded, her eyes wide. How would she ever keep everything straight and manage not to offend her five bosses?

Gretchen tossed her head. "If you have any problems, just go to my husband. He doesn't put up with their petty fights."

"O-okay."

"So, you think you can fit in here?" Gretchen leaned back in her chair, one hand on her stomach, her blue eyes sparkling.

"I'm not sure. I think I'd love it if you were staying."

Gretchen smiled. "Don't worry, kiddo. I shouldn't have told you all the bad stuff the first day. These guys are really nice. Even Brian. He just needs to loosen up a little."

"You said there were four detectives," Debra said tentatively.

"That's right."

"You didn't mention Detective Van Sant."

Gretchen's eyes widened. "I'm sure I did."

"No, no, I'm sure you didn't."

"You know him?"

27

"Well, I met him yesterday, and I saw him in the hallway here a few minutes ago—" Debra stopped in confusion, the nuisance blush returning, and she wished she hadn't spoken.

"I'm sure I mentioned Mike."

Debra sat very still as her brain clicked.

"Didn't I? He's the sergeant." Gretchen seemed to expect an answer.

"Oh, the sergeant. I guess you did." Debra looked over her shoulder at the open door to the sergeant's office. It was six feet from her chair. "He's not in there now, is he?" she asked in a small voice.

"No, he went out on a case after lunch. You must have seen him as he was leaving." Gretchen was thoughtful. "This—this isn't a problem, is it? Working with Mike, I mean?"

"I—no—I—" Debra put both hands up to her cheeks, wishing she could sink through the floor. "I didn't expect it, is all." She looked Gretchen in the eye, trying to make a decision. "He must think I'm an idiot. He probably wouldn't want me as a secretary."

"Why not?"

"I never seem to be able to say the right thing to him. It's very embarrassing. When he looks at you, it's kind of—" She groped for the right word. "Like now. I don't know what to say. That's what happens when he's around. I'm sure I come off as a certified imbecile."

Gretchen smiled slowly. "Give it some time. He's very nice to work for. Hasn't been here long, but all the men respect him."

"But when I told him I was here for the typist's job, he didn't even tell me it was actually for his secretary. Do you think he knows?"

"Yes, he and Pete have talked about it. They decided if they got someone who could type but wasn't on the ball, they'd put her in records. If they found someone with the right stuff, they'd put her in here."

"You think I have that?"

28

Gretchen nodded. "My husband would say you're a quick study."

"I don't know. I'm not what you might call aggressive."

"You don't need to be. It's more organizational skills. You seem to have that. You're single, aren't you?"

"Y-yes. But I wouldn't want to stir things up."

"Good. Pete interviewed a girl the other day who would have set off a bomb in here. To tell you the truth, she could type just fine, but her attitude and her wardrobe were a little much for the police station. Skirt to here." She measured the length against her upper thigh. "I heard one of the guys begging Pete not to hire her. He said we ought to get a grandma type like his secretary, Bernice, in here, so things wouldn't go to pieces." She smiled at Debra. "You're no grandma, but I think you'll do."

"Is that a compliment or an insult?" Debra asked with a chuckle.

"Well, just spending the last thirty minutes with you, I'd say that, while you're attractive, you're competent, fairly conservative, and professional."

"That's very flattering for someone who's never held a regular job before in her life. I worked in the college dining hall to help with my school bill. That and babysitting about complete my résumé."

Gretchen shrugged. "This will be a good first job for you. And if you decide you hate it, it will look good on your next job application. Come on, let's go tell Pete you're hired. They'll fingerprint you and take your picture for the security badge, and one of the guys will start a thorough background check. Come in Monday at eight, prepared to learn our system."

Chapter 4

Mike loosened his necktie as he walked down the corridor toward his office. It had been a hectic day, and it wasn't over yet.

When he passed the deputy chief's office door, Pete Nye yelled, "Mike! Wait!"

Mike turned and stood in the doorway. "What's up?"

Pete was grinning from ear to ear. "We've found Gretchen's replacement. A week or two of training her, and Gretchen will officially become a stay-at-home mom."

"That's terrific. Debra Griffin, I hope?"

Pete scowled. "Yeah. How did you know? I didn't show you the applications. I suppose Gretchen told you about her."

"No, she was a witness in the mom-and-pop store robbery yesterday."

"That right? What did you think of her?"

"Smart. Direct. Observant. A little short on self-esteem."

Pete laughed. "You've got her pegged, but you forgot to mention how pretty she is. Seemed very professional, but you're right, she was a little nervous."

Mike nodded in satisfaction. "I expect things in my department to go on running smoothly, then."

Pete leaned forward, turning serious. "Say, any more monkey business in your unit?"

Mike shook his head. "Nothing other than what I discussed with you. I'm wondering if I made too much of it."

"No, you keep me posted. I don't like to think one of our officers is up to something, but if there's anything out of kilter, we need to know."

"All right, I'll be sure and let you know if there are any more incidents." Mike continued down the hall wondering what it would be like to have Debra in the office every day. The secretary's job shouldn't be too stressful, but there were times when she would be under pressure to handle all sorts of calls and visitors as well as her paperwork. She'd looked petrified when Bernice had called her in for the interview.

She wasn't spectacularly beautiful, but she was pretty enough that Johnny Young would surely try to make time with her. Mike smiled to himself, remembering her neat, attractive appearance and her reserved demeanor. Somehow he had the feeling Johnny wasn't Debra's type.

Gretchen jumped up when he entered the outer office.

"Mike! I'm glad you're back. Roland Whittier's lawyer wants you to call him. Coffee coming up."

Mike plucked the memo sheet from her hand. "Thanks. I hear I was wrong—you're not irreplaceable."

She laughed. "You're going to love the new secretary. Trust me."

"I always have, Gretchen."

She was back with his coffee by the time he completed the phone call. "Thanks. I'll be in conference for about ten minutes."

"Got it. Calls on hold." She closed the door behind her.

Mike took a sip of coffee and sank back in the padded chair. He took a deep breath and closed his eyes for a moment. He'd hoped to get down to his parents' home that weekend, but there was one messy case his detectives were working on that might keep him in town.

Thank you, Lord, he prayed silently. *Sometimes I feel as if I'm barely keeping my head above water here, but everyone says we're doing fine.*

He ran mentally through the open cases the unit was pursuing. Pete Nye was a source of encouragement and practical common sense, and Mike was grateful to have men like him around to share their years of experience. But he knew the wisdom he needed for the job came from a higher source. He opened his Bible on the desk.

*****

On Sunday morning Debra sat down beside Laurie Edgecomb in the church auditorium.

32

"Debra! Welcome home," Laurie said.

"Thanks," Debra said with a smile. Laurie's husband Jack nodded to her. They had been a couple of years ahead of Debra in school, and had now been married four years and had a two-year-old son and an infant daughter.

Grant had gone off to the high school classroom, and her parents sat a few rows ahead of her. Debra wanted to just sink back in the pew and listen to the lesson, but not have to answer questions or think too hard.

"What are you doing this summer?" Laurie asked softly.

Debra slid toward her a few inches. "I've just been hired as a secretary at the police station."

"That sounds interesting." Laurie glanced toward the podium to see if the teacher was ready to begin. "Do you have a lesson book?"

"Yes, thank you." Debra turned to get it from under her Bible. Michael Van Sant was sitting down at the end of the pew.

"Well, hello again," he said evenly, meeting her eyes.

Debra opened her mouth, then closed it again. She managed a nod, and picked up her lesson book.

"I didn't realize you attended church here," Van Sant said.

"All my life." She thought that might sound rude, and tried to put warmth into her voice as she asked, "Are you visiting here today?"

"No, I've been coming here for a month."

"I didn't see you last week."

"I was out of town on business." He smiled a little, and Debra ducked her head. She'd said the wrong thing again.

"I'm sorry—I'm just surprised. If you go here, then you should know the Farnhams. I don't understand."

A blank look crossed his face. "You mean the robbery victim, Belinda Farnham, and her husband? I've never seen them here."

"They're members." Debra realized suddenly that she hadn't seen them that morning, and they had been absent the week before. "I'm really sorry. I didn't mean to be rude."

He shrugged and smiled. "I understand we'll be working together."

"I—yes. I mean—if you think—" She stopped, furious that she couldn't carry on a simple conversation with the man. She took a deep breath. "Look, Sergeant, I had no idea when I applied for the job that you would be my boss. I thought I'd be in some basement dungeon typing away in solitary confinement."

He laughed. He started to say something, but just then the class teacher stood up, and Van Sant just smiled at her and said, "It's okay," then turned his attention to the front.

When the class ended, Debra wondered if she could gracefully leave him and go sit with her parents for the church service. She was sure she wouldn't remember a word of the sermon if she sat beside Van Sant for another hour. She shifted uneasily, wondering how to execute the plan without being offensive.

"Hey, Mr. Van Sant!" Her brother Grant was standing in the aisle beside the detective, holding out his hand to him.

"Good morning, Grant!" Van Sant stood, then turned suddenly toward Debra, revelation on his face. "Of course! Grant is your brother!"

Debra nodded in acknowledgment.

"This is great. I should have put two and two together. You gave me your address on Thursday, but it never occurred to me that you were part of *the* Griffin family."

She looked questioningly past him at Grant.

"Mr. Van Sant's been playing basketball with us. He's really good." Grant pushed past Van Sant and sat down between him and Debra without apology. Debra picked up her Bible and purse and slid over closer to Laurie Edgecomb.

The organist began to play, and Debra lowered her eyes and tried to calm her emotions. After prayer, she was able to stop being put out with Grant and be thankful that he was sitting between her and her new boss. She tuned her mind to the pastor's message and was able to concentrate.

34

When the service ended, Van Sant let Grant out and waited until she approached the end of the pew.

"If memory serves, the Griffin family is usually here for the evening service," he said.

"Yes, we'll be here."

"Great."

"You know my parents?" she asked looking up at him through her eyelashes, then quickly dropping her gaze.

"Yes. I like them very much."

"My mother never said anything—I mean, when I told her about the job."

He shrugged. "I don't know them well. I've only gone to church here for a few weeks."

Debra smiled for the first time. "If you knew my mom well, you'd know she's ecstatic that I found a job. My dad is just relieved, I think."

"Well, I hope it works out well for you."

"Thank you. I hope I can do the job. Gretchen may be a hard act to follow."

"She's been excellent. Of course, I've only been here a short time, but everyone in the department seems to agree on that. I never had an office staff until I came here, and she's had to educate me on what I should do for myself and what I should let her handle."

"Well, I'll try to learn fast," Debra promised. "I hope you can—" Again she searched for the right words, but they eluded her.

Van Sant was looking at her expectantly, and her color began to rise. After a moment, he nodded and said, "I'm sure I can."

*****

"Mom, why didn't you tell me?" Debra gasped as soon as the car doors were shut and her father had started the engine.

"Tell you what, dear?" Her mother turned to stare at Debra over the back of the seat.

35

"That you know Michael Van Sant."

"Why should I—oh, dear. You're going to work at the police station."

"Yes, and three guesses who is my new boss!" Debra buried her face in her hands.

"Your new—oh, dear." Ellen looked toward her husband for support.

"You're going to work for Mr. Van Sant?" Grant asked. "Cool!"

"I don't see what the big fuss is about," her father said, easing the car into the roadway. "Van Sant seems like a nice fellow. You should be glad you have a Christian for a boss."

"Why, yes," Ellen said gently. "That's a real blessing. I was a bit apprehensive when you applied for that job."

Debra stared at her. "You were? You encouraged me to do it."

"I know, but, well, mothers always worry a little. All the criminals end up at the police station sooner or later, you know. I'm so glad it turned out this way."

"But he's—"

"He's what?" asked Grant.

Debra had nothing to say.

Chapter 5

That afternoon Debra drove to Farnham's Store.

"Where were you this morning?" She accosted Belinda in the snacks aisle, where she was stooping to restock the potato chips and popcorn.

"Right here, where else?"

"I missed you at church."

"We've been really busy. You know we're expanding the store."

"Well, yes, but that doesn't mean you can't go to church, does it?"

Belinda threw her an apologetic look. "We have so much to do."

Debra frowned. The Farnhams hired extra help to work part time weekends and evenings, but that didn't seem to keep them out of the store anymore. "You ought to close on Sunday."

"Sunday's a big day for us."

"Well, you and Mack used to take turns coming to church, at least."

Belinda sighed and stood up. "I know. It's just ... well, we have this goal."

"What kind of goal?"

"If we make a decent profit this year, we're going to—" Belinda stopped and straightened a row of barbecued potato chips.

"To what?" Debra was concerned, and she stepped closer to her friend, looking around to see if any customers were near. Mack was at the counter, and no one else was in their aisle.

"To have a baby," Belinda whispered.

Debra stared. "Wow. That's great. But, you mean, you're not going to until you meet a certain financial goal?"

"Right."

"So, what happens if you don't make it?"

"Then we wait."

"Is that what you've been doing for four years?"

"No." Belinda moved to the next section and opened a box of cheese curls. "At first we just waited because—I don't know, we weren't ready."

"But now you are."

"Yes."

"So, why don't you just go ahead?"

Belinda looked toward the counter. "Mack's afraid of going bankrupt. If we have a baby, I won't be able to work as much, and he's afraid we'll go under."

"That's ridiculous. You're not in danger of bankruptcy, are you?"

"I don't think so, not right now, but we don't want to be."

"Well, B'linda, I know I'm not an expert when it comes to family planning, but I think you ought to reconsider this. If you wait for the perfect time to have a baby, you'll end up forty and childless."

"That's not going to happen. Mack just needs to feel secure, and I'm doing everything I can to help him feel that way. If it means working twelve hours a day, seven days a week, I'll do it."

"You look exhausted."

Belinda turned back to her work, grim-faced.

"Oh, honey, come here." Debra put her hand on her friend's shoulder and turned her gently around. Belinda collapsed in her arms, her shoulders quaking. Debra held her and prayed silently, rubbing Belinda's back. She instantly regretted coming on so strong and judging Belinda's actions so harshly. "I'm sorry," she said softly.

"Everything all right?"

Debra jumped. Mack had come up behind her.

"Here, this is your job." She tried to pass Belinda over to her husband, but Belinda pulled away.

"I've got to finish this aisle," Belinda choked.

"No, you don't," Debra said firmly. She turned to Mack and pulled in a deep breath. She needed to act as a friend now, not a critic. "Mack, it seems like you're working Belinda too hard, and you're probably working yourself too hard, too. You both need a chance to unwind. And if you want her to have a baby, she needs to be rested."

"Who said anything about a baby?" Mack asked.

Belinda bent over the boxes without speaking.

"Don't you want a baby?" Debra asked, looking back and forth between them.

"Well, sure." Mack's face softened. "We just need to be on an even keel financially first, is all. Belinda agrees with that, don't you, honey?"

Belinda's mouth worked a little, but nothing came out. She turned around and began opening another carton.

"Mack." Debra laid a hand on the sleeve of his flannel shirt. "The robbery was a shock. Have you let her rest since then?"

"She said she was okay."

"Just think about what's best for your wife, and about what you really want out of this life. Do you want a huge store that takes every minute of your time, or do you want a happy wife and fat little babies who love you?"

"Oh, that's a bit much."

"Fine," said Debra. "I am your friend. I'm just telling you, you've got to decide what is really important here. Is the store more important than children? Is your financial situation more important than your spiritual life?"

"Now we're getting down to it, aren't we?" Mack asked bitterly. "You're mad because we haven't been to church for a while."

"I'm not mad. I'll admit I'm concerned. I love you both, and I don't want to see you drift away from the Lord."

Mack stared at her for a few seconds. The front door opened, and a man approached the counter. Mack turned and went to wait on him.

"Belinda—" Debra began, but Belinda kept her back to her.

Debra threw up her hands and walked out of the store.

*****

39

She sat down with her parents and Grant for the evening service, grieving inwardly for Belinda and Mack, and wishing she had taken a softer approach. They had been vocal and animated about their faith in high school, but the store had slowly drained their vitality. She realized the couple had no social life outside the business, no recreation.

As the first hymn began, a hand touched her shoulder lightly. She turned toward the aisle, and looked into Belinda's eyes. Joy flooded her face as she embraced her friend.

"Where's Mack?" she whispered.

"At the store, but he told me to come." Belinda helped hold the hymnbook, and her soprano blended with Debra's alto. Thankfulness swept over Debra, and she took courage from this sign that God had heard her prayers and begun to work in the Farnham family.

During the offering, Belinda nudged her, and she leaned closer.

"Isn't that the detective across the aisle?"

"Mm-hmm."

Belinda's eyes were huge. "He's a Christian?"

"Apparently."

"Oh, Debbie, this is too good to be true."

Debra couldn't help smiling. "There's more that you don't know."

"What? He recognized you and spoke to you this morning?"

"More than that. He's my new boss at the police station."

"I'm going to faint," Belinda whispered. "Why didn't you tell me you got the job?"

"I was going to tell you this afternoon, but I got sidetracked. I'm sorry if I caused friction between you and Mack."

"Well, the air needed to be cleared. I should probably thank you for making us face some issues we've been avoiding."

They turned their attention to the pastor then, but Debra sent silent thanks upward, a warm glow of friendship soothing her.

After church they lingered. Belinda greeted Mr. and Mrs. Griffin cheerfully and asked about Julie and Rick. As the aisle began to clear, Van Sant ambled across and stood at the end of the pew, his hands in his pockets.

"Mrs. Farnham, good to see you again," he said when there was a lull in the conversation.

Belinda turned toward him. "Detective Van Sant! How are you?"

"Fine. Everything all right at the store?"
"Yes, thanks."

"Miss Griffin told me that you and your husband are members here."

"Yes, well, we haven't been here for a while, but we are members."

"It seems like a really good church."

"Yes. Are you joining?"

"I've spoken to the pastor about it. He's going to hold a membership class." Van Sant glanced past her toward Debra. "Miss Griffin," he said, with a nod.

Debra managed a half smile, but couldn't speak. *If I don't say anything, at least I know I won't say the wrong thing*, she told herself.

"So, you live in town?" Belinda asked.

"Yes, I've got an apartment down on Riverside."

"Do you have a family?"

Debra was appalled, but Belinda said it innocently, a married woman curious about a man's family.

"No, well, not here. My folks are in Ellsworth, and I have a brother in Vermont."

Belinda nodded, smiling. "Well, it's nice to have you here. I hope you like our town."

"It's an interesting place," he said noncommittally.

Grant came up the aisle with his friend Jason and said to Van Sant, "Hey, are you playing Tuesday night?" Van Sant started to answer, but stopped and pulled a pager from his pocket.

"Sorry, guys. I've got to run." He walked quickly toward the church door.

41

Debra realized Belinda was watching her watch the detective, and her blush began again.

"What?" she asked.

"You tell me," said Belinda.

"I don't think I'll survive the first day on the job."

Belinda shook her head, looking after Van Sant. "Too good to be true."

*****

"This is not good." Mike critically surveyed the broken headlight on the passenger side of one of the city's unmarked cruisers.

"I know." Detective Jared Dore ran both hands through his sandy hair. "Sergeant, I swear I didn't hit anything. I was in the apartment building all of ten minutes. Fifteen at the most."

"Did you check for pieces?"

Jared pulled an evidence envelope from the inside pocket of his sport coat. "I didn't notice it until I got back here. Didn't see it, you know? As soon as I did, I turned around and drove back to Anson Street, and sure enough, there were fragments on the pavement where I'd parked. More than six feet from the building."

Mike took the envelope. "Anything else?"

"No. I asked some of the people if they'd seen anything. Do you think it's worth canvassing all the tenants?"

"Probably not. It's just a nuisance thing. Kids, I expect."

Jared nodded. "That's what I figure. Some tough guys who have it in for cops. They won't face up to you, but when your back is turned they'll vandalize city property without a second thought."

"All right. File your report. I'll alert the deputy chief, so we can get this taken care of."

Jared went into the police station, and Mike stood looking at the car for another long moment. He fingered the dented metal around the light bracket. A baseball bat, maybe. Was it simply criminal mischief, or was it part of a larger pattern?

Chapter 6

Monday morning was a blur for Debra. Gretchen greeted her enthusiastically and put her to work filing documents while she typed notes Van Sant needed for an upcoming court case.

"I'd have you do this, but it's a really important case, and I know you've got first-day jitters," Gretchen explained.

"Don't apologize," Debra told her. "Just let me ease into it."

Van Sant breezed through the room ten minutes later, with a brisk, "Good morning, Gretchen. Welcome, Miss Griffin." He went straight to his office, and Debra heard his voice through the doorway as he made several phone calls.

"I'd better get Mike's coffee," Gretchen said, when she had finished typing and printing his notes. "Black decaf for Mike."

"Secretaries still make coffee?" Debra asked with wonder.

"You said you weren't a feminist."

"I'm not, I'm just in mild shock."

"Well, the guys start a pot if they get in early, but I always go into the break room and get Mike a cup after he comes in. He seems to be one of these men who forgets to take care of himself."

"So, did you work for the sergeant before him?"

"Yes, and he was much more demanding. He was a good cop, though."

"What happened to him?" Debra asked.

"He's now the police chief in Harmony."

"Small town," Debra observed. "That's how cops work their way up? Go from being a sergeant in a small city to being a chief in a small town?"

"Sometimes," Gretchen said, heading for the door. "Sometimes they stay here and move up, like Pete did. But there are only so many openings in one department. You want coffee?"

"No, thanks."

Debra kept on filing. Gretchen came back a minute later with a plain blue mug of coffee and carried it straight to Van

Sant's office, picking up the folder of notes as she passed her desk.

Van Sant's voice came clearly. "Thank you, Gretchen. I'll be going out in a minute. I'll probably be at the courthouse until noon. Page me if you need me."

Relief swept over Debra, and she realized she had been tense since Van Sant entered the office. At least she could relax and learn for a few hours.

By noon she was feeling overwhelmed. Gretchen had introduced her to several procedures, which she claimed would soon become routine. Debra jotted notes on a tablet. Gretchen made her answer the telephone and taught her to transfer the calls to the detectives' offices. She showed her how to page the officers if needed and take messages for the men who were in the field. The finer points of the department's filing system and incident report forms were next, and a taste of entering data on a computerized spreadsheet.

"You'll need this for keeping track of office supplies and tracking the statistics on incidents and citations for this department. When Mike starts making his budget for next year, you'll really get a workout with the spreadsheets."

"I have to work on the budget? That's scary."

"Mike will supply all the data. You'll just have to put it where it belongs. Of course, he's never done it before, either. I'm sure Pete will walk him through it, and if you need me, don't hesitate to give me a call. The budget doesn't enter the picture until fall, and I should be able to give you some pointers when the time comes."

"That's good to know," Debra breathed, still apprehensive. "Gretchen, what if I never sort it all out?"

"You will. You're doing fine. In a month, you'll laugh at yourself for being so nervous."

"I hope you're right."

One by one, the four detectives came into Gretchen's office on one pretext or another, and Gretchen introduced them to Debra.

Leon Beaulieu came in for a case file. He had the dark features common to so many of the area's French population, and his steel-rimmed glasses gave him a studious air.

"We're so glad to know someone efficient will be in here when Gretchen leaves," he told Debra.

"How do you know she's efficient?" Gretchen asked archly.

"If she weren't, you wouldn't have let Pete hire her," Leon replied.

Johnny Young came in search of a stapler. His gaze landed on Debra. "Well, hi there. You the new secretary? Fantastic! How about lunch?"

"Leave her alone, Johnny," Gretchen scolded. "You'll make Debra regret taking this job if you give her the big rush."

"Sorry." He laughed, but he didn't sound the least bit apologetic. His unruly shock of blond hair made him look boyish. He picked up Gretchen's stapler and used it on the papers he was holding together.

"Where's *your* stapler?" Gretchen asked with annoyance.

"Haven't the foggiest. At least your husband isn't blind when he interviews job applicants. See you later, Debra." He winked at her as he turned to leave. "The lunch offer stands."

"What was that?" Debra asked, when she heard his office door close across the hall.

"That was Detective Young. He's a bit brash, but he's really a sweet guy. He's the only bachelor in the unit, though, besides Mike, and he thinks it gives him license to carry on like that. He's always flirting with Wendy, the dispatcher with the enhanced blonde hair. I should say, he's always flirting, period, but he seems to have a penchant for Wendy just now."

"I haven't met her," Debra said.

"Well, don't let Johnny bother you. Just brush him off repeatedly."

"He'll get message?"

"Probably not, but eventually you'll come to an understanding of sorts. And he can be a good friend."

45

Jared Dore was next, bringing a statement to be typed and filed electronically.

"Good, I'll have Miss Griffin do that," Gretchen told him. "She's getting used to our system, and this will be good practice."

"Miss Griffin, welcome aboard," Jared said formally.

Debra smiled. "Thank you, Mr. Dore."

Jared was older than the other detectives, in his late forties, and his haircut and clothing told Debra he was a meticulous man.

"Great on detail, very thorough, but not so good on intuition," Gretchen commented when he had left the room. She set Debra up on the computer to type Jared's document. "He hopes he's next in line for Pete's job.

"Really? Doesn't Pete plan to keep his job for some time?"

"Well, sure, for a while. But when the chief retires, he hopes to move into that slot."

"So the department is likely to promote from within?"

"Sometimes. They brought Mike in from Ellsworth, and that didn't sit too well with some."

"You said all the men like him."

"Sure. What's not to like? He's decent, and he's fair. But there's still a little resentment in some quarters. Now, for chief and deputy chief it's different. Hiring and promotion there goes through the city. Our present mayor seems agreeable to Pete moving up when the time comes."

"More politics?" Debra was wondering if she'd be comfortable trying to second-guess people's motives.

"Absolutely. If you want to be chief of police, you have to cultivate the mayor and city councilors."

"How long before the chief retires?"

"Who knows? He's 57, and has thirty-five years in as a cop. Could be anytime, could be another six or eight years."

"So if that happens, Jared Dore is hoping to become the deputy chief?"

"He and everyone else," Gretchen said with a rueful smile. "It keeps things interesting around here. I suppose having the deputy's wife in the office has been a bit unorthodox, too."

"Do they think you're a spy?"

"Oh, no, I don't think so, but they know everything that happens in this unit will get back to Pete, as long as I'm here. I get along well with these guys, but I suppose they might feel a little freer when I make my exit." Gretchen sat down next to Debra. "Know what?"

"What?"

"I'm tired."

"You'd better take a break," Debra advised. "You've been working nonstop all morning."

"I suppose so. I pride myself on being a high-energy person, but I'm beginning to remember what it's like to be seven months pregnant."

"Let me get you something."

"No, I'll be fine. Just let me sit here and watch you type that thing."

A few minutes later Brian Estes strolled in. Debra was surprised, after hearing Gretchen's previous description, to find him cordial. He was 37, with red hair and green eyes that suggested his pleasant manner could dissipate quickly.

"Gretchen, I've got Rodney Lacombe in booking, and I can't seem to find his file in the system. Oh, hello." He stopped just over the threshold and nodded in Debra's direction.

"This is Miss Griffin, Brian. She'll be taking over for me. She can check on that file for you."

Debra looked swiftly toward her, but Gretchen smiled and nodded. Debra faced the computer screen squarely and opened the data files on open cases.

"What now?" she asked softly, aware that Brian was watching her.

"Search for Lacombe," Gretchen said.

"How do you spell it?" Debra asked.

"L-A-C-K-H-A-M," said Brian.

"No, it's L-A-C-O-M-B-E," Gretchen contradicted with a soft smile.

"I don't think so," Brian said with a touch of belligerence.

"There it is," said Debra. "Rodney Lacombe."

"No wonder you couldn't find it," Gretchen said sweetly, writing quickly on a sheet from her memo cube.

Brian's face darkened.

"Here, just go back to your computer and look for it under this spelling." Gretchen held out the paper. "If you have any more problems, buzz me and I'll come in there."

Brian snatched the paper and turned on his heel.

"Ouch," Debra breathed.

"Not his best side. He needs to learn to be less helpless."

"Some of these anglicized French names are tough," Debra said.

Gretchen lowered her eyelashes. "Estes is a French name, too, so that's no excuse. He got this case from across the hall yesterday. He should know the file inside and out by now."

Michael Van Sant walked in just then. He stopped at the copier and opened his briefcase, removing a file folder and handing it to Gretchen.

"Just file that for me, please, Gretchen. We should be done with it for a while. I'm meeting Jared at the sandwich shop for lunch so we can discuss that assault case he's working on."

"Page you if needed?"

"Right. Any calls?"

"Yes, the chief asked to have you call him at your earliest convenience."

"Thank you."

Van Sant went into his office. Gretchen gave Debra the file folder and said, "Closed cases."

As Debra filed it, Van Sant came through the room again, without the briefcase.

"Chief's out to lunch," he said to Gretchen. He nodded toward Debra and left the office.

The phone rang, and Gretchen gestured toward it. Debra hesitated, then picked up the receiver. "Rushton Police Department, Detectives' Unit."

"Yes, this is Pete Nye. Is Gretchen in?"

"Oh, yes, sir." She quickly handed the receiver to Gretchen and stood up, finding herself a few more papers to file as Gretchen spoke to her husband.

"Hi, sweetheart. Yes, I'm fine. All right, that sounds nice. I'll be there in half a sec." She replaced the receiver and stood up. "My husband's taking me to lunch. Do you have plans?"

"Uh, I brought a bag lunch," Debra said. "I wasn't sure ... is it okay if I eat in here?"

"Of course. Or, you can take it into the break room. Make yourself comfy. I should be back in an hour."

"Am I supposed to take a whole hour?" Debra asked.

"Well, I usually take a half hour, but today's special," Gretchen said. "Can you handle the phone and such from 12:30 to one?"

"I—I think so. What happens if the phone rings during lunch, and nobody's in here?"

"It automatically bumps to the dispatcher after three rings, or you can set it to have voice mail pick it up. Just push ... this." Gretchen smiled broadly. "See you later. And if Mike gets back before I do, just take him a cup of coffee, okay?"

"Sure. Black decaf?"

"See? You're catching on fast."

Gretchen was out the door, pulling her long ivory cardigan on. Debra opened the desk drawer where she had stashed her purse and lunch and took out the brown paper bag. She thought about taking it outside into the park beside the police station, but it had been cool and windy that morning, and she decided to stay inside.

Johnny Young popped his head in from the hall.

"What? Having lunch alone?"

"Oh, it's—"

"I told you I'd take you out."

"No, thank you. I brought this from home, and—it's quite all right, really."

"Maybe tomorrow?" Johnny asked with a grin, but before she could answer, he was off down the hall.

49

Debra ate slowly, getting up halfway through her sandwich to fetch herself a cup of water from the break room. The detectives and Gretchen all had their own mugs, but she found Styrofoam cups in the cupboard under the coffee maker.

When she had finished eating she checked the time. It was only quarter past twelve. Gretchen had showed her how to get an outside phone line, and had assured her it was all right to make personal calls on break time. She punched in the number for Farnham's Store.

"B'linda? It's me. How ya doing?"

"Deb! Where are you?"

"At work. I'm on my first lunch hour, and I'm bored stiff."

"Really? How do you like it?"

"It's okay. There's a lot to remember, and I'm barely getting to know who's who, but I think it's going to be all right. They don't seem to care if I type fast, as long as I get it done."

"Great. Have you seen the Dutchman today?"

"Who?"

"Van Sant, silly."

"Oh, yes. He—his office is—right next to mine and Gretchen's. Connected, really."

"Wowzer. That's a perk."

"Cut it out. Besides, how do I know this phone line is secure?"

"You're in a police station."

"That's what I mean," Debra insisted. "They probably monitor all the calls."

"Oh, you're paranoid. Hold on. Gas customer."

Debra waited, wondering if the dispatchers in the com room were really listening.

"Okay," Belinda said. "Where were we?"

"I was going to ask if you and Mack had talked some things out."

"Yes, we've decided to hire a full-time employee."

"That's wonderful."

"Well, it's scary. We've got two part timers now, and Mack's afraid hiring a full timer will strain the budget, but we're going to try it and see if we can ease up on our schedule a bit. Go to church together Sunday morning, for instance, and maybe once in a while take an evening off to enjoy our friends and family."

"Sounds like a good start."

"Well, we'll see how it goes."

A button on the phone base flashed orange.

"I'd better go, a call is coming in," Debra said, and she and Belinda signed off hastily.

"Rushton Police Department, Detectives' Unit. I'm sorry, sir, Detective Beaulieu is away from his desk. Could I take a message, or would you like to leave him voice mail?"

She was beginning to feel competent. She fielded a few more calls, then Van Sant appeared in the doorway.

He nodded at her, walking toward his office. "Miss Griffin. Any calls?"

"Yes, sir. A Mrs. Langlais requested you call her about her son's hearing. Her number is on your desk."

"Thank you." He disappeared into the inner office, leaving the door open.

Debra hesitated, then went to the break room, but she didn't see his blue mug. She went back to her desk and sat down, wondering what to do. Styrofoam for the sergeant? She wished she had spirited the mug out his office when she had left the message on his desk.

The telephone rang again, and she gave her official greeting.

"This is Chief Wagner. Is Van Sant in?"

"Yes, sir, but he's on another line."

"Well, I'm in my office now. Please have him call me as soon as he can."

"Yes, sir."

Van Sant's tone indicated that he was winding up the conversation, and she thought she heard him hang up, then silence. She got up and walked slowly to the doorway between the offices.

"Sir, the chief called while you were on the phone, and he would like you to call him now if possible."

"Thank you, Miss Griffin."

"Oh, and, may I get you some coffee now, sir?"

She felt foolish saying it, but Van Sant relaxed visibly. "Thank you, that would be lovely."

She picked up his mug and went to the break room. When she returned with his coffee, he was saying, "Yes, sir, I'll take care of it. You can count on it."

He cradled the receiver and looked up at her wearily as she set the cup on the desk.

"Thank you so much, Miss Griffin. And you don't have to call me sir."

Debra swallowed and nodded.

"Actually, you don't have to bring me coffee, either. I suspect Gretchen has spoiled me."

"It's all right. I mean, it's my job to help you do your job, and—well, if coffee helps—"

He laughed outright, and Debra blushed furiously.

"I didn't mean it like that," she stumbled. "It's not like you're a caffeine addict or anything—I just meant—"

He waved one hand and shook his head, still laughing. "No, no, I understand. There is something soothing about a hot cup of ... anything. Lately, when I've felt the tension of the job mounting, and Gretchen would walk through that door with the coffee, it somehow seemed just a little bit easier. Maybe it's knowing someone's in your corner, thinking about you."

Debra nodded slowly, able to look him in the eye. His hair was less neat than usual, a dark brown lock straying toward his right eyebrow, and he had unbuttoned his suit jacket. He seemed less formidable, but the designer shirt and necktie still gave her the feeling that if he didn't work here he might have been modeling for an elite department store.

He smiled paternally. "So, Miss Griffin, how is your first day going?"

"Fine, sir."

He raised his eyebrows, but said nothing.

"I mean—Mr. Van Sant. It's going fine. It's very—" she stopped, casting about for the right word, but it eluded her.

After a few seconds, he smiled and said, "Yes, I'm sure it is." He picked up the mug and blew on the surface of the liquid, then stopped before sipping it, looking at her over the rim. "Decaf?"

"Yes, sir. Mr. Van Sant."

"Mike," he said, and took a sip.

She started to say, "Yes, sir," but realized the inanity of it, nodded briefly, and turned away.

Chapter 7

By the end of the week Debra felt at home in the office, at least when Van Sant wasn't in it. The detectives were in and out all day, and she was beginning to know their work habits. Van Sant was out more than he was in, pursuing cases of his own and supervising the other four men. Most days he spent an hour or two at his desk, making telephone calls and doing paperwork. Gretchen plied him with coffee and protected him from frivolous interruptions.

"So, do you think you're ready to fly solo on Monday?" she asked Debra as Friday afternoon waned.

"You mean you're not coming back?" Panic seized Debra.

"You're doing pretty well. I don't think you need a baby sitter any longer."

"But I don't know about the monthly reports, and you said sometimes the sergeant asks you to take him files at the courthouse, and—"

"Relax, honey." Gretchen put one hand on her arm. "Mike can explain all of those things to you. I've taught you the basics, and my feet are swelling."

"I'm sorry. I wasn't being very considerate. It's so much fun with you here!"

"It is kind of a fun job, isn't it?" Gretchen sounded satisfied. "I'll miss it. And I'll miss being down the hall from Pete all day."

"But you're right," Debra conceded. "You should be at home, where you can put your feet up and take naps when you need it."

"How about if I just come in a couple of mornings next week?" Gretchen suggested. "I can help you do the monthly reports."

"I—I guess so."

"You're getting on just fine."

Debra grimaced and ran her finger along the edge of the computer keyboard.

"What is it?" Gretchen asked. "You're not still intimidated by all these macho guys, are you?"

"Not exactly."

"Is Johnny bothering you?"

"No, I think he really likes that Wendy. He comes on to me a little, but it's not serious."

"How about the other guys?"

"Leon is fine, and so is Jared. They're both very polite. Brian has been courteous, too."

"He's all right. Don't let him bully you, though. If he gets upset, just stay out of his way for a few hours. I don't think he would get really offensive, but if it did happen, you should definitely go to Mike or Pete."

Debra nodded slowly.

"And how about Mike?" Gretchen asked quietly, glancing around at the half-closed door to Van Sant's office. "You seemed a little nervous when he came in this afternoon."

"He's—he's fine."

"Really?" Gretchen watched her speculatively, and Debra willed herself not to blush again.

"There's just something about him that makes me tongue-tied," she confessed. "When he's around I have this irrational fear of saying something stupid. So then I can't say anything at all."

"He still calls you Miss Griffin," Gretchen mused.

"Did he call you Mrs. Nye at first?"

"No, I think we've been on a first-name basis since the day he came here."

Debra shrugged, at a loss to explain the formality between them. "Maybe it's because you're married. He might be uncomfortable with a secretary who's single."

"Oh, no, I don't think so. He hasn't made any complaints, I know that. I did notice that you about strangle every time you address him."

Debra pulled her watchband and let it snap against her wrist. She leaned toward Gretchen and whispered, "He told me to call him Mike, but somehow I just can't."

"Would you feel uncomfortable if he called you Debra?"

"No, I don't think so."

"Well, he'd probably like it if you would call him by his first name."

"Are you sure?"

"Yes. Oh, I always refer to him as Sergeant Van Sant to outsiders, but here in the office, he's always been Mike."

"I'll try," Debra promised. "I'll practice over the weekend."

"Good girl. I'll ask Pete if I can just come in for a few hours Monday and Wednesday next week, all right? If everything's going smoothly, you're on your own after that." Gretchen gathered her personal things and stepped to the inner office doorway. "Good night, Mike. I'll be in Monday morning."

She turned and headed for the door, smiling. "Have a good weekend Debra. I'm heading for a bubble bath and a quiet evening with Pete and the kids."

"Good night." As Debra opened the drawer for her purse, the phone rang.

"Rushton Police Department, Detectives' Unit."

"This is Arthur Blair, of Dryden and Blair. I'd like to speak to Officer Van Sant, please."

"One moment." She keyed in Van Sant's line, and he answered immediately.

"Sir, there's an Arthur Blair on the line for you."

"Thank you, Miss Griffin."

She pushed the button to transfer the call and hung up her receiver. She shut the computer down, then put on her sweater. She picked up Gretchen's coffee cup to take it to the break room on her way out and reached for her purse. The telephone rang again. She sighed, checking the clock. It was three minutes after five.

She reached for the phone. "Rushton Police De—"

"It's me, Miss Griffin."

"Oh. Mr.—Sergeant?"

"Yes."

There was a pause.

"How can I help you, sir?" Debra asked.

"There are two things I need. I realize it's late, but I'll have to be in court at eight Monday morning, so it would really help if I could get the files in the Brewster case ready tonight. Do you think you could locate those quickly?"

"I'll try, sir. Are they in the computer?"

"No, if they were, I'd get them myself. I think they must be filed out there. It's an older case, a robbery that a couple of years ago, but it has bearing on the case I'm working on now."

"It's an open case, then?"

"No, but I think the file is still up here. I asked to have it sent up a week or so ago. If you'd just take a look, please. Marshall Brewster."

"Certainly, sir. Sergeant. Mr.—" She gave up and said, "I'll look right now." She laid the receiver down on the desk. As she crossed the room to the file cabinets, it occurred to her that she might as well have hung up. He was only yards away, in the next room. Why hadn't he come to the doorway to ask for the file?

She located it quickly, and hesitated, looking first at the telephone, then the doorway. She could see the edge of his desk, but not him.

She went back to her own desk and picked up the phone. "Sir?"

"Yes, I'm here."

"I found it, sir."

"That's great, thank you."

"Anything else, sir?" Mentally, she kicked herself, but she seemed unable to break the *sir* habit.

"Yes, just one more thing. Could you please ..."

Debra waited.

"Could you please stop calling me sir?"

The blood flooded to her cheeks, even though she knew he couldn't see her. "I—I'm sorry. I didn't mean to—please—I—" She grimaced, hating her awkwardness, and tugged at the lock of hair that hung down over her left ear.

"It's all right. I didn't mean to upset you. I thought it might be easier to ask you over the phone."

She caught her breath sharply, realizing he was nervous, too.

"Debra?"

"Y-yes."

"You're doing a great job."

"Thank you, s—" She faltered again, then said, "M-Michael."

He was silent a moment, then said softly, "Yes, that's much better. Thank you."

"Is—is that all?"

"Yes, Debra. Just leave the file on your desk. Good night."

"Good night." She hesitated, then added, "Michael." She put the receiver down quickly and picked up her purse and the cup and went swiftly to the break room, then out to the parking lot and drove home, her heart pounding.

Chapter 8

Debra went shopping on Saturday. She had decided she needed to expand her wardrobe, for a more professional look. When she had found two skirts, a pair of dressy pants, and some low-heeled navy shoes, she went to the grocery store. That afternoon she helped her mother prepare yeast rolls and apple pies for supper.

"This is really fun," Debra declared as she punched the roll dough down for its second rising. "I haven't cooked in ages."

"It's not my favorite pastime, but it's enjoyable when I have your company," her mother said.

Debra smiled. Her mother made it no secret that she hated to cook. She much preferred needlework, and produced fine embroidery and knitted articles. Her quilts won awards. But Debra hated the repetitive stitching and quickly lost patience with sewing or knitting projects. Her creative streak demanded variety.

"So, how do you like the job, after a week?" her mother asked, cutting the apples into uniform slices.

"Pretty well. I'm nervous about Monday, though. Gretchen is only coming in for the morning. She's anxious to begin her maternity leave."

"Do you feel you're ready?"

"Not really, but the men have all been patient with me so far."

"Do you see Mr. Van Sant much?" Her mom didn't look at her, and Debra thought it was by design.

"Yes, I see him every day, but he's not there all the time. He told me he'll be at the courthouse early Monday. I might not see him all day."

"He seems like a nice man."

"Y-yes."

Her mother gazed at her then, not questioning, but inviting elaboration.

"He's courteous."

"I would expect that."

"Well, yes. He's quite unobtrusive, actually." Debra tried not to analyze the ambivalent feelings the sergeant aroused in her.

*****

Debra sat through Sunday school with anticipation, ignoring Van Sant, who sat in a far corner of the auditorium.

When Mack and Belinda came in between the services, she left her family's pew to join them farther back. Finally, things seemed perfect. Except for that nagging knowledge that her boss was three rows behind her, incredibly handsome in a navy blue suit. She didn't look back, and she was relieved that Belinda didn't mention him until they were outside the church.

They stood beside Mack's pickup, talking and laughing in the warm sunshine.

"So, you're coming to our place for supper Friday night," Belinda insisted.

"I'll be there. But I'm bringing something. What should it be? Dessert?"

"How about you bring a date?" Belinda suggested.

"Oh, no, come on, there's nobody—"

"How about him?" Belinda asked, nodding back toward the church entry.

Debra glanced toward the church, then turned her back to it, her cheeks flaming.

"That's not funny," she hissed. "He's my boss."

"So?" Belinda said.

"Do they have a rule against dating your boss?" Mack asked.

"I don't know, but I don't think it's part of the picture for him," Debra said.

Belinda smiled dreamily. "He's too good looking to be single at his age."

"Cut it out!" Debra begged.

"Okay," Belinda said easily. "Well, if someone else comes to mind, bring him along."

"No one will come to mind."

"Oh, come on, you never know. You work with fifty or so men now."

"Forty-eight of whom are married," Debra replied. "I'll bring dessert. See you later." Her parents were headed for their car, and she hurried to join them.

*****

When Debra arrived at the office Monday morning Gretchen was already seated at the desk. She wore a plaid maternity dress, and her auburn hair was twisted into a knot at the back of her head.

"It's reassuring to find you here," Debra said.

"Well, thank you, but I sincerely hope I'm not irreplaceable. Mike was here earlier, but he's gone to the courthouse. Leon and Johnny are at the high school on a new case."

"So early?"

"Yes, there's been some trouble at the school, and Pete asked Mike to put a couple of detectives on it."

"What happens now?"

"Well, it's a weapons case. If they bring any students in, we might end up with parents and school officials, that sort of thing. Be prepared for anything. I hope Mike will finish with his hearing and be back here shortly."

"Okay. What should I do first?"

"Make sure there's plenty of coffee, and keep your desk clear in case they need you."

Brian Estes appeared in the doorway.

"Good morning, ladies. I need some files from Records. Who gets it?"

"Definitely Debra," Gretchen said. "I'm here solely for moral support for this confidence-challenged woman."

Brian smiled. "When you're done here, would you go pump some confidence into my wife? Sheila's trying out for a part at the community theater tonight, and she's a nervous wreck." He handed Debra a handwritten list.

"What's the play?" Gretchen asked.

"*No, No, Nanette.*"

"Oh, I'm so jealous! I love theater. I don't suppose they have any roles for pregnant women?"

Brian frowned. "I don't think so."

Debra looked up from the list. "So, three files?"

"Right. Those are suspects in a string of cottage break-ins, and they all have prior records. I want to go over the old files. I expect to question at least one of them today, and I want to know what I'm up against."

Debra went quickly down the hallway, past Pete Nye's office and into the foyer of the police station. She punched the code on the keypad beside the door that led to the basement stairway, where the records room was maintained.

The clerk who waited on her was a nineteen-year-old girl whose mascara threatened to weigh her eyelashes down so heavily she couldn't open them. She took Brian's list and went to a row of file cabinets.

"You're Debra, right?" she asked, scanning the fronts of the drawers. She pushed a lock of platinum blonde hair behind her ear. Her dark roots were beginning to show.

"Right. I'm over in the detectives' unit."

"Lucky you. That's a cushy job."

"I'm finding it a challenge," Debra replied.

"I'm Bridget. Did I hear you're having a good-bye party for Gretchen?"

"Yes, I fixed it up with Mr. Nye. Cake and coffee in the detectives' break room from eleven to noon on Wednesday. That's Gretchen's last day. Anyone can drop in and say good-bye."

"Awesome." Bridget pulled out a folder.

"How do you like working with the detectives?" a red-haired woman called across the room, from where she sat typing.

"They're nice guys."

"I'd rather be down here where we're left alone to do our job," the woman said. Debra thought she might like a job like that, too, but she didn't say so.

"Not me," said Bridget. "I put my name in for your job, but I guess the deputy chief didn't think I could do it. Tough to live up to Gretchen's reputation as a secretary."

Debra took the files she held out. "Thanks."

As she returned to the detectives' area, she passed the interview room. The door was open, and Leon and Johnny had two young men seated at the table. Debra went on past, to Brian's office. He was seated at his desk, tapping sluggishly at his keyboard.

"Here are your files, Brian."

"Oh, thanks." He reached for them. "As soon as I read these, I'm heading out. If the D.A. calls about the Merton case, could you set up an appointment for me?"

"I guess so. Is your schedule online?"

He shoved an appointment book toward her. "I keep it in that, so I don't lose it if the computer system crashes. I'm pretty much open, except when it says *court*."

She nodded and took the book back to her own office.

"You saw the boys Johnny and Leon brought in?" Gretchen asked.

"Yes. Now what?"

"Both sets of parents have been notified, and the Lassen boy asked for a lawyer."

"Do they have to get him one right away, or will his parents get one?"

"Not sure. It depends on whether the parents have someone, or if they can afford to hire someone on their own. But it puts a damper on their questioning."

"What happened, or am I allowed to ask?"

"Some kids told a teacher that a boy had a gun on the bus this morning. The principal started an inquiry, but the bus driver knew nothing about it. According to the kids on the bus, Lassen had the gun, but they found it in his buddy Nelson's locker. Loaded. It's a big deal."

"They can do locker searches like that?"

"Yes, it's tricky, but school administrators can instigate it if they think it's needed. Now Leon's going to deal with the parents while Johnny runs the gun to see who the owner is."

"The boys aren't talking?"

"Not yet. The Nelson boy says it's not his, and he must have been set up. Lassen hasn't said anything but bad words and 'I want a lawyer.' I've already checked the recent records, and there's nothing on either one of them. I don't think they're old enough to have an inactive record."

"So, what do I do?"

"Watch for the parents. Leon will probably take the ones who come first into his office to brief them, before they let them see their son. If the other parents come before he's ready, you may need to seat them in the break room and offer them coffee and reassurance."

"What do I say?"

"Nothing concrete. Don't say anything about their son or the case. Just, 'I'm sure Detective Beaulieu will be with you soon,' that sort of thing."

Debra swallowed. "Okay."

A uniformed man appeared in the doorway, and Debra recognized the day patrol sergeant.

"Hi, Zack," Gretchen called. "Can we help you?"

"Is Mike in?"

"At the courthouse."

The sergeant grimaced.

"You want Debra to page him?" Gretchen asked.

"Well, I've got a unit over at the Pleasant Days nursing home, and they need a detective." He hesitated. "Looks like your guys are pretty busy here."

"Hang on." Gretchen turned to Debra. "Page Mike."

Debra raised her eyebrows, and Gretchen nodded. "Zack wouldn't ask if it weren't a tough case."

As Debra punched in the number, Gretchen told the patrol sergeant, "Go right in and sit at Mike's desk, Zack. We'll have him call you there. It's quiet."

He went into the adjoining room and closed the door.

"What if he's in the middle of testifying?" Debra asked, but Mike responded almost immediately.

"Detective Van Sant."

"This is Debra Griffin. Sergeant Brown would like to speak to you about an urgent case. We have him in your office, sir. May I switch the call in there?"

"Yes, Debra, thank you."

She pushed the button and let out a big sigh.

"Good job," Gretchen smiled. "Did you practice saying *Mike* over the weekend?"

Debra winced. "I did it again, didn't I?"

"Yes, you did."

Sergeant Brown emerged a few minutes later.

"Thank you, ladies. Mike said to put Brian or Jared on this thing. He's pretty busy, so he asked me to make the assignment."

"Brian was at his desk a little while ago, but he was going out on field work," Debra said. "Let me try Jared first." She punched in his extension.

"Detective Dore."

"This is Debra Griffin. Sergeant Brown has an assignment. Can he come to your office?"

"Sure, send him down."

Debra hung up and nodded at Brown. "Sounds like Jared's available."

He nodded and went out the door.

"This isn't a normal day, is it?" Debra asked Gretchen.

"Not exactly. Sometimes this happens, several cases coming in at once. If Mike weren't in court, he'd probably go out to the nursing home himself. Oops. The parents are here."

A woman's strident voice rang in the hallway, and Leon's lower one, calm and soothing.

"Where is my son?"

"We have him in our interview room, ma'am, and I'll take you in there in just a minute, but I'd like you to step into my office for a moment first."

"I want to see Ricky!"

"Yes, ma'am, you will, but I'd like to talk to you—"

A door closed, and his voice was cut off.

"I think the nursing home thing is bad," Gretchen said. "Zack coming over here to see Mike is a red flag."

"How do you mean?"

"A homicide, maybe."

"Won't they call in the state police if it's homicide?"

"Yes, but our detectives would work with them, and they have to secure the scene."

The phone rang, and Debra transferred a call to Leon's office, then another call came in and she leafed through Brian's appointment book to set up his meeting with the district attorney. She was aware of Gretchen getting up and walking quickly to the hall, and when she hung up she peered out the door and saw her showing a couple into the break room. She walked down to the doorway.

"Need some help?" Debra asked quietly.

"Thanks. I'll let you take over." Gretchen turned to the couple. "Mr. and Mrs. Nelson, this is Debra. She'll get you some coffee and tell the detectives that you're here." She smiled sweetly and headed back to the secretary's office.

"May I get you some coffee, Mrs. Nelson?" Debra asked.

"No, no, I just want to see Randy." The mother held her purse on her lap, folding and twisting the strap.

"Mr. Nelson?"

"Yes, thank you. I can fix it myself." The man came over to the coffee maker, and Debra got him a Styrofoam cup. His UPS uniform told Debra he had been summoned from work to deal with his son's crisis.

"I'll speak to the detectives. It shouldn't be too long." Debra went to the closed door of the interview room and knocked. Johnny opened it.

"Randy Nelson's parents are in the break room," she said.

"Thank you. I've asked for a patrolman to come stay with Randy. As soon as he shows up, I'll go talk to them."

Debra turned back toward the break room, and almost collided with Van Sant.

"Excuse me, Miss Griffin!" He stepped backward.

"Oh, I'm sorry—my fault."

"I'm sure it wasn't," he said with a smile. "Are things under control?"

"I—I think so. Jared has gone to the nursing home, and Johnny's asked for a patrolman to help them with the two boys they—" She stopped, and gestured toward the interview room.

"Great." He shifted his briefcase to his other hand and knocked briskly on the door of the interview room.

Debra went on to the break room.

"Detective Young will be with you shortly. Can I do anything for you folks?"

"No, thanks," Mr. Nelson said. His wife was dabbing tears from her cheeks with a tissue.

Debra hesitated. "I'm just down the hall. If you need anything, I'd be happy to help you. The door to my office is open, second on the right."

"Thank you," Mrs. Nelson choked.

Gretchen smiled at her as she entered the office. She was speaking into the phone, and Debra retrieved Brian's appointment book from the desk and took it back to his office. When she got back, Gretchen had moved to the second chair, and Debra sat down.

"Those poor parents," she sighed.

"It's always a shock the first time your little dear crosses the line," Gretchen agreed.

"They seem like decent people."

"They probably are."

Van Sant came through a moment later and closed the door to his office for about ten minutes. When he emerged, he paused beside Debra's desk.

"I'm heading over to the nursing home to touch base with Jared. Two residents were assaulted, and they've been taken to the hospital by ambulance. No one saw it happen, but there's a strong suspect. You might get some calls from the media. If you would just refer them to me and take messages, I promise I'll call them back before 2 p.m."

"All right," Debra said gravely.

"Are the state police involved?" Gretchen asked.

"No, we're handling this. Jared has three patrolmen over there, but he has so many people to interview that I may put Brian on it, too. I'm going over there and see just how complicated it is." He turned his attention back to Debra. "Remember, I'll be back by two, and I *will* return calls."

She nodded.

"The last sergeant was infamous for not returning media calls," Gretchen said when he was gone. "Mike's been trying hard to live that down. Now, if any reporters do call, don't say a word about the case. Just tell them they'll have to speak to Sergeant Van Sant, and he'll return the call as soon as possible. The local reporters will go to the scene, but out-of-towners will call the police station, and the dispatcher will forward the calls to you."

It was the last chance Debra had to talk to Gretchen that morning. The phone rang almost constantly after that. She spoke to reporters, attorneys, the mayor, worried parents of high school students, the daughter of a nursing home patient, and the nursing home administrator.

At ten minutes past twelve, Pete Nye strolled into the office.

"Ready to go home, beautiful?" he asked Gretchen.

"I'm exhausted, just from watching Debra this morning. You picked the right one for this office, honey. Now that she's gotten past her jitters, she's terrific."

"Glad to hear it." Pete smiled at her, and Debra smiled back as she answered another call.

When she hung up, Gretchen called from the doorway, "Don't forget to eat lunch."

"What about the phone?"

"Let the voice mail pick it up. You need a break. I'll see you Wednesday."

Debra got her lunch out and forced herself not to pick up the receiver the next time it rang. After three rings, the recording clicked on. She took a bite of her sandwich, but it drove her crazy to think she would just have to rewind the tape and listen to all the messages after her lunch hour. The next time the phone rang, she picked it up.

She was talking to a frenzied woman when Van Sant came in. The noon news report had carried a story saying a student took a loaded gun to the high school that morning.

"Ma'am, please, you don't have to be upset. If you can't get through, it's probably because so many parents are trying to call the school for information, just like you. One of our detectives will be available soon."

"I'll take it," Van Sant offered.

She threw him a grateful glance. "Ma'am, our detective sergeant just came through the door. Would you like to speak to him? All right, hold just one second." She pushed the transfer in and sighed.

Another parent's call made it in through the dispatcher, and she transferred that one to Johnny, whose line had cleared. A minute later, he appeared in her doorway.

"I'm going over and log some evidence, then I'm going to lunch. If these parents keep calling, tell them there were no students injured at the school."

"I can say that? I wanted to, but I wasn't sure if I should."

"Well, I'm telling you. Nobody was hurt."

"What if they ask who was involved, or if the gun's been recovered?"

"Don't tell them anything else. We're holding a press conference at 2:30, outside. You can tell that to any reporters that call. We want to make sure they have it straight on the news tonight. But don't tell parents anything except that nobody was hurt, okay?"

"Got it," Debra agreed.

71

Van Sant opened his door. "Johnny! You fellows all set?"

"Yeah, we're going to lunch. We'll talk to reporters at 2:30. We let the Nelson kid go with his parents. The gun belongs to Lassen's stepfather. He admits taking it to school, but not ditching it in the other kid's locker. Randy Nelson may have let him, or Lassen may have intimidated him. Anyway, they'll probably both be expelled."

"Did the Lassen boy walk?"

"His mum brought a lawyer in. Anyhow, he's eighteen. We booked him and let her bail him out for five hundred. Hearing tomorrow."

"Okay," Van Sant told him. "Get your lunch. Debra can handle the phone calls for a while. Good job."

Johnny nodded and left the room, pulling at his necktie.

Van Sant turned to Debra. "You understand all of that information is confidential?"

"Yes, sir."

He nodded. "I'll take the calls on the nursing home incident until Jared gets back. Any messages?"

She held up the list. "Only fifteen."

He took it and headed for his office. The phone rang again, and Debra picked it up. Van Sant's line was busy for the next half hour, as he returned calls. Debra started a new list of messages for him.

At one o'clock, he came out. "I'm going to get a bite to eat, Miss—Debra."

"I have five more messages for you, sir."

He took the list and scanned it. "All right, I'll do these as soon as I get back. Something tells me you haven't had a break."

"I—" she stopped.

"State law, you know."

"Yes, sir—Mr.—" She turned away from him and put her hand to her forehead.

"Yes, well, busy morning," he murmured, and went quietly out the door.

Debra collapsed with her head on her arms. The phone rang. One, two. When the third rang began, she snatched it up. It infuriated her that she couldn't let it ring.

"Detectives' unit."

"I'd like Sergeant Van Sant, please."

"He just stepped out. May I take a message?"

When she had jotted the number on her list, she grabbed her lunch and went out, closing the office door behind her. The phone rang. She stood trembling outside the door, her hand on the knob.

"What's up?"

She jumped.

Brian Estes stood in the doorway to his office.

Debra leaned back against the door. "I can't let the phone ring. I've become an obsessive-compulsive receptionist. It drives me crazy to let it ring." Beyond her door, the ringing stopped.

"That's what we have voice mail for," Brian said.

"I know, but I keep thinking about all those people out there today, afraid their child was shot or their grandmother was bludgeoned, and I can't make them wait to talk to someone."

Brian cocked his head to one side. "Go out to the park. It's nice out today. Sit on a bench and eat your lunch and watch a pigeon for a while."

She nodded. "Thanks."

The muffled ringing began again. She stiffened.

"Better go now," Brian said.

Debra straightened her back and walked quickly down the hallway.

Half an hour later she returned to her desk refreshed. The maple trees in the park had leafed out, and the grass was bright green. She had rediscovered the healing power of praying outside, with the sun warming her shoulders and the breeze ruffling her hair.

She heard the phone ringing as she entered the unit hallway. The office door was open, and as she came into the room, she could hear Van Sant's voice coming from beyond the partition.

73

The phone stopped before she reached her desk, and she put away her lunch bag and punched in the code to retrieve the voice mail. Seven calls had come in while she was gone, and she sat with her pen poised, writing down the names and phone numbers. Two were for Johnny, one for Leon, four for Van Sant.

When she finished, she looked up and caught her breath. Michael was standing in the doorway to the inner office, watching her.

"Get your lunch?" he asked.

"Yes, thank you."

He nodded.

She looked at him, wondering again what it was that unnerved her so when he was around. She could talk to the detectives now without any qualms, even Brian, and it was far easier to talk to the faceless callers than to leave them at the mercy of a machine. But Van Sant was another story.

The first time she had seen him, at Farnham's Store, she had talked to him fairly easily, but it seemed to have gotten harder since.

The phone trilled at her elbow, and she turned toward it, realizing they had been watching each other, motionless, for ten seconds. When she had transferred the call to Brian, Van Sant's lean frame was no longer in the doorway, and his deep brown eyes were no longer fixed on her.

He came out at 2:25, tying a fresh necktie.

"I'm going out to observe the detectives' press conference," he said. "Should be back in half an hour."

Debra nodded without saying anything. It was quiet for a few minutes, and she opened the mail that had sat untouched on her desk for four hours. There were a few documents to file and an item to type for Brian. The phone rang, and it struck her that it had not rung for some time. It was the nursing home director, and Debra was able to forward the call to Jared, who had recently returned to his desk.

She sat back with a sigh and reminded herself that this was not a typical day.

Chapter 9

Tuesday was less hectic, but Debra sorely missed Gretchen. She called the bakery to order the cake for the farewell party. There was enough work to keep her busy, but not frantic. Van Sant was out of the building most of the day, and she typed and filed and took messages. It seemed simple compared to the day before.

Still, she wondered if she could continue with the job. Her nerves were on edge continually, as long as the sergeant was in. When he left the office, she felt guilty because she was relieved. When he returned, her anxiety returned.

She was able to perform her duties for the most part without the smallest hitch, but whenever Van Sant spoke to her she stammered and blushed. Her fingers were steadier now when she punched the telephone buttons to transfer his calls, but in person he still had a tsunami effect. She avoided speaking to him whenever possible, and she had dropped a file that afternoon when he walked in the door. She was certain he thought her clumsy and inefficient.

At five o'clock she went gladly into the cool, fresh air and drove home. Her mother was putting supper on the table. Grant came to the dining room in sweat pants and a T-shirt.

"You look spiffy," Debra said sarcastically.

"Basketball tonight."

Her father came in from his job as a millwright, and the four of them sat down together.

Debra wondered how Grant could eat as much as he did and then go play basketball.

"Are you taking the car?" Ellen asked, passing a dish of baked potatoes to her son.

"No, Mike's picking me up."

"You mean Mr. Van Sant," Henry said, opening his potato with his fork.

"Aw, Dad, when you're playing ball and you wanna make a pass, you can't yell, *Mr. Vant Sant!* He's told me five thousand times to call him Mike."

Me, too, thought Debra. *Why can't I just yell, hey, Mike, and throw him the ball?*

"I suppose that makes sense on the basketball court," Henry conceded, "but when you're not playing ball, son, you should still address him as Mr. Van Sant."

"Or Sergeant," Ellen put in.

Debra frowned.

"Why so glum tonight, Debbie?" her father asked.

"Oh, I'm just tired."

"Busy again today?"

"Not as bad as yesterday. I don't think I've recovered yet, though. And tomorrow is Gretchen's last day. I'm starting to think I—I can't do it."

"Do what?" her mother asked, startled.

"This job."

"Is it so difficult?" Henry asked.

"Not physically. I can handle the phones pretty well, and the computer stuff."

"Do the men behave themselves?" Ellen asked.

"Yes. They're fine."

"Then what is it?" Henry asked.

She shook her head slowly, unwilling to admit that her nerves were shattered. If the detective sergeant were anyone but Michael Van Sant, she was sure she could handle the position. Her anxiety to please him made her so shaky when he was around that she ended up botching the smallest task.

Her mother snapped her fingers. "I forgot. You know that doctor's office where you interviewed a couple of weeks ago?"

"Yes."

"They called today. Wanted to know if you were still interested in the job."

Debra stared at her. Perhaps it was an answer to her prayers for peace. "Did you tell them I took something else?"

"No, I said you'd call tomorrow."

"Thanks. I will." She ate silently then, wondering if she should pursue the job at the doctor's office. The doctor was fifty-five and married. And his eyes were light blue and placid.

"Why don't you go over and visit with Belinda for a while?" Ellen suggested.

"No, I think I'll just stay here and go to bed early."

She was helping her mother with the dishes when Van Sant came for Grant.

"You should go speak to him, dear," Ellen said.

"Mom, I see him every day."

"But still, out of respect."

Grant rushed through the door from the dining room.

"Hey, Mom, okay if I'm a little late tonight? Mike's taking us out to McDonald's after."

Ellen turned toward him. "Well, it's a school night—"

Van Sant had followed Grant into the kitchen.

"Hello, Mrs. Griffin. I won't keep him out late. Nine-thirty, tops. I promise."

"All right."

Debra had kept her eyes on the salad bowl she was drying, but when she sneaked a look toward Michael, he was watching her.

He smiled. "Hello, Debra."

She nearly dropped the glass bowl. The suit was always part of his image, for work, for church. She hadn't thought about him changing into jeans and a T-shirt after hours, although she had known about the basketball games. *Stupid, did you think he played ball in a suit?*

"H-hello."

"Say, some of the wives and sisters and—well, sometimes the ladies come and watch. Why don't you come tonight?"

Debra couldn't deal with that. She turned around and swallowed, then turned back, opening her mouth, still unsure how to couch her refusal.

"She won't," Grant said dismissively.

77

"Oh." Van Sant shrugged. "Maybe another time."

"Yeah, let's go," Grant said, heading for the door.

"Okay, he'll be home by 9:30," Van Sant said again, over his shoulder.

The front door closed and an engine started.

"Why didn't you go along?" Ellen asked.

Debra picked up a plate and wiped it methodically. "Grant didn't give me a chance."

"Did you want to go?"

"No." But she felt a pang of regret as she carefully stacked the china plates. It might have been fun. There would be other women from the church there. Had Michael meant she should go watch the game as Grant's sister, or as something else?

*****

Wednesday morning was easier, with Gretchen there. The detectives were deep into their cases, but the frenzy of the media had cooled. The high school boys were under suspension, and Lassen had had his hearing. The nursing home residents were recovering from their wounds, and Jared was piecing together the evidence, hoping to arrest the assailant soon. Brian had wound up his case on the cottage break-ins, and Van Sant had handed him a new file—ingenious shoplifting of high-priced merchandise. Gretchen tutored Debra on the monthly statistics report for the unit.

At mid-morning, Johnny entered their office scowling.

"Is Mike in?"

"Yes," Gretchen said serenely. "You want to see him?"

Johnny ignored her and strode to Van Sant's door. He rapped on the jamb and kept walking into his office.

"Johnny, what's up?"

The door closed.

Gretchen arched her eyebrows. "Seemed a little tense."

Debra said nothing, but her stomach was churning. She sent up a silent prayer for peace, knowing she was picking up Johnny's agitation. The men's voices went on for some time, muted, with Johnny's rising occasionally. She tried to ignore them.

At 10:45 she took a call from the dispatcher.

"Your cake and six pizzas are here. Shall I send them in?"

"Six—I don't understand." Debra glanced toward Gretchen.

"The deputy chief ordered the pizza."

"Oh, well, yes, please."

"Great, it will be right there."

She pushed back her chair. "Could you mind the phone for a few minutes, please, Gretchen?"

"Certainly."

Debra went quickly to the break room. Margaret Karter, a patrol officer, was just setting the boxed cake on the table, and a young man from the pizza shop set down his stack of boxes. Debra directed him to Pete's office for payment.

"Thanks for carrying the cake in," she said to Margaret.

"Does Gretchen know?"

"Not a clue," Debra said. "I need to get the decorations pronto."

"Need some help? I haven't taken my break yet."

"Sure! Leon Beaulieu's got balloons in his office, and Brian Estes has a banner. Want to get them? That way, Gretchen won't see me in the hall. But don't let her see the balloons!"

"I can handle it," Margaret assured her. They had soon transformed the break room into a party hall, and patrol officers and typists began coming quietly in from the main part of the police station.

"There's a lot of traffic out there," Gretchen said with a frown when Debra went back to her office.

"It's nothing, but you know what? I forgot to get Michael his coffee again." Debra was proud that she had said his name without flinching in front of Gretchen.

"He's still talking to Johnny."

"Well, why don't you get it for him? He won't mind, and it's your last day as his secretary."

"No, you're wrong there. You've been his secretary for over a week now, but I'll get it. Don't know why you let Mike scare you."

"He doesn't scare me."

"Yeah, right." Gretchen smiled and stood up, rubbing her abdomen. "The little guy's kicking like crazy today. It's gotta be a boy. Where's Mike's mug?"

"I think it's in the break room by the coffee maker."

Gretchen went off down the hall. Debra sat still and listened.

"Surprise!"

She smiled and answered the phone, knowing the break room was full, and more officers would drift in as their lunch hours approached.

"Rushton Police Department, Detectives' Unit."

"Hi, this is Pete Nye. Party started?"

"Yes, sir, your wife is in the middle of it."

"Great. I'll get down there. Thanks for doing that, Debra."

"You're welcome. Enjoy."

As she cradled the receiver, Van Sant's door opened and Johnny came out, carrying his necktie. The top two buttons of his shirt were undone, and his hair was tousled.

Van Sant, still impeccably groomed, followed him into the outer office.

"Just keep quiet and let me handle this," he told Johnny firmly.

Johnny nodded, grimacing. "All right, but I don't like it one bit."

"Neither do I. But don't stir things up."

Johnny glanced at Debra.

"Cake in the break room," she said brightly.

"Cool," he said disinterestedly, and walked slowly out, stuffing his necktie into his pocket.

Van Sant stood gazing after him for a moment, then turned toward Debra.

"So, Gretchen's party is under way?"

"Yes."

"Have you been down there?"

"Not yet."

"Well, come on," he said with a smile. "You're the one who organized it. You ought to be there."

The phone rang, and she reached toward it.

Van Sant took a step toward her. "Don't touch it."

She turned wide eyes on him.

"Come on, Debra, walk away." He was smiling, just a little.

It rang again.

"Yes, sir," she whispered.

He looked at her with raised eyebrows.

She closed her eyes, wishing she could just laugh and say, *Sorry, Mike. Let's go get a piece of that cake.*

The phone rang the third time, then stopped.

"I confess Brian told me about your telephone compulsion," he said gently. "It's perfectly all right to leave it once in a while."

She nodded, unable to return his smile. It was a simple thing, to let the voice mail answer the phone, but it still unsettled her, and having Van Sant see that made it worse.

He jerked his head toward the doorway. "Come on. Gretchen will expect us."

Chapter 10

The party lasted well into the lunch hour. When Pete took Gretchen home, Debra felt bereft. Bridget stayed and helped her clean up the break room, then Debra plodded slowly back to the office.

As usual, the phone was ringing.

"This is Mayor Krell. Is the sergeant in?"

"Yes, sir. One moment, please," Debra said smoothly. She transferred the call and sighed. She could even talk to the mayor without getting the jitters now. Why not with Michael? It was only with him that she felt incompetent and clumsy now. Well, she might as well face it. If she was experiencing some misguided attraction for her boss, it was time to do something about it.

She bowed her head and sought the peace she had in every area except where Michael Van Sant was concerned. Things couldn't go on the way they were.

Lord, show me what to do, she prayed. Whenever Mike entered the room, her heart raced. It was silly, it was childish. How could she run an efficient office for the detectives if she reacted like a schoolgirl to her boss's presence?

She went about her tasks diligently that afternoon, but the plan was solidifying in her mind. She was sure she could handle calls and appointments for a physician's patients without the heart-pounding, breath-snatching moments she experienced in the detectives' office. She told herself over and over it would be simple. One phone call, then the letter of resignation. She could put it on Michael's desk after he left.

At four o'clock she knew she couldn't put the call off any longer.

"Dr. Lee's office."

"Hi, this is Debra Griffin. My mother said you called me yesterday."

"Yes, Debra, I'm glad you called. Are you still interested in the receptionist's job here?"

"Well, I—I think I might be."

"Great. Did you have any questions?"

"Is the doctor hard to work for?"

"Dr. Lee? No! Not at all."

"I—could I just have one more day to think about it?"

There was a pause. "Sure. Why not?" the woman said. "See, it's my job, and I can't stay longer than the twenty-first. My husband's been transferred to Connecticut. You'd have to start by then. It would really help if you could tell me now."

Debra hesitated. "I'll let you know for sure tomorrow. Before noon."

"All right. I'll expect your call."

*****

An hour later she took the perfect letter from the printer. The need to pray, uninterrupted by the telephone, nagged at her. Michael was still in his office, and she couldn't slip in there with it. Maybe she should wait until morning. She could come in early and place it on his blotter.

I won't sleep tonight if I don't get this over with. Please, Lord. I'm going to get an ulcer if I keep working with him. I've got to leave here before I make an absolute fool of myself and him. If you don't want me to do this ...

What? She couldn't think what to ask for, and didn't feel that she had a right to ask anything just then. Her hand trembled as she pushed the button for Mike's extension.

"Detective Van Sant."

He always referred to himself as detective, not sergeant. At first she had thought he just wasn't used to his new title, after years as a detective in Ellsworth. Now it hit her differently, as an unconscious humility.

"I—this is—"

"Debra?"

"Yes, s—"

84

"What can I do for you?"

Her heart plummeted. She was about to do something *to* him, and he wanted to do something *for* her.

"I—I have a document here for you, s—"

There was a pause.

"Would you like to bring it in?"

"I—no."

"All right. Would you rather leave it on your desk? I can pick it up when I leave."

"I—yes, sir. Sorry. I—it's—"

"Debra, are you all right?"

"Yes. No." She sighed. "It's my r-resignation, sir."

Silence.

She closed her eyes. *Lord, show me this is the right thing. The doctor's office will be quieter, and it's a dollar more an hour, and he won't be there in the next room.*

"Debra, I'm stunned. Could you please explain?"

"I—I don't know if I—"

"Well, can we talk about it?"

If we can, it will be the first thing we've ever been able to talk about since the robbery, she thought.

"I—I just don't think I'm right for this job," she said weakly.

"Is it too strenuous? Is the work too demanding?"

"No, I think I could get used to the pace, and Gretchen was very good at making me learn to do things myself and—" She never seemed able to finish a sentence with him.

"Please tell me it's not the men. Has someone been rude to you?"

"N-no. It's not that."

"Then it must be ... me."

She tried to swallow the huge lump in her throat, but she couldn't, and tears were filling her eyes. Her breath came fast, and she knew she was going to cry seriously. She reached for a tissue and wiped her eyes, then managed, "It's not—you don't—" and stopped. There was nowhere to go with the explanation.

"Debra."

She jumped and whirled around. He was standing behind her in the doorway.

*****

Mike walked slowly around in front of her desk, pulled over an extra chair, and sat down facing her.

She put the receiver carefully back on the base, threw the tissue away, and folded her hands in front of her, on top of a sheet of paper.

"What's this about?" he asked softly.

"I—I had another job offer, and I—" She couldn't look at him.

"Hm. I'm having a hard time with that. I don't think you're the type who would take a new job and quit ten days later because another one that looked a little better came along."

Debra swallowed.

He leaned forward, his hands on the desk top, trying to see into her evasive eyes. "If I've done anything—*anything*—to offend you, you have to tell me. So I won't make the same mistake again."

Debra looked toward the doorway, and he wondered what he had done.

He waited.

At last she said, "You haven't. It's just—"

"Just what?"

"Just—I—don't seem to be able to work with you."

"Your work has been fine."

She sat silent, fingering the edge of the letter, and he thought about what she had said.

"You can't work with me," he repeated. "I know you can work. The key phrase is *with me*."

She kept her eyes lowered. "I shouldn't have come here," she whispered.

She was serious, and that bothered him. He liked Debra, and he didn't want her to leave. "I know you're new at this, but I thought things were going well. Is there something about my personality, or my manner toward you ...?"

"No. N-no."

"Something spiritual? If it's a matter of conscience, please tell me."

"No, that's not a problem. I know it's unusual to have a Christian for a boss, a blessing, really, and—I've tried to—" She stopped again, and shrugged. He could see that her turmoil was still there.

"Something physical, then? The way I look? I could grow a beard or change my aftershave."

She looked at him then, with wide, startled gray eyes. "Do you wear aftershave?"

"No."

Her unintentional laugh was minuscule.

"What was that sound?" Mike leaned forward slightly. "I thought it was Debra, laughing. Something I don't think I've ever heard before. Do you hate my neckties?"

She couldn't help smiling then. "It's nothing like that."

"The coffee? Because I've been thinking about putting a coffee maker right beside my desk. Save you running down the hall for it."

"That doesn't bother me."

Just delivering it to my desk does, he thought. "What, then? Because I would be absolutely helpless if you left now, and have you thought about poor Pete? How would he feel if I told him he had to hire me another secretary? And Gretchen wouldn't want to come back and train a new person. She's too close to her due date."

"I—I hadn't thought about—" That seemed to hit the mark. The thought of causing Pete and Gretchen more headaches was clearly troubling to her.

She met his gaze and inhaled deeply. "It's me," she said in a small voice. "It's not you. I know it's silly, but I seem to go to pieces whenever you're—"

She couldn't say it, so he finished the thought for her, something he realized he did often with Debra. "You mean, it's just the fact of my being here?"

"Well …"

He leaned back in the chair and was silent a moment. "I wonder if I could move my desk into the break room or something. Then you'd hardly ever have to see me."

She looked at him quickly, as though wondering if he were serious.

"It's the name thing, too, isn't it?" He asked with certainty. "I shouldn't have pushed you on that. Some people require more personal space. I didn't mean to force familiarity on you. I can call you Miss Griffin." He could see that she was about to deny that, and he hurried on, "If it will help, I'll even change my name. You can pick something that just rolls off your tongue. Reginald, or Harry, maybe. You don't have to call me Mike. Just don't call me John. That's my brother's name, and it could get confusing at home."

Debra bit her lower lip, but a lopsided smile came out anyway. "There's nothing wrong with your name. I just—choke on it."

"Did you know someone despicable named Michael?"

"No, no."

"Then call me sir, or sergeant, or whatever. I'll grit my teeth and bear it. Please, Debra, don't quit." He reached tentatively for the letter, and she lifted her hands. He picked it up and scanned it. Regret and contrition washed over him. He had caused her untold discomfort, just by existing. If she left now, she might be more at ease, but he realized suddenly that he would feel bereft. He wanted her to stay, and to find a serenity here, but apparently it was his fault that she couldn't. "This will never do. Debra, I'm so sorry I've upset you. Please don't leave."

She swallowed. "I must be the least efficient secretary ever."

"Hardly. I did wonder, when you didn't want to bring the document in, but I understand now."

She nodded. "I can try—if you—" She looked off toward the file cabinets, blinking at her tears.

"I do. I definitely do. Thank you."

She nodded, and made a dive for the tissue box.

"So, I can shred this now?" He stood up holding the letter, waiting for her response.

She nodded again. The weight on his heart lightened. He could be patient, and in time she would get used to the job and even him, and then her awkwardness would disappear.

He walked to the shredder in the corner near the copier and slid the paper into the slot.

"Uh, I told you I was helpless. How does this thing work?"

"Oh, it's on the side."

He bent down to look, fumbling for the switch. Debra got up and came to him.

"Here." She reached out and pushed the button. The machine began to chatter, and her resignation disappeared slowly into it. Through a small plastic window, he saw fine strips of paper dropping into the bin.

They were standing very close together. Debra's eyes were a bit puffy, and her cheeks were red, but it didn't matter. They'd had a breakthrough in communication. He wanted to reassure her further, to comfort her and himself, but he knew immediately that time would be Debra's best remedy to this situation. She stepped away from him.

"I'll try," she said again. "That's all I can—" It trailed off, and she shrugged.

"It's enough."

She went to the desk and opened a drawer. Mike thought quickly about her position in the unit. If she was going to stay and work with the detectives, she needed to know what was happening. He hesitated. It might frighten her into trying to resign again, but it wouldn't be right to keep her in ignorance. That might endanger her.

"Debra, there's something else I need to talk to you about."

She raised her eyes to his.

"It's business," he said, "but not the usual kind of business."

"Do you want to— ?" She gestured toward the chair opposite her.

"Yes, thanks." He sat down again, and she sank into her chair. "Debra, I don't want to worry you, but there's something going on in this department that I don't like, and I think you should be aware of it." He linked his fingers, frowning at them. "I talked to Pete about it this afternoon, and you need to know, too. It's a matter of you being aware of what's happening, alert to anything unusual going on."

Debra waited in uneasy silence.

"I also think I can trust you." He glanced up at her. "You're new here, and you came in after it all started. Besides that, I know you're a Christian, and I'm letting that count for a lot, I guess, but … well, I just trust you, and I need someone in this office whom I know I can trust."

"What is it? Something dangerous?"

"Maybe. So far, it's been nuisance things. Missing reports, men being delayed. Today, something more serious happened. You remember when Johnny was in here before lunch?"

"Yes."

"Well, he was very upset, and justifiably so. A piece of evidence he had filed on the high school case disappeared."

"Disappeared? How? From his office?"

"No, that's what's a little scary." Mike shifted in his chair and looked deep into her eyes. She wasn't stuttering and avoiding his gaze now. She was intrigued. "This is confidential."

"Of course."

Mike nodded. "Johnny logged the gun they took from Nelson's school locker into the evidence locker Monday afternoon. The normal procedure is for the officer to put the evidence in the locker and log it on the computer in the duty room over there beside the patrol sergeant's office. Johnny swears he followed procedure. But when Zack Brown went to move it from the locker to the evidence room, the clip was missing."

"Out of the locker?"

"Apparently. The gun was there, but no clip."

"How could that happen?"

"I don't know. Zack and Pete are the only two with keys to the lockers."

"Then how do the men put stuff in there?"

"The lockers are left open when they're empty. When a man puts something in, he shuts the door, and it locks. Then Zack comes along later with the keys and opens the lockers and makes sure everything is logged properly, and transfers the items to the evidence room."

"And nobody else has keys?"

Mike watched her, recognizing that her mind was whirling. "Just the patrol sergeant and the deputy chief."

"Not you?"

"Nope. Zack's desk is right between the duty room and the evidence room, and he handles most of it. If he's not available, Pete does it."

Debra's brow furrowed. "I only see three possibilities, then."

He smiled. "Which are?"

"Either Johnny messed up somehow, or Sergeant Brown did, or some third party somehow accessed the locker. You said you talked to Pete about this?"

"Yes, and he hasn't been near the lockers in days. His key is safe on his key ring."

"Well, if Johnny was in a hurry, he might have put the gun in and forgotten the clip was separate."

"I thought of that, but he insists he had both in there."

"Then, let's think about Sergeant Brown. Could he have made a mistake—dropped the clip or something?"

"I hardly think so, and he did check twice, after seeing it listed on the computer."

"So, were his keys secure?"

"Always a difficult question. Of course, he says they are. But if someone else has a key to the lockers, it's bad news. We'll have to get all new locks."

"It had to be someone within the department," Debra mused.

"Definitely."

"If a third person could have somehow gotten a copy of the key, or if the clip was misplaced and someone else picked it up …"

"You have an analytical mind, Debra. We need you here."

She smiled briefly. "I love puzzles. And I think Johnny's the weak link."

He shook his head slightly. "I don't like to think it, but you may be right. The worst part is, if this wasn't an accident, it's just one more in a series of incidents aimed at the men in this unit."

"You mean someone is trying to make the detectives look bad?"

"Individually, I think, not as a group."

"Why?"

"Politics, maybe. Future promotions."

"Gretchen mentioned that. A lot of guys here are hoping to have Pete's job if he becomes chief some day?"

"Well, it might not be so far away. Rumors have surfaced that the chief might retire as early as September."

"And who's in line?"

"Just about everybody who's higher in rank than a patrolman. All four of my men, and Zack, at least. I don't fancy myself aspiring to it, especially since I'm still settling into this job, but some folks might think I'm in the running. The city could hire someone from outside. But these pranks, if you want to call them that, are coming from within the department."

The phone rang. Debra looked at it, then at Mike.

"It's after hours," she said. "We're not here."

He smiled. They waited until the ringing stopped.

"I'm proud of you," he said.

"So, have these malicious things been done to all of the people on the short list?"

Once more he was conscious of his growing admiration for her. She was thinking the whole situation through, and she was determined to understand it and unravel the cause.

"Well, there hasn't been anything this bad so far. A headlight was broken on a car Jared was using last weekend. He was out on a case, and he said it happened while he was in a building trying to locate a witness. But I only have his word. Brian's report on a holdup was deleted from his computer before it was filed in the system. Could be he pushed the wrong button. Just little things that make a guy look bad, you know?"

"Have you been targeted?"

"Something happened a couple of weeks ago, and at the time I didn't think much about it, but now I wonder. I was out on a case with Brian, and the dispatcher paged me. Said I had a call from the managing editor at the paper, and it was important. I returned the call, and no one there seemed to know anything about it. I felt pretty foolish, and I'm wondering if the motive was to make the local media think I'm stupid."

"So, nuisance stuff."

"Yeah."

"But they're getting more serious?"

"Well, this evidence thing is definitely a black mark against Johnny, or Zack, or both."

"And you think someone wants to keep stacking up black marks against all these men so that when promotion time comes, they'll look too sloppy to be named deputy chief."

"That's my theory," he agreed. "All except one, of course."

"Right, the one who's behind it."

He eyed her speculatively. "Do you realize what we're doing?"

She stared at him. "Working together?"

"Even more basic than that. We're talking in complete sentences."

She blushed crimson. "You're right."

"This is progress." He smiled, then glanced at his watch and did a double take. "Good grief, it's quarter past six, and it's Wednesday!"

Debra gasped. "Prayer meeting night. That last phone call—it was probably my mother. She must be worried about me."

"Sorry. I shouldn't have egged you on to ignore it. You'd better call home now."

Debra quickly punched in a number.

"Mom?"

"Yes, dear, where are you?"

"I'm still at the office. I should have called. I didn't mean to worry you."

"As long as you're all right. You're usually punctual."

"I know, but something came up here, and I stayed late. I'll just meet you all at church tonight."

"Fine, dear."

"Come on," Mike said as she hung up. "If we hurry, we can drive through McDonald's on the way to church.

"No, I'm not really hungry," Debra said.

"Well, I'm starved. Is there any of that cake left?"

"As a matter of fact, there is. I put it in the refrigerator in the break room."

"What are we waiting for?"

He closed the office door, and they went down the hall. "Look at that," he said, opening the refrigerator. A pizza box was inside. He flipped up the cover. "Sausage pizza and chocolate cake. The perfect meal."

Debra laughed. "You'll take that with decaf, I suppose?"

"You got it."

They sat down at the small table.

"You're going to eat that cold?" Debra asked. "Stick it in the microwave for a minute."

"Cold pizza is gourmet food," he replied. "Want some?"

"No, thanks. I'll stick with the cake."

There was half a quart of milk in the refrigerator, left from the coffee service during the party. She poured some into a Styrofoam cup for herself.

"What about your dog?" She asked. "Will he be hungry?"

"You know about Skipper?" Mike asked in surprise.

Debra's flush returned and she took a sip of milk. "Belinda told me the paper said you had a dog."

"Oh, that article. That was ages ago."

"She told me the day of the robbery, because she recognized you, but all she could remember was the dog."

He laughed. "Well, I took Skipper back to my parents' last weekend. It wasn't working out at the apartment. If he had a place to run outside it would be all right. I tried tying him up out behind the building, but the landlady called me at work and told me he was loose, and I had to go home and find him and put him inside. It was just too stressful for him. For me, too, I guess. He's better off with my folks."

"Any chance someone let him loose deliberately?"

"Hadn't thought about that. Could be. It made me leave work for almost an hour, in the middle of a busy day."

At quarter to seven, they hastily cleaned up the break room.

"I don't have pizza sauce on my face or anything, do I?" Mike asked.

"No, you're fine. How about me? Frosting alert?"

He stood looking down at her, thinking about how far they had come in the last hour. "No, you're fine, too. Very fine."

She looked away and said quietly, "We ought to get going, Michael."

He smiled and gestured toward the door. She walked beside him, not looking at him. It was still light outside, and he walked with her to her car door.

"I'll be right behind you," he said.

She drove to the lot exit, and he followed her out into the street. When they arrived at the church, he parked beside her and walked toward the building with her. The muffled strains of "Amazing Grace" came from within the church.

"Sounds like we're a teensy bit late," he observed. "Will it upset you if I sit beside you?"

She took a deep breath and looked up at him. He wondered if she would choose mundane safety or opt for the sweet hazard of vulnerability.

"Probably, but don't let that stop you."

He hesitated, his hand on the door knob. "If you'd rather I didn't—"

"No, Michael. I'd rather you did."

Chapter 11

The next morning she found a mug on her desk. It was cream colored, with purple iris splashed profusely around it, and a yellow sticky memo on one side. She pulled the memo sheet off.

Since you're going to stick around, you shouldn't have to drink out of Styrofoam. MVS.

She walked slowly to the doorway that separated their offices.

He looked up and smiled, a padlock in his hand. "Hi."

"Hi. What are you doing?"

"This is the padlock from the locker Johnny used. I was thinking maybe it didn't lock when he put the gun in."

"So was I," Debra cried eagerly. "Last night, it came to me. If someone could jam the lock somehow, so it wouldn't close all the way—but I wasn't sure what kind of locks they were."

"Well, they're better than the ones they give kids for school lockers, but still ..." he looked at it critically.

"Anyone could pick the lock?"

"Well ... probably, but they'd need a few minutes, and the evidence lockers are in a high-traffic area. It had to happen within a few hours after Johnny logged the gun in Monday. If it had happened overnight, I'd be more inclined to think the lock was picked, but there's always someone in there. Zack can see the lockers from his desk."

"But Zack wasn't there when Johnny logged the gun in."

"No, you're right, or Johnny would have given him the gun and the clip, and Zack would have put them right into the evidence room. They only use the lockers when the sergeant's not available. Mostly the night shift uses them."

"Did you ask Zack about that?"

"Yes, he was out to lunch, and he had a meeting with Pete Nye about scheduling that afternoon. But still, there's almost always an officer or two in the duty room or the hallway. I can't see anyone having time to stand there and pick the lock."

"Hm. Well, what if the perpetrator stuffed something into the lock, so that when Johnny closed it, it didn't latch all the way?"

He smiled, but shook his head. "It would still be jammed now. This one works perfectly."

"What if they switched the locks after?"

"It just wouldn't work. If they jammed it, the lock wouldn't close all the way, and Johnny would have noticed. And it was locked when Zack went to get the gun. He's positive about that."

"So, no bubble gum or paper wads stuffed in it?"

"Right."

"It couldn't just kind of close part way and wedge, but not lock? Because then the perpetrator could have sneaked in there and taken the clip out and—"

"Afraid not. If it didn't latch securely, I'd have to say Johnny was extremely careless not to notice. Most likely it would just fall open again."

"Rats."

He laughed. "Keep thinking."

It struck her at that moment how easy it was to talk to him about the missing evidence. She'd forgotten her anxiety for the moment. As he opened his desk drawer, she couldn't help noticing the object he reached for.

"Wow! You really have a magnifying glass in there?"

"A very useful tool in this business." He held the lens over the keyhole on the padlock. "I can't see any scratches. I really don't think anyone had time to pick the lock Monday."

Debra's mind leaped onward, following the chain of events. "So, getting back to the fact that Sergeant Brown wasn't available when Johnny logged the gun in. Didn't Johnny stop in here Monday and say he was going to log it before he went to lunch?"

"Yes, I remember. He had run the serial number to see if it was reported stolen."

"How long was it in the locker?"

"All afternoon. Zack's shift overlaps the night shift, so he's here later than we are. He said he'd been busy all afternoon, and he emptied the lockers the last thing before he left Monday night."

"So why didn't Johnny hear about it until yesterday?"

"I wasn't very happy about that, either. Zack said he tried to catch up with Johnny Tuesday, but he was out of the building a lot. He just didn't connect with him until Wednesday morning."

"Doesn't that seem a little—I don't know—"

Michael sighed. "Between you and me, yes. For something that important, I'd have had Johnny paged. No, I'd have called him at home Monday night, as soon as I discovered the discrepancy."

"You know what I'm thinking?"

"That Zack deliberately lost the clip to make Johnny look bad?"

She waited, watching him digest the thought.

"I don't know. I hate to think the sergeant would do something like that. He's worked hard to get where he is, I'm sure. Everyone seems to like him and respect him."

"But his delay in telling Johnny speaks poorly of him," Debra pointed out. "If he couldn't reach Johnny yesterday, he could have come to you."

Michael shrugged. "I was gone a lot, too."

"But he didn't even call this office looking for you or Johnny."

"He tried Johnny's line direct. But you're right, this whole thing is casting a shadow over both of them."

"Maybe it *was* a third party, and that's what he wanted." Debra sighed. She remembered her errand and swallowed down the butterflies that kicked up on principle. "Anyway, I came in to say thank you for the mug. That was very thoughtful."

He smiled, looked up at the row of phone books and law books above his desk, then looked back at her, still smiling.

"You're welcome."

"You ready for some coffee?"

"Love some."

She picked up his mug and started toward the door, then turned back. "What if they switched around the numbers on the lockers? No, that wouldn't work."

He shook his head regretfully. "They're riveted on. And the gun would have been missing, too, if the locker number was wrong. Sorry."

"I just didn't think that one through," she admitted.

"It's okay, sometimes thinking out loud helps. If you get any more theories, you know how to find me."

She nodded, wondering suddenly if her amateur sleuthing seemed silly to the professional. "I hope I haven't been a nuisance, talking about this. You don't mind—"

"Not in the least. Our session last night inspired me to take a closer look at the locks." He stood up, hesitating. "There's not really anyone else I can talk to about this, except Pete. And I meant what I said. Keep thinking."

Debra's pulse accelerated, but she realized it had been easier to talk to him this morning than ever before. The fact that he valued her input on the locker mystery was rewarding. She turned with a fleeting smile and headed for the break room with his coffee mug.

*****

The tension in the detectives' area was palpable that day. Johnny scowled at everyone. Michael spent an hour closeted with Pete Nye and returned to his office as baffled as before.

"Pete can't make any sense of it either," he said quietly to Debra on his return. "We've just got to stay alert. Whoever's doing this might strike again anytime."

"And pray about it," she said.

Mike smiled. "Absolutely. Thanks for reminding me."

She seemed to be settling into the routine of the office, and Mike was grateful. Another week, and she'd be confident in her position as his secretary, he was sure.

He assigned Brian to a new case that afternoon and spent several hours in the field with him. Leon was busy preparing documents on an abuse case that was coming to trial soon. Jared was meticulously building his case against the suspect in the nursing home assault, while Johnny worked on an auto theft case. Keeping track of all his men was tedious, but in light of the recent incidents targeting the detectives, Mike felt he had to supervise them all more closely.

He slept fitfully that night, going over and over the locker incident in his mind. At five a.m. he rose and showered and went to the office.

Debra arrived at eight and found him slumped wearily in the chair before his desk.

"Did you sleep?" she asked from the doorway.

He turned his chair slowly toward her and smiled.

"Not enough."

"Maybe you need some real coffee this morning?" She reached for his mug.

"No, the decaf's fine, thanks."

When she came back with it, he said, "Can you sit down for a minute?"

"Should I check the voice mail first?"

"Sure."

It was twenty minutes before she came back. Mike had finished his first cup of coffee and was reading his men's reports from the previous day.

"I brought the whole pot," Debra said with a tentative smile, holding up the coffee pot and her mug.

"I knew you were brilliant." He held his mug out for a refill. "I'm serious about putting a coffee maker in here, just for us. I think I'll buy one this weekend."

Debra smiled, not quite looking at him. She set the pot carefully on the desk and pulled a chair over. "Okay, sergeant, what's up?"

"I'm just trying to get a handle on this sabotage thing, and I think two heads are better than one." He sipped his coffee and leaned back, looking at her. "If it really is sabotage, which we haven't proved, there are five suspects."

"Johnny, Leon, Brian, Jared, and Zack," Debra agreed readily.

Mike's pulse quickened, and he sent up a quick, silent prayer of thanks for Debra. His confidence in her analytical ability was not misplaced, and for some reason that made him happier than he'd felt in weeks. "Right. Johnny's had the worst thing done to him, the clip disappearing."

"Yes, so if he's the culprit, he did a real biggy on himself."

Mike nodded. "I can't believe any one of them would do something that bad to himself, muddy his own record like that, even to throw off suspicion."

"Well, he could have done the other things."

"What, the headlight, and Brian's report?"

"Yes," said Debra, "and faked the editor's phone call for you, maybe even turned your dog loose."

"There may be other things we don't know about. Things that slow them down, but they haven't reported, just thinking it was bad luck or something." He watched her face closely for her reaction.

"Well, suppose Zack were the one," Debra said. "That would be tougher. He had the best chance to take the clip from the locker, but what about Brian's report? He'd have had to come over here to do that, wouldn't he?"

"I think so. But maybe not, if he's a computer whiz."

"I suppose it's possible ..." The phone rang in her office, and Debra hopped up to go answer it. He heard her crisp, pleasant voice as she transferred the call to Leon's office. When she was all business, Debra's nerves were under control.

She came back and sat down, and he determined to skip over the awkward stage and get right back into their discussion of the sabotage. "If Jared is the one, he could have broken his own headlight, killed the report, and faked the phone call, but what about the locker incident?"

"The same goes for Leon and Brian. The disappearing clip is the stickler. Whoever could do that could do all the other things." Debra picked up her mug, smiling at the bright iris that decorated it. She looked shyly at him. "I really love this mug."

He smiled back.

"You and Brian were out late last night," she said.

"Well, yeah. It's that so-called 'adult book store' on Outer Maple Street. We're going to do our best to close it down. We took about half a ton of pornographic material out of there last night. The evidence room is bulging."

"Isn't that a judgment call? I mean, who decides what's pornography?"

"A court will, and until they do, we're invoking the city ordinance. This department has apparently looked the other way since they lost a battle two years ago. Well, the retailer may win again, but not without a fight from me." He shook his head. "This stuff is bad. I advised Brian to wait until he had something he could really nail them on."

"And?"

"He paged me when he saw a couple of kids go in. They were fifteen and sixteen, and they came out with—well, let's just call it contraband."

The telephone rang again.

"I'd better go man my own desk," she said reluctantly.

"If you think of anything else, or hear of any more pranks, tell me."

Mike went back to work for half an hour, then went out with Brian again for the better part of the day. It was four o'clock when he returned to the police station.

"Did you eat?" Debra asked when he greeted her.

"Yes, we got a bite."

"You look—" she stopped, and her face colored.

He smiled. "Shall I fill in the blank? I look awful?"

"I was going to say exhausted."

"I am tired." He headed for his office, but stopped in the doorway and turned back. "Debra, do you have plans for tonight?"

His heart began to hammer. Had he really said it? He'd thought about it for two days, but wasn't sure the timing was right.

She frowned. "Well, actually, yes, I'm going to the Farnhams'." She was biting her lip, and he wondered if he'd just set her back severely into anxiety.

He shrugged. "Just as well. I was going to head home tonight. To Ellsworth, I mean."

"It's a long weekend," Debra said.

"That's right. Memorial Day. I'll probably come back Sunday. Does your family celebrate the holiday?"

"We usually go to the cemetery, and my brother Rick will come up from Portland for a cookout. How about your family?"

"Well, we don't have anyone buried here. My father and his brother came over from the Netherlands as students. All of his ancestors are in the old country."

"What about your mother?"

"Her family's mostly in Ohio."

"So, it's just another day off."

"Yeah."

"Kind of sad," Debra said. "Do you feel rootless?"

"Not really. I've been over to the Netherlands twice and met my grandparents and a bunch of cousins."

"That's neat."

She took a deep breath as though she were about to say something important. The phone rang and she blinked, then turned to answer it. Mike turned away, disappointed. There was no doubt, he wanted to be part of Debra's personal life, not just her coworker. If she had extended an invitation, he would have pounced on it.

Chapter 12

On Sunday afternoon, Debra sat cross-legged on her quilt, frowning over a list she had written in a notebook.

> Johnny—Could have done everything, but the clip is too serious for him to have done it intentionally.
>
> Leon—No pranks on him so far. Worked with Johnny on the school case. Could he have somehow taken the clip?
>
> Brian—Lost his report. Could have done everything but the clip.
>
> Jared—Headlight broken. Ditto.
>
> Zack—Could have taken the clip, but could he have accessed Brian's computer?

She racked her brain, trying to think who else with access to the detectives' area and the duty room could possibly benefit from the sabotage. Pete Nye? He was the logical choice for the next police chief, and he wouldn't want to do anything that might jeopardize that. She couldn't see a motive. His secretary? No, Bernice Watson, the chic grandmother who coddled Pete and the chief seemed a very unlikely saboteur. Certainly not Chief Wagner. No one else had the security codes to their hallway.

Reluctantly, she made herself write:

> Michael—Could have made up the phone call and dog incident. Could have killed Brian's

report and broken the headlight.
Claims he can't access the lockers.

She stared at what she had written. No, she would never believe Michael was behind it. She believed his faith was genuine, and his statement that he didn't covet Pete's job was true. She tore the page from the notebook and crumpled it.

*****

He came into the church that evening looking around for her. Debra knew he was looking for her before his gaze landed on her and his eyes lit up. She was sitting two thirds of the way back, with Belinda. She smiled and turned her head, so the whole congregation would not see her staring and smiling at him, but the smile wouldn't go away.

He dropped into the pew beside her.

Belinda leaned forward and greeted him with a bright smile. "Mr. Van Sant! Hello."

"Hello, Mrs. Farnham." He glanced toward Debra and smiled, but they didn't speak to each other.

When they stood for the first hymn, Belinda whispered in Debra's ear, "Funny sort of relationship you two have, where you never talk."

"We talk," Debra whispered.

"Sure. At first you couldn't, now you don't have to."

Debra smiled and glanced up at Michael, then down at the book.

The dark smudges were gone from beneath his eyes, and contentment radiated from him. His dark hair shone. She was glad there were enough hymnbooks for them each to hold their own. Standing beside him was electrifying enough.

*****

It was her mother who invited him to the cookout. She and Henry came after the service to where Debra and Michael stood talking quietly in the aisle.

"Mr. Van Sant! We missed you this morning," Ellen exclaimed.

"Hello, Mrs. Griffin. I went to my parents' this weekend."

"That's nice." Ellen eyed her daughter, as Henry shook Michael's hand.

Debra still couldn't put the smile away, as much as she tried.

"Where's home?" Henry asked.

"Ellsworth. They've got a place on Green Lake."

"That must be beautiful," said Ellen.

"It was a wonderful place to grow up."

"Are you going back tomorrow for the holiday?"

"No, I'm staying here."

"Why don't you join us for lunch?" Ellen asked. "We're having an informal cookout. Our older son, Rick, will be here."

"Sure," said Henry. "Go to the parade with us after if you want."

"We always go to the cemetery to decorate the graves," Ellen added.

Debra stood by, blushing, wanting to protest. Lunch was more than enough, let alone the cemetery and the parade.

"I'd really like that," Michael said. "Thank you. What time should I arrive?"

Debra's breathing was becoming more painful. Why couldn't she react like a normal person? But she couldn't. *I will die tomorrow. I will absolutely die.*

"Oh, elevenish? The parade is at two. We'll eat first, then go to the cemetery."

"Sounds good." His eyes darted toward Debra, and concern crossed his face. "That is, if Debra doesn't mind."

Breathe, stupid! You can't asphyxiate in front of him.

"That would be fine," she managed.

*****

Debra braided her hair Monday morning and dressed in denim capris and a red-and-white striped shirt. Patriotic, but not overdone. Rick arrived at 10:30 and lounged in the back yard with his father, catching Henry up on his job and city life in Portland.

Debra watched the hands of the kitchen clock creep closer and closer to eleven as she helped her mother prepare the food, and each minute the pressure doubled. At eleven o'clock, she would explode.

Michael arrived at one minute before eleven, in jeans and a plaid sports shirt, just in time to save her from disintegrating. She was very grateful to him for not being late. When he shook hands with Rick, Debra could see them sizing each other up, and pride ran through her for both of them.

The two young men seemed to hit it off, and Debra tried not to analyze the slight letdown she felt when her father, Rick, and Grant kept Michael deep in a male-oriented conversation until Ellen called Henry to start cooking the chicken.

Somehow she survived the barbecue, Rick's teasing, her father's guided tour of the cemetery, and the parade complete with majorettes, fire trucks, and firing squad. When they were home again and she saw herself in the bathroom mirror, she wasn't sure whether she'd been sunburned or her blush had become permanent, but she was still breathing.

The family exhibited more tact than usual by leaving her and Michael in the lawn chairs in the shade of the overgrown lilac bushes, apart from the badminton game.

Ellen and Henry played against their sons after Debra flatly refused, and Michael declined in deference to her. Debra thought that physical exertion was the last thing she needed. It was hard enough to exert her mental faculties when Michael was about.

Ellen surprised the men with her agility, slamming the birdie into Rick's back court, then Grant's, and the boys were soon struggling to keep the score even.

Debra looked sideways at Michael. "My mom never does this."

"Never?"

"Well, hardly ever."

"We sound like Gilbert and Sullivan."

She smiled. "Don't ask me to rhyme and alliterate."

"What, never?"

She swatted at him half-heartedly.

He critically examined her face. "I think you've got a little sunburn."

"Maybe."

"Your folks are great," he said.

"Daddy didn't bore you to death with the family saga at the cemetery?"

"No, it was interesting. I had no idea you came from such staunch pioneer stock."

"At least we got good weather today."

"Beautiful." He settled back in his chair.

They sat in silence for a while. Deborah was surprised to find she was comfortable with the interlude, and her pulse had slowed at last. She let herself enjoy the moment. She hadn't felt so happy in a long, long time. Belinda's words came to her mind. *At first you couldn't talk, and now you don't have to.* She looked cautiously toward Michael again, and he was watching her. Her heartbeat picked up again, and she looked toward the badminton court on the lawn.

"Your sunburn gets worse when you look at me," he observed.

Debra tried to think of a witty comeback, but she'd never mastered the art.

"I thought a lot about Mr. X this weekend," she said at last.

"Mr. X?"

"You know—at the office." She wondered if he thought she sounded childish, referring to the saboteur as Mr. X.

"Oh. Right. Me, too."

"I don't think it's Johnny."

"Me either. He may have been careless, but he's not stupid."

"I hope it's not Leon."

109

"I don't want to think it about any of my men, or about Zack, but I don't see how it could be anyone else."

"I've ruled out Pete and Bernice and you," Debra admitted.

He shifted in his chair and bent toward her, forcing her to make eye contact.

"You actually put me under the microscope?"

"I—I felt I had to."

"And?"

"You couldn't do this. Ever."

He reached for her hand, and Debra caught her breath. The calm was gone, and her heart raced. The scent of the lilacs was suddenly overpowering, and she felt a bit dizzy.

"Michael, I think I'm having an anxiety attack. Is that foolish?"

"No, but—are you serious?"

She pulled her hand away and closed her eyes, knowing her face was now scarlet, and it wasn't sunburn.

"I read something the other day about people who feel the way I do. Their heartbeats accelerate, and they can't breathe, and they think they're dying. Only there's nothing wrong."

"How long has this been going on?"

"Since the robbery at Farnhams'."

He was quiet.

She opened her eyes. "I put that verse on my mirror—be anxious for nothing—you know. I say it every morning, but—"

"Do you think you should see a doctor?" he asked. "Maybe you should talk to a psychologist about the robbery. I didn't realize—"

"It's not the robbery," she said.

"That's the day we met."

"Mm-hm."

"You mean I'm doing this to you? I knew you were nervous around me, but I thought we'd dealt with that. Should I be flattered or scared?"

"I don't know. I can't believe I'm telling you. This morning I thought I'd have a heart attack. I was so stressed before you got here! First I was afraid you wouldn't show up, then I was more afraid that you would. I just thought I couldn't—"

She closed her eyes again, and breathed deeply.

"Couldn't what?"

"Couldn't possibly spend the day with you like this and live through it."

"Did you ever feel this way before?"

"Well, yes, in school."

"Speech class?"

She eyed him sharply. "Yes, I guess it actually started then. But the mock trial was worse than Speech. That's when I decided not to go to law school."

"Law school?" He was startled.

"I was going this fall."

"I had no idea."

She shrugged. "Well, I found out I panicked every time I had to get up and talk in front of people."

"That happens to everyone at first," he said soothingly. "You could get over it, with practice."

"No, this was major. Not just butterflies. I went to pieces and ran out of the classroom. And lately I've been having those feelings again. Job interviews, starting the new job at the police station ... Until we sat down and talked about my resignation letter, I truly thought I couldn't do it."

"But you're not terrified of me anymore?"

She swallowed hard. "I thought about it a lot last night. I'm wondering if it has anything to do with the federal judge who came in to preside at the mock trial."

"A real dragon?"

Debra gritted her teeth. "He scared me out of my wits. I couldn't get my arguments out. Every time I looked at him, I froze."

"A traumatic experience."

"Cataclysmic."

His brown eyes softened. "Debra, you can still go to law school. Not that I want to encourage you to leave the P.D., but you could. You have the brains for it. You could—"

She shook her head adamantly.

"Was he that bad?"

"He ruled that my client had inadequate counsel."

"Ouch."

"You look a little bit like him."

"I'm sorry."

They sat in silence for a long moment, watching the badminton game.

"Small doses," Michael said.

"What?"

"Isn't that what they recommend? People who are afraid of elevators go practice getting on one without going up."

"That's right. The article I read told about classes for people scared of flying. They would go visit the airport without—" She halted and breathed again.

"Without getting on a plane?"

"Yes. Then after a while they'd get a tour of a plane, and the next time they'd taxi down the runway without taking off."

"So ... "

She opened one eye. He was looking at her.

"I guess today was a pretty big dose," he said.

"Nearly lethal."

"You want me to leave?"

"N-no." She sat up quickly, suddenly afraid he would. "Unless you want to."

"Do you think it's less severe than, say, your first day at work? Because Friday we were able to sit and talk."

"I know. Like normal—"

"Yes. Did we lose ground over the weekend?"

"I think maybe I'm getting used to you at work, but having you transported into my private world was a little unnerving. Like the night you came to get Grant."

"I thought you hated me that night."

"Hated—?" She bowed her head. "I'm sorry. I've been rude to you a lot, and there's no excuse. But I never hated you, Michael."

"Then, let's just keep taking it in small doses."

The game ended with Rick slamming the birdie viciously past his father, to within two yards of Debra's chair.

"Game point," Henry said ruefully, trotting over to retrieve it.

"Rematch?" Grant called.

"I need a break," Henry said. "That about killed me."

"Lemonade time!" Ellen handed her racquet to her husband and headed for the house.

"Grant, give your mother a hand." Henry pulled another lawn chair over and sat down. "Whew, that was a workout."

Rick came over, twirling his racquet. "Good game, Dad." He sank down on the grass, sweeping his damp blond hair back from his forehead. "So, Mike, you play basketball with the boys Tuesdays?"

"Yeah, it's something they had going last winter, I guess, and they told me they needed another player. The boys are a lot of fun. Good sports."

Debra let the words flow around her and tried to breathe deeply and slowly. It wasn't so bad when other people were around her, behaving normally, without reacting to Michael as if he were a bomb. By the time her mother brought out the lemonade, she was able to join in without betraying her anxiety.

Rick brought another lawn chair for his mother, and Grant plopped down on the grass beside Michael's chair.

"So, think we'll win tomorrow?" Grant reached for a paper cup.

"I'd say we have a chance," Michael said.

"Who you playing?" Rick asked.

"The Methodist Church." Grant drank down the lemonade and held the cup out for more.

"They beat us the last time we played them," Michael admitted.

"But we've been working hard," Grant said. "Weren't they, like, the first team we played after you came?"

"I think so."

"Well, we're a lot better now. We've got strategy."

Debra smiled.

"You ought to come watch," Grant said eagerly to his father.

"Sure, I'll go. How about you, Mum?"

"Well, I don't know," Ellen said. "Those bleachers..."

"Bring your lawn chair," Michael suggested.

"I'll go if Debra will."

Suddenly they were all looking at Debra. She opened her mouth, but nothing came out.

"I'm not sure she's ready for that," Michael said. Then they were all looking at him.

Debra swallowed hard.

"Well, Henry can go, and you come here after for ice cream," Ellen said.

"All right," Michael agreed, and Debra breathed again.

He kept one eye on her as he chatted with her family. Debra sat silent, holding the paper cup of lemonade on the arm of her chair.

"Guess I'd better hit the road," Rick said at five o'clock.

"I thought you were staying for supper," Ellen protested.

"Sorry. I have a date."

Debra stared at him. Rick had given the family no indication there was a girl in the picture.

"Well," said his father.

Ellen said, "Just have a sandwich. We've got salad and chips left from noon. You'll have to stop on the way to Portland if you don't." She hesitated, then said, "Or is it a dinner date?"

"No, but I really do have to go soon. Just make it quick," Rick said.

"I'll help." Debra jumped up before anyone could protest and went into the cool kitchen with her mother. She made sandwiches while Ellen laid the table buffet style. Michael was absorbed into the family as they all came for the blessing, then filled their plates.

"Want to sit outside again?" he asked Debra. "The bugs aren't too bad yet."

They went back to the lawn chairs. No one followed.

"Are you okay?" Michael asked when they were settled.

"Yes, thank you. Sorry I'm so irrational."

"Not the word I would have used."

"Well, this ... reaction ... isn't rational."

"No, but I think it will pass, if you take your medicine faithfully. Small doses, of course."

The companionship descended again as they ate and the sun sank behind the trees. A mosquito buzzed around Debra, but she ignored it.

"You've got the mind for a lawyer," Michael said, watching her carefully. "You could get over this anxiety, I'm sure you could."

"Maybe. But I don't think I'll go back to school. I just—that last semester, I could hardly stand it. It seemed to happen more often, and—well, I don't think I want to struggle with that for three more years. It's really good being home."

He nodded. They ate in silence for a few minutes, then he asked, "What's happening at work tomorrow?"

"You have an appointment with the chief at nine."

"Right. Pete and I usually meet with him on Monday, to bring him up to speed, but it's Tuesday this week because of the holiday."

"Then you have to be in court at one."

"Oh, yeah. In between, I'll probably work with Brian on the adult bookstore thing. We need to get the owners held over."

"Probable cause hearing?"

"I'm hoping. Because we can prove they provided salacious material to minors. I'm sure it's not the first time. I'd really like to shut them down." He bit into a chocolate chip cookie. "Your mother's a fantastic cook."

"She hates to cook."

"Really? These cookies are great."

She looked at him through lowered lashes. "I made those."

The satisfaction in his look as he chewed made her absurdly happy.

Rick came out of the house calling, "Catch you next time, Debbie."

"Hey, wait." She set her plate on the ground and ran over to his car, throwing her arms around his neck. "Don't stay away so long."

"Okay." Rick glanced toward Michael, who was picking up Debra's dishes, stacking them with his own. "Is this guy a keeper?"

She bit her lip. "Don't know yet. I get awfully ... nervous."

"So I noticed. Any particular reason?"

She shook her head. "He's just—well, I never dated an adult before. Just guys at school. You know what I mean?"

"I think so. Take it slow." He kissed her on the cheek. "For what it's worth, I like him."

She smiled. "When do we get to meet the girl?"

He hesitated. "Don't say a word?"

"Sure."

"Tonight's our first date. I've got some butterflies myself. But if I don't get going now, I'll be late."

Michael came and stood beside her as she waved, watching Rick drive out.

"I'd better get going, too."

She didn't protest, although it was early. He carried the dishes in and said good-bye to her folks, then said to Debra, "I'll see you at work."

She put a bag of chocolate chip cookies in his hand. He smiled and went out. She sighed and leaned against the door when he had closed it.

Chapter 13

The next morning the smell of coffee was potent in the office. Debra put her things away and tiptoed to Michael's door.

He looked up from his computer screen and flashed her a smile.

"Want some decaf?"

On top of his file cabinet, a coffee maker was at work. Her mug was waiting beside it.

"Thanks." She poured herself a cup. "I have a new theory."

"On the sabotage?"

"Yes—oh, there's the phone." She carried the cup quickly into the other room and grabbed the receiver before the third ring ended.

"Rushton Police Department, Detectives' Unit."

"The mayor would like to speak with Sergeant Van Sant."

"One moment please."

She buzzed Michael.

"Hi. The mayor is on the line."

"Okay, thanks."

She transferred the call. In between more incoming calls, she located a file for Jared and copied a report for Leon.

Ten minutes later, Michael came out with his coffee mug and pulled the extra chair up to the other side of her desk.

"Tell me quick, before the phone rings again," he said.

She smiled. "Well, you'll probably shoot my theory full of holes, but it's an idea."

"I'm all ears."

"What if Mr. X has an accomplice?"

"You mean, two of them are working together?"

"Not necessarily. Think about it."

Michael's brow furrowed. "Mr. X inside, and an accomplice outside?"

"Possibly."

"Like a wife?"

"Possibly."

He sipped his coffee and put the mug down. "I don't want to be indelicate, but a lover, perhaps?"

"Possibly. I was thinking of a second person who might be able to pull some of the stunts while Mr. X had an alibi."

"But you are thinking a woman, am I right?"

"Yes. I can't see two men working on this together. It would backfire, wouldn't it? I mean, two of them can't have the deputy chief's job."

"One of them could have mine if they got rid of me."

"Michael, don't. You can't be serious."

He shrugged. "I don't know how badly Mr. X wants it, you know? There are some here who really wanted this job."

"They were angry when they didn't get it?"

"Well, they haven't said it straight out, but things have been implied. Pete told me himself not to be surprised if I took some flak at first."

"Were the men offensive when you came on?"

"No. Well, Brian's a little abrasive, but I think that's part of his package. Johnny can say things when he's upset, but I don't think it goes deep. Jared—well, it's hard to say. Still waters run deep."

"He's the senior detective," Debra noted.

"Yes. He's never been discourteous to me, but I'm not sure he's happy to work under me, either."

"Gretchen said they all like you and respect you."

"I hope so. I'd like to think so. Still, when they first heard I'd been picked over all of them, how did they feel? They might not vent all their feelings in front of the deputy chief's wife."

*****

At 2:30 that afternoon, Debra took a call from an irate businessman.

"This is Ralph Bainbridge at Bainbridge Electronics. I called Detective Estes forty-five minutes ago, and he's not here yet.

We're holding a prisoner in the store office, and we need an officer now!"

"One moment please." Debra's hand trembled in reaction to the man's anger. She punched Brian's extension, but he didn't answer. She called Michael, who had returned from the courthouse minutes earlier.

"There's a man on the phone for Brian, but Brian's not here, and he's really upset."

"Transfer the call to me."

She opened the line again and said, "Sir, Sergeant Van Sant will speak to you," and pressed the button to transfer the call before Bainbridge could respond.

She couldn't help hearing Michael's voice, louder than normal, through the open doorway. "All right, sir, all right, just calm down. I don't know what the problem is with Estes, but I'll come right over there myself. Yes, I'll be there in five minutes."

He came from his office, pulling his jacket on over his shoulder holster.

"Where's Brian, Debra?"

"I don't know."

"Check his office. Ask the dispatcher if he's checked in with them. If not, page him."

He was out the door.

Debra rose and went quickly down the hall and knocked lightly on Brian's door. There was no response, and she opened the door, but the room was empty.

As she turned away, Leon came toward her from the break room.

"Have you seen Brian?" she asked him.

"Not since lunch."

She went back to her desk and buzzed the com room. The dispatchers electronically monitored officers in high-risk situations. If the men didn't check in every twenty minutes, they were called. If they didn't respond immediately, backup was sent out.

"Wendy, this is Debra Griffin. Are you tracking Detective Estes?"

"No, we tracked him and the sergeant this morning, but he hasn't asked us to this afternoon."

"Have you heard from him since noon?"

"No. Someone called for him a couple of minutes ago, and I transferred the call to your unit."

"We got that. Thanks."

"Is there a problem?"

"Not really, I just need to page him for one of his contacts."

"Well, let me know if you need assistance."

"Thank you. Sergeant Van Sant is aware of the situation."

She looked up Brian's pager number and keyed it in, then made herself work on a statement she was typing, instead of waiting for him to return her call, but he phoned in less than a minute later.

"Brian, where are you?"

"At the D.A.'s office."

"Well, a Mr. Bainbridge called, and Michael had to go and take his prisoner at the electronics store."

"What?"

"This man said he had asked you to come get the prisoner, and you weren't there yet."

"He didn't talk to me."

"Well, he said he had. Would he have your office number?"

"Yes, I gave him my business card last week, in case he needed to reach me in a hurry. They've been losing expensive stuff, electronic organizers and GPS locaters, gadgets like that. Small, but high-priced."

"Well, I guess they caught somebody."

"Oh, man! Should I go over there?"

"I don't know. Michael went."

Brian swore. "I'm going over."

Debra threw herself into a frenzy of work. She finished typing the statement, her fingers faster than Squidman had ever seen them move. She polished off the monthly reports, then printed them and took them to Michael's desk for his approval before copies went to the deputy chief. Between phone calls, she filed documents and electronically archived reports.

After an hour, Brian and Michael came in together. Michael nodded grimly at her and went into his office with Brian, glowering, on his heels.

Debra fidgeted, then went down the hall to the ladies' room, where she couldn't hear their voices. As she went back to her desk Michael opened his office door. "Debra, could I see you for a moment, please?"

She went to the doorway. Brian was sitting in the padded black chair Michael kept for visitors, unhappiness etched on his face.

Michael turned toward her. His eyes were warm, but his voice was formal.

"Debra, we're trying to sort out what happened with Mr. Bainbridge. His security man had collared a shoplifter at the store just after 1:30. Bainbridge told me he called Detective Estes on his direct line. I questioned him specifically about that, and he showed me the business card Brian gave him Wednesday."

Debra nodded.

"But I wasn't here at 1:30," Brian snapped.

"Right," said Michael. "Brian and I took lunch at the Pizza Hut, then I went to the courthouse, and Brian tells me he went straight to the district attorney's office. He says there's no way Ralph Bainbridge spoke to him on the phone this afternoon."

"The call didn't come through me," Debra said.

"No, it couldn't have, unless he'd dialed 911 or the police station number and the dispatcher transferred the call. I've checked their logs, and that didn't happen. I just wanted your input on this, to make sure there hasn't been a mix-up somewhere."

"You'd better believe there was a mix-up," Brian said angrily. "If I'd gotten the call, I'd have been there. I've been waiting for this. I talked to him and his security people last Wednesday and told them how to set the guy up, for crying out loud."

"All right," Michael said quietly. "Go arrange the bail hearing and transport for the prisoner to the county jail, then file your paperwork."

Brian stalked out, not looking at either of them. Seconds later, the door to his office down the hall slammed.

Debra looked unhappily at Michael. "So, what really happened?"

"You got me. Bainbridge swears he talked to Brian. Brian swears he didn't."

"So, Mr. Bainbridge talked to someone, who he *thought* was Brian."

Michael shoved his hands in his pockets and walked over to his lone eye-level window and looked out toward the park. Debra waited. He jingled his keys in his pocket, then faced her.

"That's got to be it, but who did he talk to?"

"If he's telling the truth and he dialed the number correctly, someone else had to pick up Brian's phone at his desk. Unless Brian's just plain lying."

Michael nodded. "It wasn't me. I was at the courthouse then, anyway."

"So, Johnny, Leon, or Jared."

"It could have been someone else."

"Who else would have been in here?"

"Any other officer *could* have been in here," he insisted. "Think. Did anyone from across the hall come over here after lunch?"

"I don't remember seeing anyone. Well, I saw Pete, but that was down near his office, not up here in our area."

"No uniformed officers?"

"I didn't see any. I realize that doesn't mean there weren't any."

"Dispatchers? Records clerks?"

"No."

"How about Zack?"

"I haven't seen him at all today."

"All right, listen to me." Michael walked toward her and glanced into the outer office, then closed the door. "We are going to try to establish where every one of those men was between 1:30 and 1:45. Check the detectives' reports first. If they were out on field work, the reports will say so. I'll see if I can find out about Zack without stirring anything up across the hall. I'll also call the DA and find out what time Brian arrived at his office."

Debra nodded.

"If this is another sabotage attempt, it's working." Michael checked his watch. "We've only got an hour, and I—" he broke off and stepped quickly to his desk, running his finger down the page on his open appointment book. "Whew! I thought I was late for an appointment, but it's tomorrow." He turned beseeching eyes on her. "Debra, do you think you could take on one more duty and keep my appointment book for me?"

"Yes, I'd be glad to."

"Thanks. Gretchen offered when I first came, but I thought I could do it myself. It seemed too stuffed-shirt, somehow. But the way things are going around here, I'm having trouble remembering where I'm supposed to be when. And now Brian tells me he had this meeting with the district attorney in his appointment book, and he didn't so much as mention it to me this morning while we were working on the case. We need a better system."

"You know, we really don't have very tight security here," Debra said thoughtfully. "We have badges and electronic doors and all that, but anyone who got access to this part of the building would pretty much have free rein. The men don't lock their offices half the time, and if I stepped into the break room, anyone could just walk in here and take a look at your appointment book or delve into our open case files."

"You're right. Anyone could have looked at Brian's appointment book and known he'd be out this afternoon. I've been depending on the department's security measures, but we're facing danger from within now, and they don't allow for that."

"If someone wants to make you look bad, all they need to do is pick up a file you've left on your desk and lose it."

"I'd have said that's ridiculous, but now it's totally believable." He paced to the window and back. "All right. We proceed with the investigation. I'll speak to all the men about security. Make sure your office door is locked when you leave, and I'll make sure mine is. If you're leaving the office during the day and I'm not here, lock the door."

"All right, and I'll lock your appointment book in my desk when I'm out of the room. Gretchen gave me keys to the file cabinets out there, but she said they're never locked."

Michael nodded. "Start using those keys. I'm sorry to involve you in this intrigue, Debra."

She was able to look into his penetrating brown eyes without panicking. Instead she wanted to grow closer to him and, if possible, protect him from danger. "I'm not sorry, Michael. If all this was happening and you didn't explain it to me, I'd be terrified."

The telephone rang in the outer office, and he quickly punched a button to transfer it to his phone before she could move toward the door.

"Detectives' Unit. Yes, Pete." He glanced toward Debra.

She gave him a slight smile and went out to her desk, where she checked the computer to see if the men had filed reports for the day yet. They hadn't. She glanced up as someone passed the doorway and saw Jared going toward his office, down the hall. She picked up her empty mug and sauntered out there, hoping she appeared casual as she stopped in his doorway.

"Hey, Jared. Busy this afternoon?"

"Yeah, kinda. I finally arrested the guy."

"What guy?"

"The one who clobbered those two elderly women at the nursing home last week."

"The nursing home people must be glad."

"Yes. It's going to be the top story on the evening news. I just got done with the reporters."

"I'll have to tape it. Channel 5?"

"And 2."

"So, you're a celebrity."

"For a minute or two."

"Was it someone who worked at the nursing home?"

"No, it was another resident. A disturbed old man. Beat them up with a cane. They were pretty sure he did it all along, but nobody actually saw him do it, except the victims. So I had to wait for them to recover to take their testimony. Meanwhile, the man's family were all upset because the nursing home director wanted to isolate him. The other residents were afraid of him, but I didn't have the evidence yet. But I've got things tied up pretty tight, now that old Mrs. Gunter's out of the hospital."

"So you booked the guy and sent him to Augusta?"

"Yes. Hearing at 10 a.m. tomorrow."

"Great. Congratulations. I can hardly wait to see your report."

Michael came out of their office and passed her in the hallway. He stopped a few paces down the hall and turned toward her. Debra went to join him.

"I'm going over to talk to Zack. Find out anything yet?"

"Well, Jared brought in his man from the nursing home after lunch."

"I'll check with Zack and see what time he was booked."

"Great. And listen, I wondered if we should go to an electronic calendar that you and the other detectives can all access online. I know it has some disadvantages. Brian's afraid of losing his calendar if the computers go down. But if it was password protected, only the five of you and I could see it, and you wouldn't be leaving your schedules lying around."

"That might be a good idea," Michael said, "but if it's one of my four men doing this, it wouldn't help."

"True." Debra made a face. "Maybe the paper version is better, but we'll need to keep yours locked up."

Michael went off to his meeting, and Debra glanced into Leon's office, but he wasn't there. She stopped in Johnny's doorway, almost across the hall from her own.

"Hi, Johnny."

"Hi, Debra." He was back to his upbeat self.

"How's it going?"

"Good. A trooper called and told me they found the stolen car I was looking for."

"So, your victim will be happy."

"Yup. The car's okay, the thief just ran it out of gas. It was down in Richmond, so the troopers will take fingerprints."

"You didn't have to go to Richmond?"

"Nope."

"What are you working on now?"

"Missing persons case."

"Guess I didn't hear about that."

Johnny reached for the coffee mug that said *I'm available.* "It's a fifteen-year-old girl, missing since yesterday. Didn't show up at school this morning. The parents are agitated."

"So, you had them in here?"

"No, I went over to their house. They let the daughter go to her friend's yesterday, and she never came back. The friend says she never arrived at her house. Could be a runaway, I don't know." He sipped his coffee and put the mug down. "I hope it's a runaway."

"Well, I'll let you do your paperwork."

He looked at his watch. "Maybe I'll get my reports done and be out of here on time, for once."

Debra returned to her office and wrapped up her tasks for the day. It was ten past five when Michael returned.

"Good, you're still here." He stopped beside her desk and pulled out his pocket notebook. "Perkins says Brian was definitely at his office by 1:30. Zack claims he was at his desk or in the duty room during the time Bainbridge's phone call came in."

"So he couldn't have been over here in our area."

"Probably not, but not proven one hundred percent. Jared made a video while he was booking his prisoner, time 1:20 to 1:35 p.m."

Debra frowned. "So...could he have been back over here in time to intercept the phone call?"

"I doubt it. It's iffy. The prisoner was taken to the county jail after that."

"Did Jared stay with him?"

"Actually, no. After booking, he turned him over to Zack, and Zack assigned a patrolman to watch the prisoner until the transportation was ready."

"Why don't we have a holding cell? I've wondered about that before."

"They used to have cells, but the state and federal regulations on holding someone in a lockup have gotten so complicated that it's simpler for a small department to avoid it. You'd have to have someone check on the prisoner every fifteen minutes, and the liability issues are enormous. So we either bail them out or send them to the county jail."

"Who took Jared's prisoner to Augusta?"

"Two of Zack's officers."

"Where was Jared?"

"That's the iffy part. If he came straight back here—to start paperwork, or whatever—he might just possibly have been able to pick up Brian's phone when Bainbridge called."

Debra picked up a pen and chewed the end of it. "If I could just remember who went through the hallway around that time, but there's so much coming and going! If my phone's busy, I don't notice who's in the hall."

"And we don't have security cameras in this hallway. Maybe we should."

"You said Jared taped the booking?"

"Yes, the officers usually do that. It's optional, but it's for their own protection, especially if the prisoner is violent. The guy can't turn around and sue the officer for brutality if we've got the whole thing on tape."

"Well, Johnny tells me he was in and out, interviewing and such. He filed his report and left. Everyone's gone but Leon, I think. He came in late, and I think he's still working on his reports."

Michael put his notebook away. "I'll take a look at Johnny and Jared's reports. I didn't get to speak to the men about security. Maybe we should schedule a unit meeting for 8 a.m."

Debra unlocked her desk drawer and took out his appointment book.

"Done," she said, writing *Unit meeting on security* as the first item on Wednesday's page. Michael went into the inner office, leaving the door open.

As she checked to make sure all the file cabinets were locked, Leon looked in from the hallway.

"I'm heading home. Just filed my report."

"Leon, wait a sec." Michael appeared in his doorway. "Did you lock up tonight?"

"No, do I need to?"

"Well, yes, I think so. We've had a few incidents lately. I'm calling a meeting in the morning to talk about it, but I think you fellows need to exercise a little caution right now."

"I heard what happened to Brian. Did that get straightened out?" Leon's dark eyes were somber behind his glasses.

"Not really, and I don't want it happening again. Have you noticed any of these incidents—pranks or nuisances, things that slowed you down, maybe?"

"Not unless you count losing my pager."

"When did this happen?"

"This morning. I thought I left it on my desk, but—" Leon nodded. "Right. I'll lock my office."

He left, and Debra gathered her purse, sweater, and lunch bag.

"I'm ready to go home, Michael. Did you look at the reports?"

"All but Leon's. So far, I don't see an airtight alibi for anyone but Brian for this phone call thing."

She sighed. "Well, I'll see you later. I've locked my desk drawer and the files."

"Fine, I'll get the door when I leave." He stood with one hand on the door jamb, looking at her, and she thought for a moment he was going to say something else. Maybe he would ask her to go to the basketball game, after all. Debra toyed with accepting, but, no, she didn't think she could sit on the bleachers watching him play while the other church members watched her and speculated. He smiled and nodded briefly, and Debra went out.

Chapter 14

"Debra, the boys are home."

"You're so funny, Mom."

"All right, the men are home."

Debra put aside her letter to Julie and stood up. "I'm sure Grant, at least, would appreciate being referred to as a man."

She went downstairs and greeted her father, Grant, and Michael as they came in.

"You should have been there, Debra," Henry said. "They pulled it out at the last minute. Mike passed to Jason, and Jason passed to Grant, and Grant just drove right in for a lay-up." He pulled three cartons of ice cream from the freezer and set them on the kitchen table.

"It was awesome," Grant agreed, taking bowls from the cupboard. His damp hair clung to his forehead. "We really had teamwork tonight, right, Mike?"

Michael leaned against the counter, smiling. "Yeah. We did it right tonight."

Debra tried not to stare at him, snatching glances now and then. The casual Michael, in khaki slacks and a black pullover, was very distracting. His hair wasn't as disciplined as usual, sticking up boyishly in the back. She was glad Belinda wasn't there, whispering, "He is *too* cute!"

"So, who are you playing next week?" she asked, opening a drawer for spoons.

"Nobody, we just practice next week," Grant said. "But the week after, we're playing Clinton Baptist, and they have a really good team."

"You ought to go, Debbie," Henry said.

"Maybe I'll wait until they're facing another team they have a chance to beat."

"You're cruel." Grant heaped his bowl with rocky road ice cream, and put just a dab of cherry vanilla on the side.

Ellen opened a plastic box of cookies. "There are a few of Debra's cookies left. I don't suppose you boys would eat them?"

Debra gave her a pointed look.

"Men," said her mother hastily. "Men love chocolate chip cookies, right?"

Debra smiled and shook her head. "What will you have, Michael?"

"Definitely a cookie."

"What kind of ice cream? Rocky road, cherry vanilla, or coffee?"

"Is it decaf?" he asked with a grin.

"No, it's high-test."

"Cherry vanilla, I guess."

She fixed his dish for him, and they all sat down in the kitchen. Grant continued giving the highlights of the game between bites, until he scraped the bottom of his bowl.

"Better get ready for bed, son," Henry said.

"Okay, but I need to show Mike the specs for the science fair."

"All right, but make it snappy."

"I took my shower at the gym, Dad."

"I know. Go get your stuff."

Grant bounded out of the kitchen.

"I apologize, Mike, I've tried to remind Grant to address you properly—"

"It's all right, Mr. Griffin," Michael assured him. "I don't mind if the boys call me Mike. I'm not *that* old, and I think there's some good in a boy being on a first-name basis with a police officer."

"You've got a point there." Henry stood up and reached for Ellen's empty dish, taking it with his to the sink.

"More ice cream?" Debra asked.

"No, I'm stuffed." Michael surrendered his bowl to her.

"So, what's the science fair thing?" she asked, rinsing all the bowls.

"Well, Grant has an interest in ballistics, and I told him I'd get him some research material, if your parents don't mind him going in this direction."

"What sort of project does he have in mind?" Henry asked.

"We have an electronic system that will match spent bullets to the guns that fired them. Grant wants to fire several bullets, then examine them and show how the computer tells they were fired from the same gun. He'll do a report explaining how the system works, and the criteria the program uses for matching the bullets. It's quite complex, and virtually foolproof."

Grant came back into the room with several sheets of paper.

"This is what Mr. Blaine gave us. You have to have an exhibit, a demonstration, and a report."

Michael scanned the papers. "Pretty thorough."

"Yeah. Do you think I can do it? I asked Mr. Blaine, and he said if I could get enough material the topic was okay."

"I think I could take you into the station, say some evening, and demonstrate the system to you, if we provided our own bullets," Michael said.

"Well, Dad has a deer rifle. Could we use that?"

"It would be easier to recover .22 bullets, I think." Michael laid the papers on the table. "We could set that up without going to a shooting range."

Henry picked up the papers and squinted at them. "There's a gravel pit just down the road. A lot of people sight in their rifles there."

"Can we do our shooting there?" Grant asked eagerly.

"Sure," said Michael. "Tell you what, are you free Saturday?"

"I'm working from eight to two at the grocery store, but after that I could do it."

"Great. I'll bring my .22 over around three Saturday afternoon, and we'll go do some shooting. That all right, Mr. Griffin?" He turned to Henry.

"Guess so. I might even tag along, if you don't mind."

"That would be great." Michael looked at Debra, and she thought for a moment he was going to suggest she go, too, but he just smiled at her.

Her heart lurched a little, but the panicky feeling was at bay.

"Well, it's getting late, Grant," his father said.

"Okay. Thanks, Mike." Grant picked up his papers and headed for the stairs. "Good night."

"Empty your laundry," his mother called after him.

"Well, Ellen, are we going to read tonight?" Henry asked.

"I suppose so. We left off at a very exciting place."

"You'll excuse us?" Henry asked, standing up.

After they had left the room, Michael noted, "Your father's very tactful. What are they reading?"

Debra tried to quell the embarrassment her parents' obvious retreat caused her. "They always read out loud to each other. I think right now it's a Zane Grey, but they must have read five hundred books out loud since they got married."

"Do you listen?"

"Sometimes. They've read all kinds of things to us kids over the years. *Hans Brinker* and *Robinson Crusoe*, lots of children's books and classics. As we got older, they moved into biographies and mysteries."

"Do you mind me helping Grant?"

"Not at all."

"I'll supply him with books and help him do the test firing and identification. I'll show him how it works, but I'll make him do it himself."

She nodded. "It should make a very interesting project."

"So, my encroaching on your private life is ... acceptable?"

"I think it's becoming less cataclysmic."

"Merely calamitous?"

He reached for her hand, and she let him hold it, their fingers interlaced on the table.

"I'm still breathing." She was startled that she'd said it out loud. "Sorry."

Michael smiled. "It's a good sign."

"Any progress on Mr. X?"

"Well, I looked at Leon's report. I couldn't nail down his whereabouts between 1:30 and 1:45 from that. He was probably in the office."

"So, another suspect without an alibi."

"Yes. I think at tomorrow's meeting I'll lay it all on the table. Mr. X must know I'm after him. He can't think I'm too stupid to know what he's up to."

Debra looked at him carefully. "Do you think you'll be in danger if you bring it out in the open?"

He squeezed her hand. "No more than I am already. So far there hasn't been an actual physical attack."

"You think he'd go that far?"

"It seems unlikely. Let's talk about something more pleasant."

"Like what?"

"Can I come get you for prayer meeting tomorrow night?"

"I can see you there."

"I'd rather come get you."

She hesitated.

"You're still breathing," he reminded her, although her breath was choppier than it had been.

She looked up at him and swallowed. "All right."

His smile always affected her, but now instead of terrifying her, it melted her resistance, and she knew she wanted to go with him the next evening. She wanted him to come for her so he could spend a little extra time with her, and escort her, take care of her, and bring her home afterward to her family.

"I'm going to put my bid in early this week for Friday, too. Do you have plans?"

"No."

"Not going to Belinda's?"

"Not this week."

"Will you go with me?"

"Where?"

"Anywhere." His brown eyes were magnetic, and she couldn't look away. "You choose," he invited.

She took a deep breath. "*No, No, Nanette.*"

"At the community theater?"

"Yes. Brian's wife, Sheila, has a part."

"Terrific. Dinner first?"

"If you want."

He smiled. "I'll have to ask my secretary to make us a reservation tomorrow."

"What if she's jealous?"

He laughed. "No, I'll do it myself. Debra, I—" He stopped and looked deep into her eyes. "How's the anxiety level?"

"Not calm, exactly, but manageable, I think." Her voice was very low.

He touched her cheek gently with his fingertips. "And now?"

"Rising rapidly."

Slowly, he lowered his hand. "Okay, we'll leave it at that." His other hand still held hers on the table, and he gave it a soft squeeze. "I'd better go, so we can get some rest and be fresh in the morning."

"Thanks for coming," she whispered.

He hesitated, then leaned toward her and kissed her cheek, where his fingers had touched it. She knew she could be in his arms in half a second, and her heart began to pound. She raised her eyes to his and caught her breath.

"G-good night."

He sat there another moment, his eyes teeming with unspoken thoughts.

"Really rising now," she whispered.

He nodded. "Good night."

She stayed where she was, and heard him pause in the living room doorway and speak to her parents.

"Good night, Mike," her father said cordially.

"Come again," Ellen called.

Debra waited until the door had closed. She imagined him walking to his car. She heard the car door close and the engine start. When he had driven away and she couldn't hear the motor any longer, she rose and walked slowly to the living room.

"Well, dear, did you have a nice visit?" Ellen asked. She sat on the couch, piecing a quilt block by hand, with her scissors, thread, and calico patches set out before her on the coffee table.

Debra nodded.

"He's a nice young man," Henry said, laying Zane Grey upside down on his lap.

"He—he's picking me up tomorrow for prayer meeting."

"What, he can't wait until he gets to church to see you?" her father asked with a laugh. "He sees you all day."

"Hush, Henry. You remember how it is." Ellen eyed him anxiously. "Don't you?"

"Yes, dear, I remember."

"You look worried, Debra."

Slowly, the smile came out. "I'm very happy, Mom. Can you be worried and happy at the same time?"

"Can't see why you'd want to." Ellen reached for the scissors.

"Why can't you just be happy?" Henry picked up the book.

"Maybe I can. I hope so. But I think if I let myself, I'll burst."

Henry shook his head. "Don't know why Michael would worry you. He's made of good steel. The deacons are meeting with him Sunday before the evening service about his application for membership. Pastor says he's solid right down the line."

"Thanks, Daddy."

"God doesn't want you worrying, honey."

"I know." She bent and kissed both her parents, then went up the stairs, hugging to herself the memory of his nearness and his touch.

137

Chapter 15

Debra notified each of the detectives Wednesday morning that Michael had called for a meeting in the interview room. By ten past eight they all were assembled, Brian testily eyeing his watch because of the shoplifter's arraignment he was expected to appear at that morning.

Michael entered and set his briefcase on the oak table. "I'll keep this short because we're all busy." He glanced toward Debra. "You'll stay, please, Debra." She sat in one of the straight chairs with an open notebook, and he faced the four detectives.

"We've had some incidents in the unit lately that concern me, and I want to urge you all to be cautious. Someone is trying to make us look bad, and we can't afford it. Until I find out who's behind it, we need to be extremely careful. I don't want any of you to have his reputation impugned, but it's gone beyond that. Things are happening that keep us from doing our best. We not only look incompetent, but if we can't get the job done, we *are* incompetent. I'm concerned that next someone's going to be injured." He looked each of them in the eye in turn.

"Watch out for nuisance pranks, and report anything unusual to me. I'm going to get to the bottom of this, and I need your help. I need to know everything that goes on in this unit. If something happens for no apparent reason—your pen disappears, or you're delayed unexpectedly—tell me. If you get a suspicious phone call, or your reports are tampered with, I need to know. Understood?"

They stirred and gazed at each other.

"You think someone intercepted Brian's call yesterday?" Johnny asked.

"Yes, I do. I also think there may be sabotage behind the clip missing from the evidence locker in your school case."

"Well, thanks, Sarge," said Johnny. "I thought you had me pegged as just plain stupid."

"No, you're not stupid. None of you is stupid, or you wouldn't have made it this far. I want to keep you functioning in top form. That means no more disappearing reports and pagers, no more minor squad car damage, no fake phone calls. We need to work together to keep this unit at its best."

"Hold it," said Brian. He looked hard at Michael. "You think one of us is doing these things?"

"I honestly don't know. What do you think?"

"Well, what happened to me with Bainbridge made me pretty mad, I'll tell you. But I wouldn't expect one these guys to do it."

"Maybe someone took the message and forgot to contact you," Jared suggested.

"Who, you for instance?" Brian snapped.

"Don't look at me. I'm just saying, if someone *did* make a mistake, maybe they're embarrassed to admit it."

"How about your headlight?" Brian asked. "Was that a mistake one of us won't admit? When it's a reprimand in your file, you won't be so calm."

"Settle down, Brian." Michael held his gaze for a moment. "I know you've got court this morning, and you're also working on the bookstore case, so you've got plenty of places to channel your energy today. I'm just saying, everybody be careful. And watch out for each other. If you see anything out of the ordinary, tell me, and make sure your offices are secure when you go out. Lock up."

"All the time?"

"Quit whining, Johnny," said Jared.

"I think that would be best, at least until this business stops," Michael said. "That way, we'll be certain no one has come in here—whether it's an officer, a civilian employee, or a visitor—and accessed your equipment or your files."

Leon said, "Since you mention it, has anyone seen my pager?"

"Someone took it?" Brian asked.

Leon shrugged. "Maybe I dropped it somewhere."

140

"I'll give a quick rundown on suspicious events so far, and if anyone can shed any light on them, speak up now." Michael opened his briefcase and took out a notepad. "I had a phony telephone message, and my dog got loose. Could have been accidental, or could have been intentional. Jared had a headlight knocked out. Leon's pager has disappeared, as did an ammo clip Johnny logged as evidence. A report of Brian's was tampered with, probably on his computer. You all know about Brian's headache yesterday with the phone message that went astray."

They looked at each other.

"Could it be coincidental?" Leon asked.

"Man, I hope not," Michael said earnestly. "That's way too many goof-ups in so short a time. If we're really that careless, we're not the cops I thought we were."

"So, what can we do?" Johnny asked.

"I want you all to keep Debra posted on your whereabouts. I know it's constricting, but under the circumstances, I think it's necessary. You don't have to keep checking in, but give us a general idea of where you're going to be. I'll help Debra set up a schedule in her office so that I can look at it in there anytime and have a pretty good idea where all of you are. Brian, you'd better get over to the courthouse. Check in with Debra when you get back."

Brian rose. "Do you have any idea what the motive is on this?"

Michael paused. "I do have an idea, but there's no proof. It could be something totally unrelated, but ... given the nature of the incidents, I think they're being instigated by someone within the department."

"Why?" Jared asked.

"Who hates us that much?" Leon took his glasses off and held them critically up to the light, examining the lenses.

"Either this person's a phenomenal hacker, or someone came inside this area to delete Brian's report," Michael said.

"Unless his computer just ate it," said Johnny.

"I left the room for two minutes, and when I came back it was gone," Brian said belligerently.

"Enough," said Michael. "Brian, get going. Jared, I think you have some work to do on your case from Pleasant Days?"

"Yes, there's a hearing at ten. I need to make some phone calls and pull my file together."

"All right, go."

Jared followed Brian out the door, and Debra jotted down their plans.

"Johnny, what's on your agenda today?" Michael asked.

"I'm going to check with S.P. on the stolen car. If they've got a match on the fingerprints, I might have to follow up on that. And there's the missing girl."

"Anything come in overnight on that?"

"I didn't have a chance to check yet."

"Better make that a top priority. Call the State Police after you check on the girl's status."

"Okay."

"And tell Debra if you're leaving the building," Michael instructed.

Johnny nodded, but he didn't look happy.

"Leon, can you take a new case?"

"Well, there are a couple of open cases I've been working on, but nothing urgent."

"Good. I need you this morning. Two patrolmen went to River Street on a domestic last night. Things had calmed down by the time they got there, but they got the feeling something wasn't right. The night sergeant left Zack a detailed report, and he asked me to put a man on it this morning. Come into my office, and I'll brief you."

Johnny went into his office, and Leon followed Michael into his. Debra went to her desk and retrieved e-mail and voice mail messages.

A few minutes later, Leon came out of Mike's office.

"Do a background on this guy," Michael said, following him to the hallway door. "Zack feels there's cause for further investigation."

"Right," said Leon.

Michael turned to Debra as Leon left. "I talked to Pete, and we decided it's vital to keep track of where each of our men is. The best solution we could come up with was a tracking board."

"Do you think it will help?"

"I hope so. It surely would have helped yesterday. Hang on."

He stepped back into his office and returned with a wipe-off white board.

"You've thought this out," she said.

"Yes." He produced a black marker and drew a grid on the board. Across the top he wrote Beaulieu, Dore, Estes, Young, and Van Sant. Down the side he blocked out time periods: 8 a.m., 10 a.m., noon, 1 p.m., 3 p.m.

"You can put exact times in the squares," he said to Debra, and she nodded. "Okay, so what have we got today?"

She took the marker from him, and under Beaulieu, for the first block wrote *office*. Under Dore, she wrote *office*, and at 10 a.m., *court*. Under Estes, in the first block, she wrote *9 a.m. court*. For Young, she wrote *office* in the first square, and for Van Sant, *office* in the first block, and *4 p.m. mtg w/ DA* in the last.

"Good, it's a start," Michael said with satisfaction. He nodded at the side wall. "Can I take that landscape down and hang it there?"

"Sure, but I'm thinking this might make us less secure in a way. Anyone who looks in here can immediately see where all our detectives are, and know who's out of the way for an hour. It might make sabotage easier."

"True. But it's never a secret within the unit where the guys are. If someone is going to lie about it to us, it won't be any different if it's on the board. But remember to lock the door when you're out."

The phone rang, and as Debra answered it, Michael replaced the nondescript landscape print with the white board.

"One moment, please." Debra put the caller on hold. "Michael, the Lions Club wants you to speak at their meeting next Thursday."

"When and where?"

"Six o'clock, at their clubhouse on Park Street."

"I guess I can. Try to find out what they expect."

"Do you want to talk to him?"

"Not really. My secretary can set it up. You can write the speech, too. Just kidding," he assured her, as she stared at him wildly. He went into his office smiling, and Debra clicked back to her caller's line.

"Yes, sir, the sergeant is available. Did you have a topic you wanted him to address?"

Johnny came to the doorway. "Mike in?"

Debra nodded, scribbling frantically on her notepad, *Current crime level in Rushton.* Johnny walked past her to the communicating door and rapped on the jamb.

"I'll make the suggestion to him, but it's all right if he wants to go a different direction? All right. Twenty minutes. Got it. You're welcome."

Johnny addressed the sergeant from the doorway. "Mike, the state police ID'd the car thief from the fingerprints, and I'm going over to his address on Lark Street with some uniforms, but my vest is gone from my locker."

Michael came to the doorway.

"What do you mean, it's gone from your locker?"

"It's not there."

"When did you see it last?"

"Well, I wore it when we went to the school last week. I guess that was the last time. But it was in my locker yesterday."

"You're sure?"

"Yes. I got something out of there before I left, and it was there."

"And you locked the locker."

"Well ..." Johnny winced and glanced toward Debra.

144

"Come on, Johnny, that's why they call them lockers."
Michael's perturbation was evident.

"I never lock it. I mean, who's going to steal a bulletproof vest? They've all got their own."

"Don't you keep other stuff in there?"

"Sometimes. An extra shirt, or my jacket when it's cold."

"And you never lock it?"

"Only if I put something important in there."

Michael ran a finger under the side of his shirt collar, looking toward the new white board. "You know how much those things cost?"

"Well ... yeah." Johnny shrugged. "If it counts, I locked my office door just now."

Michael shook his head. "What about the other guys? Do they lock their lockers?"

"I'm thinking not."

"Come on."

Michael left the room with Johnny following contritely. Debra took Michael's appointment book out of the drawer and entered his engagement for the Lions Club meeting.

Her telephone rang. "This is Brian. I'm done at court, and I'm going over to the adult bookstore to make sure they're obeying the injunction we got. Am I supposed to tell you that?"

"Yes, thank you. When do you expect to be back?"

"I don't know. Before noon."

"I'll page you if we need you."

Michael and Johnny came back from the locker room.

"So, Jared and Brian get brownie points for locking their lockers," Johnny said. "What do I do about my vest?"

"Report it to the deputy chief and use mine today," said Michael, walking briskly into his office. The detective sergeant had his own washroom and kept his extra clothing and equipment in there, rather than in the men's locker room. Johnny lounged, frowning, in the doorway until Michael came back and handed him the Kevlar vest.

"Bring it back," Mike said.

"Right."

"You said this is the car thief you're going after?"

"Well, his prints were all over the stolen vehicle."

"I'd better go with you."

"Then you need your vest." Johnny held it out.

Debra thought Michael was counting silently to ten. He took the vest and said through his teeth, "Go to the deputy chief's office. Tell Pete you lost your vest and ask him if he can issue you another one. Come get me when you're ready to go to Lark Street."

Johnny's face brightened. "Leon's vest was in his locker when you checked it."

Michael stared at him.

"Yes, sir." Johnny turned away.

Michael looked at Debra. She put her hand over her mouth to smother a laugh.

"I'm sorry," she gasped. "It's not funny. His vest is missing, and maybe it's Mr. X again. Johnny's in danger without it, not to mention the cost, but—"

Michael smiled. "There's one in every unit, I guess. I'm overdue for coffee. Tell me when he comes back, but I don't want to see him unless he's wearing body armor."

"You *did* lock Leon's locker, didn't you?" Debra asked.

"What do you think?"

He disappeared in search of coffee, and Debra turned her attention to her work. Leon arrived a few minutes later.

"Debra, I'm heading out on this domestic case Mike gave me."

"All right." She walked to the white board and wrote in Leon's second block *River St. domestic.*

Leon hesitated. "A funny thing happened just now. I guess I should tell Mike."

Michael came to his doorway with the blue mug in his hand. "What's up, Leon?"

"Oh, hi. Well, I went to the locker room just now, and my locker was locked. I know I didn't lock it, so somebody else did."

Michael tried to keep a straight face, and Debra turned away to hide her smile.

"That was me," Michael admitted. "One of the men had something taken from his locker, so I went in and locked the ones that weren't locked."

"Oh."

"I noticed your vest was in your locker when I checked it."

"Well, yeah, but it's not in there now," Leon said.

Michael's face paled, the humor vaporized. "It's gone?"

"No, I'm wearing it." Leon opened the front of his jacket to display the vest. "I'm going out on this domestic, and—"

Michael stepped forward and clapped him on the shoulder. "You just gave me a turn. I thought you meant someone stole it."

"No, but you know what?"

"What?"

"When I went to get my vest, my pager was in the locker."

"The pager you lost yesterday?"

"Uh-huh."

Michael's eyes narrowed. "So … you put it in the locker and forgot about it?"

"No, I don't think so. I was thinking maybe someone took it as a joke, but your lecture this morning sobered everyone up, and whoever took it stuck it in my locker so I'd get it back without me knowing who did it."

"You may be right, but I don't think it was a joke. I think it was meant to inconvenience you. Keep your locker locked from now on, all right?"

"Sure, Mike."

"Now, you said you're going over to River Street? What did you find out?"

"Zilch. I think the name's an alias. No DMV record for that name in this area. I thought I'd talk to a few neighbors, and maybe shake the tree."

"Take someone with you," Michael said firmly.

"You think?"

"Yes, I do. I'd go with you myself, but there's another matter I have to tend to. Go over to Zack Brown. I'll call him right now and tell him you're coming, and that you need a patrolman."

"I hate to take a guy in uniform. What if the subject's a runner?"

Michael caught Debra's eye. "Is Brian out of court yet?"

"Yes, he called in. He was going to check the bookstore."

"How about Jared?"

"No, his hearing's at ten." They all looked toward the clock. It was quarter to ten.

"Page Brian," Michael said, turning back toward his office. "If he hasn't got his vest on, he needs it."

Debra paged Brian, and he called in two minutes later. Meanwhile, Leon paced and hummed.

"Detective Estes."

"Brian, the sergeant wants you to back Leon up on River Street. Body armor required."

"He's over there now?"

"No, Leon's here. Would you like to speak to him?"

She handed the phone to Leon and took a handful of documents to the filing cabinets.

"Yeah, Brian, it started as a domestic, but we think the guy's using an alias, and the patrolmen who were there last night thought they were hiding something. I want to check him out, get a look at him if I can. Okay, I'll wait."

Leon hung up and said, "He's coming back here to get his vest, then going with me."

"Good." Debra wrote on the white board in Brian's 10 a.m. block *River St. domestic.*

At that moment, Johnny came in sheepishly, sporting a bulletproof vest over his dress shirt, carrying his suit jacket, and went directly to Michael's door.

"All set, Sarge."

Michael came out, putting his jacket on. "Did you check on that missing girl?"

"Oh, yeah," Johnny said with a grin. "She's home. Spent the night with another friend. She was mad at Mom and Dad, I think; wanted to scare them a little. It worked."

Michael nodded and turned to Debra. "Ask the dispatcher to track us, please. We'll take Johnny's car to Lark Street. Did you get Brian?"

"Yes, he's coming in to assist Leon."

Leon nodded at Mike.

"All right. Be careful." Michael hesitated, looking back at Debra. She smiled at him in spite of the fear that grabbed her when she saw him wearing the protective vest. He nodded, and she knew there were things he would have said if they were alone.

She called the com room.

"Wendy, Sergeant Van Sant and Detective Young are on a case on Lark Street. The sergeant has requested tracking."

"So." Leon leaned on the edge of her desk as she began typing. "You and the sergeant are pretty friendly now?"

The blush began.

"What do you mean?"

"He seems to think highly of you."

Her face was scarlet. She continued typing. "Leon, I'm his secretary."

"Well, yeah, but ... tell me I didn't see something there."

Debra kept typing. "Becoming an object of gossip in this office would upset me very much."

"Oh, you're too much of a lady for that, I think." He looked down at her, and she bit her bottom lip. Leon persisted, "Mike seems to have loosened up a little. Do you think he'd accept a dinner invitation if Calla and I issued one?"

"I really don't know."

"I just wasn't sure if he wanted to socialize. He's seemed a little—I dunno, aloof."

"I think he's just a private person," Debra said, still blushing.

"Well, that's okay, but it can be lonely, you know?"

She said nothing.

"So, maybe we'll ask him to supper some night, and he could … bring a friend?" It was definitely a question.

"We—we haven't been on an actual date, Leon," Debra faltered.

"Oh. Okay. Well, maybe later on."

Her hands stopped typing. She looked up at him, blushing even harder.

Leon said, "I figure it's a matter of time. I mean, the way he looked at you."

"Please—" Debra stood up abruptly.

"I didn't mean anything. I think it's nice."

She wondered suddenly if Leon were the saboteur, intent on distracting her from her work.

"You know how Calla and I met?" he asked.

She took a deep breath and met his eyes. "How?"

"I was a patrolman, and I got called for a 10-55. Car accident. Guess who was driving the white Saab."

"Calla?"

"Nope. Her mother. I met Calla in the hospital waiting room."

"Was her mother all right?"

"Broken collar bone."

"So, not too serious?"

"No, but I got to do some comforting until she found out for sure."

"That's very sweet, Leon." Debra sat down and returned to her typing.

"Guess I'll wait in the break room," Leon said.

Chapter 16

As noon approached, Debra looked more and more often at the clock. Neither team had returned from its field assignment, and she was staving off worry by working hard and throwing prayers upward whenever she found herself dwelling on possibilities.

Jared had called in from the courthouse and told her he was having lunch at home. She pulled her brown bag from the drawer and ate at her desk, pouncing on the phone each time it rang. She considered calling dispatch to see if Johnny and Michael were checking in on schedule, but resisted the urge. Instead, she took the iris mug into Michael's office and made a new pot of decaf.

At 12:45 Trina, one of the dispatchers, called her.

"Debra, Sergeant Van Sant asked me to tell you that he and Johnny Young are coming back to the station with a subject in custody, so you can adjust their schedule if you need to."

"Thank you, Trina." Debra hoped she sounded cool, and that Trina had no inkling of the relief her call brought.

Half an hour later, Michael came in. Debra stood up, looking anxiously for signs of strain.

"Been worried?" he asked, walking toward her with a smile.

"No. Well, yes. This is the first time I've had to sit here while you were on a case like that, where you thought tracking was needed. Trina called."

"Good. I asked her to. Thought you might be wondering and fretting a little."

"I prayed a lot."

He nodded, and stepped closer to her. "I didn't want you to worry, so as soon as we had the suspect in custody, I asked dispatch to call you."

"Thank you. He didn't give you any trouble?"

"No, Johnny's booking him now, and his lawyer's on the way." He peeled off his suit jacket and opened the Velcro at the side of the bulletproof vest. "By the way, Leon and Brian came in just behind us. The man on River Street was using an alias, all

151

right. They found out he's wanted on a warrant in Auburn. I called the courthouse for a search warrant, and they're going back and search the apartment."

"What's he wanted for?" Debra asked, very aware of Michael's nearness.

"Drugs. That was a good call. Leon and Zack and the patrolmen who first smelled a rat all deserve a citation."

"Will it outweigh the sabotage?"

"I don't know."

"Seems like Zack is the only one Mr. X hasn't bothered," she mused.

"That we know of. Did you eat?"

"Sort of. There are oodles of phone messages on your desk."

"Okay, I'll look at them, then I'll get some lunch."

She nodded. "Maybe now that they all know you're alert, the sabotage will stop."

*****

Debra was content as she prepared for prayer meeting that evening, with only an occasional stab of nerves when she thought of Michael coming to pick her up. In her imagination, she couldn't get past the moment of his arrival. First she pictured her father opening the door, saying, "Come right in, Sergeant. What are your intentions?" Then she imagined Grant letting him in, asking, "What do you see in my sister, anyway? She doesn't know anything about sports." Or her mother, fussing over Michael and telling him, "You should have come for supper. Debra made the most scrumptious casserole!"

She chose a checked jumper that she had never worn to work, and a crisp white blouse with an eyelet collar. She took pains over her hair, wishing Julie were home to do the job.

Before she felt ready, she heard his car in the driveway. She grabbed her Bible and purse and ran down the stairs, but her father was already in the entry, swinging the door open.

"Mike, come right in," he said heartily. "I'll see if Debra's—"

152

"I'm right here, Dad." She stepped up behind him. "Hello, Michael." His dark eyes glittered, and her shyness returned, making her look away.

"All set?" he asked.

"Yes." They went out to his car, and she knew they would be early, but she didn't care. He was wearing the suit he had worn to work, with a clean light blue shirt and a snappy gray print necktie she didn't recognize. She wondered if he had an innate sense of fashion, or if someone else had picked it out. Or maybe it was his bearing that lent a flair to his appearance, no matter what he wore.

It was warm, and Michael switched on the air conditioning. "Tomorrow's the first of June."

Debra nodded. "It's just about my favorite time of year, except for the bugs."

"I like fall," he said.

"It's pretty, but it's too close to winter."

He parked under an oak tree in the farthest corner of the empty church parking lot, put the windows down, and sat looking at her. She felt the color infusing her face and wished she could will it away.

"Any panicky moments today?" he asked quietly.

"Besides now?"

He chuckled, and she was able to laugh with him.

"No, just—when you were out with Johnny." She traced a line in the design of her jumper with one finger. "I *was* worried."

"Things went peacefully. You just never know. Better to take precautions."

"I know. It was sobering, though, to see you put on the vest."

"The patrolmen wear them all the time."

She nodded. "I'll just have to get used to it. I don't think like a cop, I guess." She wondered if she would ever be able to watch him put on the protective gear without imagining the worst.

"Not nervous now?"

"Maybe just a bit, but ... nothing like before."

153

He smiled. "Good. I'm hoping for a complete cure, you know." The breeze ruffled his hair. "I talked to Zack again this afternoon. I decided to tell him what I think is going on. If it's him, maybe it will deter him, just knowing I'm on it. If it's not him, well, I thought he ought to be watching out for himself."

"What did he say?"

"He seemed surprised at first. Of course, he knew about the ammo clip. But after he heard about the other stuff, he told me he'd had a strange call the other day. Someone reported an accident, and he sent two patrolmen out, but there was nothing there. Of course, we get a false report every once in a while. But he also had a requisition form disappear. He'd been filling it out at his desk one day last week and stepped away for a minute. When he came back, it was gone, and no one in the duty room or the com room could account for it." He sighed and gripped the steering wheel. "He could have made those things up to throw me off, but Zack seems like a genuinely nice guy. I hope it's not him."

"I was thinking the same today about Leon. He asked me if I thought you would go to supper at his house if he and his wife asked you. He's likable, but he didn't want to seem pushy. And I've never heard him say anything bad about anyone. How could he do bad things to people?"

Michael shook his head. "What if it's all in my mind, and no one's being malicious?"

"You said there were too many coincidences. Besides, we know someone intercepted Brian's call yesterday, and Johnny's vest and the clip did disappear."

"I talked it out with Pete tonight."

"You went back to the office?" she asked in surprise.

"Yes. I updated him. Leon's pager, Johnny's vest …"

"What did he say?"

Michael winced. "He said that if he has input on promotions for this gang, he'll have to knock Johnny out of the running, just for carelessness. Not locking his locker, and losing that clip."

"But if someone else took it out of the evidence locker—"

"No one could do that except Zack or Pete. I don't for a second believe it was Pete. If Zack didn't take it, then Johnny was somehow careless. Again."

"I suppose you're right."

"He's a good detective, has good instincts, but to be in management you have to stay on top of details. And Brian's too hot-headed. The deputy chief has to deal with personnel problems a lot. I just can't picture Brian handling that position with dignity."

Debra sat considering for several seconds, then raised her eyes to Michael's. "Maybe Mr. X doesn't need to do anything. If he's just patient, these men will betray themselves. The best man will be appointed."

"That's assuming Mr. X is a man without a fatal flaw. But he has to be somehow aberrant, or he wouldn't be doing these things."

"Hmm. I don't like to think about the evil Mr. X sitting back from now on and letting all the honest but imperfect candidates destroy themselves."

Michael shrugged. "Maybe the best thing would be to hire a deputy chief from outside when needed. Period."

"That wouldn't be fair to our men, would it? They're not all disqualified already, are they?"

"No, but, Debra, we may never find out who did these things."

Cars were gradually filling the church lot. "Time to go in," she said softly.

"Yes. Keep praying about this." He got out and went around to Debra's door and opened it for her.

Other parishioners greeted them and smiled. No eyebrows were raised, no surprise was displayed when they sat down together. Overnight, it seemed to Debra, they had become a couple. Her parents and Grant came in, and Grant went around the pew and came in the other end to sit beside Debra. Her parents smiled and sat on the other side of the aisle. Debra felt her apprehension drain away. She glanced up at Michael, and he

155

was smiling at her. In sharp contrast to her recurring panic, she felt very safe with him now. If her pulse was rapid, it was from anticipation, not fear.

"Are you okay?" he whispered.

"Yes. I was just wondering ... " She leaned toward him slightly. "Michael, what was I afraid of?"

*****

The office was quiet for the next two days. The detectives bent to Michael's discipline, keeping Debra apprised of their movements. She charted their activity on the white board and kept Michael informed. All were absorbed with their cases, and the competition for Pete Nye's job seemed to have been forgotten.

Debra's trepidation had eased into a subdued excitement when Michael was in the office. Her senses seemed more receptive when she knew he was in the next room. She heard him type and open drawers, smelled the coffee she usually ignored. The quiet murmur of his voice when he was on the telephone came to her through the open doorway. She could go for hours without seeing him, but still feel the consolation of his nearness. When he was in the same room, her pulse quickened, but without bringing apprehension.

On days when he was in the field for hours, she worked steadily and prayed for him, envisioning herself as his support system, performing the mundane chores that enabled him to be at his peak when pursuing a suspect, briefing reporters, or laying evidence before the district attorney. She began to take great satisfaction from the role she played in the unit, knowing at last that her work was valuable to all of the detectives.

But on Friday evening Debra was determined not to think about the police station or the saboteur. As she hurried home to prepare for the evening, she knew Michael was looking forward to their date as much as she was.

"Debra, look," Ellen cried when she entered the kitchen after work. Resplendent on the dining room table was a bouquet of yellow roses. "They came about an hour ago."

"For me?" She pulled the tiny card from its envelope. *Forgot to have you write it on the board—between city hall and the courthouse, I stopped at the florist. Michael.*

She held one bloom to her nose and shivered a little as she inhaled its sweetness. Her treatment had reached the stage where it was time to step into the elevator.

"Mom, can you help me with my hair?"

"Certainly, but it looks fine."

"No, it's got to be special tonight."

Debra was almost, but not quite, certain Michael would approve of the simple but elegant upsweep her mother achieved with her fine, dark blonde hair. She was sure when she opened the door to him and his eyes flared in admiration.

She sat across from him in *Le Chat Noir*, the town's finest restaurant, with delicate music in the background and light gleaming softly on his hair. She wore a single rose on her shoulder. Her midnight blue dress, shot through with a silver thread, sparkled subtly when she moved.

She hadn't had the dress out of its plastic wrapping since an evening of opera at college that spring. She knew it flattered her; her roommates had told her so, and her escort to the opera had practically drooled that evening. Afterward, Debra had felt let down that she had wasted the dress on her first and last date with a fellow who had turned out to be very disappointing. Somehow it had seemed that the perfect dress would ensure a perfect evening. It was her last date before she had gone home, disillusioned, with the extraneous diploma.

Michael's gaze never seemed to leave her face. They placed their order, and he reached across the table for her hand.

"You are beautiful." It was the first time anyone had said that to her, except her mother, and Debra hadn't really believed it then. Ellen was always trying to buck up her confidence. Self-

157

assurance had never been a problem for Julie and Rick, and Grant, the baby, seemed to have been born dauntless.

"It's the dress, I think," she faltered.

"No, the dress is nice, but it's you, Debra. I'm not talking about what you're wearing."

She pressed her lips firmly together and swallowed. "Thank you." It seemed inadequate, but he rewarded her with the smile that melted her.

"I'm so glad you came to work at the police station."

"We'd probably be strangers, nodding to each other occasionally at church functions if I hadn't," she said.

"No, I don't think I'd put up with that for long."

The food was well prepared, but she couldn't eat much with him watching her. Although she wasn't frightened, she was too excited to be comfortable. It was a relief when they left for the community theater, where she could sit beside him and he wouldn't be looking at her constantly with those arresting eyes. *He's too good looking to be single,* Belinda had said. Debra wondered how many broken-hearted women there were in Ellsworth, waiting for news that Michael Van Sant was back in town.

"Michael," she ventured as he drove out of the restaurant's parking lot, "have you ever—"

"What?" He threw a glance at her, then looked back at the road ahead.

She lost her courage. "Never mind. It doesn't matter." She didn't need to know about the hearts he had broken, might be better off without that knowledge.

"If you're thinking about it, it matters."

She put that away to treasure later.

He parked outside the old stone building, a former convent a hundred years old. As he helped her from the car, he asked, "What was it you wondered about?"

"Nothing."

"Yes, something. Have I ever—what?"

"I'm not sure I want to know."

He looked deep into her eyes. The sun was below the building behind him, but the light was still good. Her stomach flipped, and she took a shaky breath.

Michael smiled slowly. "Come on." He took her hand firmly and guided her up the steps and inside. Debra looked up into the old beams and arches, where there might be bats high above. Their seats were in the center of the fourth row. On either side were stained glass windows. The light from the sinking sun touched the ones on the west, bringing a brilliant glow to the mosaics of Paul on the Damascus road and the angel guarding the way to the tree of life. Debra had seen them many times from outside, but the splendor brought by the back lighting made her catch her breath.

As they sat down Michael took her hand again, and she looked at their fingers, clasped over the armrest that separated them. She memorized the faint stripe in his dark suit, and the way the buttons lined up on the cuff. The edge of his shirt cuff showed light against his wrist, and her hand was pale compared to his. They sat there not speaking for half a minute, and Debra knew he was looking at her. She couldn't look up, but her happiness grew until it enveloped her, and she wanted everything to stay exactly the same for a long time.

"Hey, Mike!"

She jumped and turned, instinctively tugging her hand away, but Michael held it tightly in place. Brian and two teenagers were settling into the seats in front of them.

"Good to see you, Brian." Michael stood up, and Debra stood, too. He released her hand then, shaking Brian's, but reclaimed hers immediately. "Don't tell me these are your kids."

"Yeah, David and Michelle." The boy had his father's red hair, but Michelle's was a dark auburn. Brian's eyes swept over Debra approvingly. "Hi, Debra."

"Hello, Brian. We thought we'd come see Sheila perform."

"Well, she's gonna be great. Right, Shelly?"

His daughter smiled shyly.

"This is Sergeant Van Sant and Miss Griffin," Brian said.

The youngsters nodded and murmured, "Hi."

"Your mother has been working hard on this, I'm sure," Michael prompted.

David rolled his eyes. "She drives us nuts. I'll be so glad when this is over and we don't have to hear *I want to be happy, but I won't be happy, 'til I make you happy, too* anymore." He strummed an imaginary ukulele as he sang the line, and Debra laughed in delight.

"You should have tried out for the show!"

"Me? Uh-uh."

"Well, Mom's decided to do another show this summer, anyhow," Shelly said.

"Yeah, when this is over next week, she starts rehearsal for *Much Ado About Nothing*," Brian said with a touch of pride.

"They're doing Shakespeare?" Debra asked. "That's ambitious."

"Well, at least it doesn't have songs," David put in.

"We'll have to come," Michael said, looking at Debra, and she didn't protest.

The lights flickered, and they all sat down. The sunlight was gone, and the stained glass windows were darkened. Debra could just make out the apostle Paul, lying helpless in the road, beneath the lighter beam that streamed from heaven.

Brian turned around and leaned toward Michael, and Michael leaned forward, squeezing Debra's hand a little.

Brian whispered, but not so low Debra couldn't hear him, "Hey, Mike, I didn't know you two were—uh—"

"First date," Michael said conspiratorially. "How are we doing?"

"I'd say pretty good." Brian winked at him and turned around as the house lights went down. By the end of Act I, Debra's blush had faded.

Chapter 17

"So, what was the question?" Michael asked again. He had parked his car at the town boat landing, where Rushton residents and "summer people" crowded all day in the summer, launching their boats and swimming at the public beach a hundred yards down the shore. Debra walked dreamily beside him, onto the deserted dock that jutted out fifty feet into the lake. The moon, just past full, reflected in a long, shimmering path over the smooth water.

"What question?"

"In the car, before. Have I ever——?"

"It's insignificant."

"I doubt it."

"Really. It's——"

"Trivial?"

"Paltry."

"Good one. How about inconsequential?"

"That, too."

"Let me guess." He stopped and looked out over the lake. "Have I ever been, A. married, B. engaged, C. in love, or D. arrested."

She chuckled. "Or E., none of the above?"

"Well, no, I guess I'd have to plead guilty to C. But that's debatable, really."

"So, no tragic past." She shook her head in mock solemnity. "I am so disappointed. I was sure there was a story there."

"Not much of a story, especially if you like happy endings."

She hesitated, then repeated her earlier statement. "I don't think I want to know."

Her lack of confidence prompted him to stop walking and face her in the moonlight. "It was ages ago. Just a bump in the road, looking back now. Really ... insignificant. But it kept me from wanting to drive for a while."

"Just tell me one thing," Debra said quietly.

"Anything."

"Am I likely to come face to face with her?"

"No."

She nodded. "Then don't tell me any more."

He put his arm around her waist. "So, how about you?"

"No."

"No? That's it?"

"Do crushes count?"

"Not unless you went out at least ... oh, three times."

"Then I stand by my answer."

He shook his head. "Incredible. You were at a co-ed college four years, and no A., B., or C.?"

"I was a study-aholic. Didn't socialize much."

He drew her closer to him and brought his other hand up to her cheek, sliding his fingers back over her ear, into her hair, where it was pulled smoothly back. There was anticipation in her face, not fear, and his heart thudded.

"Debra—" His pager went off and he froze for an instant, then sighed. He pulled it out of his jacket pocket and squinted at it. "Come on."

They walked quickly back toward the car, their footsteps hollow on the dock. When they reached the vehicle, he opened the passenger door for her, keenly disappointed.

"It's dispatch at the police station. I've got to phone in."

Debra climbed in without question, and he went around to the driver's side. As he reached for his cell phone, another car turned in at the access road. Michael peered toward it as it came toward them, and laughed in recognition. "It's a prowl car."

"What are they doing here?"

"Probably looking for kids down here necking." He wished he hadn't said it as soon as the words left his mouth. It was the type of reference that would set off Debra's insecurities and embarrassment. She certainly wouldn't want half the police department to know he'd brought her down to the boat landing on their first date. "Sorry."

He put his window down, waiting for the squad car to come even with him and stop. When the driver had opened his window, Michael called, "Hi, I'm Sergeant Van Sant."

"Oh, hi, Sarge. Didn't recognize your vehicle."

"That you, Jimmy?"

"Yeah. Bob Gagnon and I are patrolling tonight. Just hitting the usual spots."

"Well, I've been paged by dispatch, and I was about to call in."

"Use our radio if you want." The patrolman got out of the car, and Michael opened his door and stepped across to the patrol car. He sat in Jimmy's seat and took the radio. Debra was looking out the passenger window of his car on the other side. She was probably mortified, not to be seen with him, but to be seen in one of "the usual spots."

Mike made the radio contact and said, "This is Sergeant Van Sant. You paged me?"

The dispatcher responded with an urgent call, and Mike's heart sank. "10-4, Call Leon Beaulieu. Have him meet me there."

He exchanged brief pleasantries with the two officers and rejoined Debra in his car. "I've got to go over to the Riley complex. There's an unattended death. Could be a suicide, but they're not sure yet. I'll take you home."

"You ought to go straight there," she protested.

"They'll send Leon."

"Still, you're in charge."

He hesitated, hating the fact that he had put her in an embarrassing situation. "Would you want to ride home with these guys? They're good fellows, Jimmy Whelan and Bob Gagnon."

"I've met Bob. Sure, I guess so."

"Or you could take my car, and I'll have them drive me to the apartment complex."

"No, take your own car. I'll ride with them."

He stepped out of the car to speak to Whelan, then went around to open Debra's door. The police car headed toward the lake.

"They're going down to the landing to turn around. I'm really sorry," he said. "Not quite the ending I had in mind for this evening."

"It's all right." She laid her hand lightly on his shoulder.

Michael glanced down the road toward the lights of the patrol car. The car was still facing the water. He leaned toward her and kissed her on the cheek. She caught her breath, and he pulled her into his arms, holding her close for a moment. "Debra, there's a lot I wanted to say."

"There's time," she whispered. The lights swept along the trees at the edge of the gravel road. When the beam washed over them, Debra and Michael were standing apart again.

He put her in the back seat of the squad car, and squeezed her hand before shutting the door.

"You take good care of Miss Griffin," he charged the officers.

"That's affirmative," said Whelan, and they pulled away.

Chapter 18

Michael came on Saturday afternoon, ready to do some shooting with Grant and Henry. Debra watched with amusement as her father assembled ear protectors, paper plates for targets, and a length of two-by-eight lumber to hold them for target practice. Michael supplied a cardboard box, which he told Grant was packed tightly with cotton batting to stop the bullets without distorting them.

"You want to go along?" Michael asked Debra.

"No, thanks. I think it's a guy outing."

"You'll stay for supper after, Michael?" Ellen asked. "Mack and Belinda are coming."

"Sure, I'd like that."

When they came back from the gravel pit, Belinda was in the kitchen with Debra, timing the spaghetti while Debra tossed the salad. Mack strolled outside and met the men on the porch. Grant was charged up about his project, and the dinner conversation ran heavily to ballistics and police work.

"He is perfect for you," Belinda whispered to Debra as they rinsed dishes and stacked the dishwasher afterward, while Ellen put away the leftovers.

Debra smiled.

"So, you had a big date last night," her friend prompted.

"It was wonderful, until Michael was paged for an emergency."

"Bummer."

"Yes, I had a ride home in a squad car."

"So, Prince Charming went off to fight crime while you rode home in the pumpkin. Sounds like a mix-up between Superman and Cinderella."

Debra laughed. "At least I didn't drop a slipper in front of a reporter from the *Daily Planet.*"

"I haven't seen you so happy in years," Belinda said.

"Is it that obvious?"

"Well, it's not overblown, but you're content."

When the kitchen was clean, they joined the men in the living room. Grant and Mack were setting up the Tri-Bonds board. They formed teams and played a heated game, wrangling over Grant's interpretation of the rules.

Michael and Debra didn't have a moment alone until he was leaving, and she went to the entry with him. Mack and Belinda's pickup truck was just pulling out of the yard.

"I love your family, and your friends are great, too," Michael said.

Debra smiled. "I didn't get a chance to tell you how much fun I had last night."

"Well, we're going to have to try that again soon, only I'll leave the pager home." He reached for her hand.

"What happened last night, anyway?" she asked. "It wasn't in today's paper."

"It was too late for their deadline, I guess. It will be in tomorrow. A guy went out a third-story window."

"Fell or jumped?"

"Not sure. We haven't ruled out the third option yet, either."

"You mean, he might have been pushed?"

"I put Leon in charge and told him to treat it as a homicide until he's sure. There were at least four other people in the apartment, but they were all drinking, and the stories don't exactly match up."

"So, Leon's on it again today?"

"Right. I went back over there before I came here. He's trying to sort it out, now that the witnesses are sober."

"Did you guys get any sleep?"

"I got home around 3 a.m. Leon said he got about four hours. I told him to knock off early tonight and get rested. You know, he's got a lot of potential."

Debra agreed. "He's very methodical, and he seems to have some intuition."

166

"The funny thing is, he told me last night he has no interest in Pete's job."

"Really?"

"He's so happy to be in our unit, he just wants to make good and be a detective. No aspirations to management."

"Do you think he was serious, or would he say that to avoid suspicion?"

"I think all the acting ability is in the Estes family. Leon is an open book. Either that, or he's *so* good that ... well, I really like him. I want to trust him."

"But you don't?"

He sighed. "I can't trust anyone right now. Well, I trust you and Pete. But it's awfully hard to picture Leon doing those things."

She nodded thoughtfully, then darted a wary glance up at him. "You realize the whole department knows we went on a date last night."

He smiled. "Is that so bad?"

"Not if you're—"

"In love with you?" Michael asked softly.

Her eyes snapped up to his. "I think I was going to say *supportive*."

"Oh, I'm very supportive."

Debra swallowed hard. "Good, because there will be speculation, I'm sure."

"Well, let them speculate. I'm more of an investment man myself. Long-term investment."

Grant came clattering down the stairs, and the mood was broken.

"Hey, Mike! We forgot to set a time to do the ballistics tests."

"You're right. Can you come to the police station at five o'clock one day next week? Or I could take you in next Saturday."

"I'd hate to wait that long," Grant said. "That's only a week before the science fair, and I have to do the report."

"Well, how about tomorrow afternoon?"

"Sure, I think so."

"All right. I'll see you at church tomorrow."

"Cool." Grant stood there smiling.

Debra tried to catch her brother's eye, but Grant was oblivious. She was too embarrassed to ask him to leave them alone, and she thought Michael was too polite. She knew he liked Grant, and she was glad, but there were times when little brothers were superfluous.

Michael turned to her and said wistfully, "Well, good night."

"Good night."

He opened the door.

"'Night, Mike," Grant called. When the door closed, he said to Debra, "I'm really glad you like him. Forget about all the times I ever teased you about the subnormal guys you liked before."

She stood looking at him for a long moment. "Thanks, Grant. I'm glad you like him."

Chapter 19

Michael left the church with an apology immediately after the Sunday evening service.

"It's this case of Leon's. He's leaning toward accident, but he wants me to go over it before he makes that his official opinion."

"It's all right. He needs you."

"I'll see you tomorrow."

She nodded, wondering when the demands on Michael's time would taper off. Perhaps she should be scheduling his appointments for the weekend, too. At least he'd had time to take Grant to the office in the afternoon to complete his ballistics tests.

She purposely arrived early at the office Monday morning and started his pot of decaf. Michael came in at 8:30.

"I'm behind schedule," was his rueful greeting. "What did I miss?"

"Nothing, but you're due to meet with Pete and the chief at nine."

"Right." He stared at the white board. "I told Leon not to come in until ten. He was up late again."

"So were you, I guess. Your coffee's ready." She stepped into the inner office and poured his mug full, bringing it back to him.

"Thanks. Looks like the other guys have plenty to work on. Anything I need to know about?"

She shook her head. "Just the usual collection of messages. We're very tranquil this morning."

"Secretary included?"

"Yes. Very tranquil."

"Good."

He went into his office and worked down his list of messages, coming out at five minutes to nine.

"I'll be in the chief's office. Could you just get this information into the system for me?" He handed her a file and was gone. Debra opened the folder and recognized it as notes and statements from Leon's weekend case. She decided to take care of it right away and opened a new computer file.

"Hi there, Debra!"

She looked up as Bridget, the records clerk, entered with a stack of files. Bridget's short suede skirt displayed her legs well, and the top three buttons of her blouse were undone. Debra was glad Michael had left the office.

"Detective Beaulieu called down for these, but he's not in his office. Can I leave them here?"

"Sure. Leon's not in yet."

"Well, he called and asked specifically for these files." She piled them on the edge of Debra's desk, and Debra moved her coffee mug aside just in time.

"He must have called from home. I'll see that he gets them." Debra picked up her letter opener, prepared to attack the morning's mail, but Bridget lingered.

"So, I heard you and Mike Van Sant went out this weekend."

Debra's face reddened. "We went to see the play at the community theater. Brian Estes's wife is in it."

"So, did you have fun?" Bridget lowered her mascara-clumped lashes coyly.

"Yes, the play was good."

"Jimmy Whelan said you had a killer dress."

Her blush deepened. "Well, that's flattering. Excuse me, Bridget." She slit the first envelope and took the letter out, scanning it.

Bridget hovered a few seconds longer.

"So, does this mean Mike's out of circulation now?"

Debra slowly brought her gaze up to Bridget's. "I wasn't aware that he was circulating."

"Well, you know. One less available bachelor. There's Rick Parker and Terry Hofses, of course. Wendy seems to have her hooks deep into Johnny Young."

"I wouldn't know about that."

"Well, they've been—"

"Bridget, please, I don't think I *want* to know. I've got a lot to do this morning." She looked pointedly at Bridget, whose deep brown eyes were incongruous with the nearly white hair. Her glittery green eye shadow completed the garish look.

Bridget sniffed. "Well, excuse me. It's hard to have a social life when you work down in the cell block. Now, if the detectives would come down to get their own files, it might be a different story."

"Cell block?" Debra couldn't resist asking.

"Oh, you know. The old cells were down there. Then they remodeled and turned it into our lovely suite. It was probably more cheerful before they did it over for the records room." She looked appraisingly at Debra's French braids. "You ought to cut your hair."

"I beg your pardon?"

"You'd look good in a blunt cut."

Debra was nonplused. "Thanks for the input."

Bridget turned away.

*****

When Michael returned from his meeting, he paused by Debra's desk.

"Can I see you in my office when you have a few minutes?"

"Is now all right?"

"Perfect."

She followed him in and sat in the visitors' chair.

"What is it? Not the gossip mill, I hope?" she asked anxiously.

"It's begun to grind?" he asked.

"Bridget was full of tales."

"Who's Bridget?"

"The bleached blonde in records."

"Can't place her."

"Well, she knows who you are, trust me."

171

"She must be the girl who wanted your job, but she didn't have the brains. Gretchen told me about her."

"She wants a social life, and she's not getting it in the basement. But she knows about everybody else's."

"I'm sorry, Debra. I know you like your privacy." Michael's contrition over exposing her as a target for gossip was genuine. Being the center of attention was torture for Debra, and the better he knew her, the more he wanted to protect her. "I shouldn't have taken you to the landing the other night. It seemed like a good idea at the time."

She looked down at her hands. "It's all right, as long as you're still feeling ... supportive."

He smiled. "Definitely. But that's not what I wanted to talk about. Well, I do, but it will have to be some other time. This is business."

She sat up to attention. "Yes, sir. Should I take notes?"

"No need. It's just that the chief is going to officially announce his upcoming retirement this week."

"So soon?"

"Yes. His brother had a heart attack, and it seems he wants to retire and enjoy it before that happens to him."

"Can't say as I blame him, but what does this mean to us?"

Mike shrugged. "Chief Wagner has already talked to the mayor. The city council will meet with Pete tomorrow night. Pete and Wagner both think they'll tap Pete as the next chief. They want a smooth transition."

"And Pete's job?"

"They'll advertise right away. Take applications for a few weeks, then start interviewing."

"Whew. So this will all be settled."

"If all goes well. I was hoping to find out who Mr. X was, but if he stops his hijinks, we may never know." He watched Debra, and he couldn't help the tenderness that flooded him. "You are so ..." He took a deep breath. "Well, maybe this isn't the right time or place."

172

Debra smiled and said quietly, "No, I don't think so. Keep being supportive, though."

*****

Brian came into the office carrying a briefcase. "Debra, could you get me some files?"

"Sure. What do you need?"

"These first two should be up here, but the others I think would be downstairs."

Debra glanced at his list, took her keys from her desk drawer, and headed for the file cabinets.

"Sheila was fantastic Friday night, Brian."

"Thanks, I thought so, too. I'll tell her you said so." He grinned, and Debra thought he wasn't half bad when his temper was in check. He said, "I was really glad you and Mike came."

"We enjoyed it." She pulled out the first file on the list and opened another drawer for the second. "Your son looks like you."

"Yeah, everybody says that. He's a good kid."

"What year is he?"

"A sophomore."

She handed the folders to Brian. "I'll go right down for these others."

"Thanks. It's for a big court case, and I have to meet with Perkins tomorrow morning."

"What time?"

"10:30."

Debra jotted a note on her memo pad, so she could fill it in on the white board the next day.

"Great. You guys have been doing really well keeping me posted."

"No funny business for a few days," Brian noted. "Maybe it's really working."

"Seems like it. I hope it's over." Debra stepped to Michael's doorway. "I'm going to run down to records. Just so you know … the office is open."

He nodded. "I'll try to keep an ear open."

*****

Mona, the red-haired clerk, came to the divider and took the list from Debra's hand. Debra was glad Bridget was deep in a filing project at the other end of the large room. Mona walked slowly down an aisle between rows of metal file cabinets, peering at the drawer tags through bifocals and muttering to herself. She stopped, yanked open a drawer, and thumbed through the folders inside.

"This one's out," she called to Debra.

"You mean someone's using it?"

"Apparently. I can check and see who logged it out. Let me get these others."

She stopped before another cabinet and opened a drawer.

"That's funny. Detective Estes is the investigating officer?"

"Yes, he brought me the list himself."

Mona went to her desk and sat down at the computer, frowning.

"Uh-huh, uh-huh." She consulted Brian's list, comparing it to her computer screen. "These files were all logged out for Detective Beaulieu this morning. Are they working on it together?"

"I don't think so. Leon's not even—" Debra stopped in confusion.

"Bridget," Mona called.

"Yo?"

"You took a stack of files up to Leon Beaulieu an hour or so ago?"

Bridget looked toward them. "I left them on Debra's desk."

"Wait a minute," Debra said, "these are all the files you brought up to my office this morning?"

174

Bridget sighed and put down her armful of papers, came to Mona's desk and picked up the list.

"Yup. Those are the ones. Not the top two."

"Right, I had those upstairs. I'm sorry, it seems to be a mix-up. I didn't realize Brian was asking for the same files you'd brought up. Sorry to bother you."

She plucked the list from Bridget's hand and went quickly up the stairs and into the foyer, where she punched in the security code at the door to the detectives' side of the building.

"Michael!"

He rose and came quickly to her.

"What is it?"

"Something weird. Leon's not in yet, is he? I just tried the door to his office, and it's locked."

"No, I haven't seen him. I told him to come in late."

"I know, but Bridget said he called her this morning and asked for a bunch of files. A few minutes ago, Brian was in here asking for files. When I went down to Records, they told me they're the same ones Bridget brought up here for Leon."

Mike frowned. "Where are they now?"

"On my desk, where Bridget left them."

"Let me see."

They went to her desk, and Debra indicated the stack of folders.

"This is the list Brian gave me a few minutes ago." She gave him the paper, and he compared the folder numbers to the list.

"All right, if Brian's in his office, ask him to come see me."

"All—all right."

"Are you okay?"

"I'm frightened," Debra admitted.

"It could be nothing."

"I know. I'm sorry."

He stepped close to her and brushed her cheek with the back of his fingers. "I'm here."

"Yes." She smiled at him a little shakily. "It helps."

He nodded. "All right, then, ask Brian to come in here." He went into his office.

Debra punched in Brian's extension.

"Detective Estes."

"Brian, the sergeant wants to see you for a moment."

"Be right there."

In seconds he was at the door. "Got my files yet?"

"Uh, yes. You can pick them up—after—" She gestured vaguely toward Michael's office. Her pulse pounded in her temples.

Brian walked toward the door, watching her. Debra realized she was holding her breath.

"Brian, come in," Michael said heartily.

Debra breathed.

"Seems you and Leon asked for the same files this morning. A girl brought them up from the records room for him." Michael's voice was calm and soothing.

"I don't understand," Brian said, louder.

"I thought maybe Leon was helping you and ordered the files so you could get a head start this morning."

"No. Leon's got nothing to do with this case. I don't even know where he is this morning."

"Well, he worked a lot this weekend on the falling death, and I told him to come in late today."

"The one where the guy defenestrated himself?"

"Well, yes, actually."

"That's a word I learned in my rookie days, when a freshman at the college jumped out a window during a frat party," Brian said. "The D.A. was throwing it around, and I thought it was a euphemism at first, but I found out it was a real word. So what is going on here?"

"I'm not sure yet," Michael said. "You didn't call records and ask for the files? Because the clerk could have written down the wrong detective's name. Simple mistake."

"No, I went into Debra's office and asked her if she could get them. I didn't call anybody about it."

"Okay, I'll check with Leon, and just see if he knows anything about this. Meanwhile, you take the files and get to work."

Brian came out and stopped at her desk.

"Strange thing," he muttered.

"Yes," Debra agreed, with a tight smile. She picked up the stack of folders and placed it in his hands.

When he had gone she could hear Michael on the telephone, and she went about her work until he came out and leaned on the desk beside her.

She looked up at him. "So?"

"Leon just got up. Says he knows nothing about it. He'll be in soon, and I'll talk to him again, but I want to believe him."

"What do we do?"

"You just keep being the perfect secretary."

She smiled and looked away from his piercing eyes.

"I, on the other hand, will ask Brian when he made that list, and if he left it lying around anywhere. Then I might have to descend to the basement and question—did you say Bridget?"

"Yes," Debra said uneasily. "I'm—"

"What?"

She shrugged. "Nothing."

"When you say *nothing*, Debra, it's always something," he said gently.

"It's just that I'm certain she'll be glad to see you. She's very frank about—Michael, we've thought about there being a woman in this."

He glanced toward the open doorway and said softly, "You're thinking Bridget could be part of this?"

"If she's not, then some man called her this morning, claiming to be Leon."

"Hm. I'd thought you meant Wendy when you advised me to *cherches la femme.*"

"I did think of Wendy, perhaps helping Johnny with the phone calls and things. But you don't think it's Johnny—"

He nodded. "If Johnny is Mr. X, I'm afraid he's shot himself in the foot."

"What if it's Bridget and ... somebody?"

"Who? All the other men on the list are married." Michael's dark eyes were troubled.

"I know, but—"

There were footsteps in the hall, and he stepped back.

"All right, I'll get right on this. Keep thinking. And let me know if you need more ... support."

Chapter 20

The files remained a mystery, but by the end of the week Mike was thinking of them as Mr. X's swan song. Things had run smoothly after that. The chief had announced his impending retirement, and Pete had spoken to the detectives, telling them that anyone interested in the deputy's position should submit a résumé to him. Mike rode herd on the men, and all their cases progressed without major setbacks.

"All set for the Lions Club?" Debra stopped in his doorway at quitting time on Thursday.

His spirits always lifted when she was in the room. He stood up with a wary smile. "I think so, thanks. I've been trying not to think about it too much. I haven't done much public speaking."

"You'll be great."

"What time am I supposed to be there?"

"At six. Dinner, boring business meeting, then you."

"I have to sit through their business meeting?"

"I'm sorry."

He shrugged. "Guess it comes with the job. Are you sure they didn't say I could bring a date?"

She smiled and looked toward the window. "Michael, it's a men's club."

"I thought they had Lionesses."

"Well, all I know is, when I set up the appointment for you, I wasn't invited."

"Too bad. Did they ask if I was married?"

"No."

He sighed. "I hope they serve decaf. If they give me real coffee I'll be awake all night." He brushed a hair from the sleeve of his suit coat. "Do I look all right? Should I run home and change?"

"You look great."

"Not unduly rumpled from a day in the office? I'd better at least get a clean shirt, I think. I'm representing the city."

"You look fine, but if it will make you feel better, get a quick shower. You have clean shirts here, don't you?"

"Yes." He reached out and tweaked her braid. "Sure you don't want to come hear the Lions roar?"

"I'm sure. I'll see you tomorrow." She turned to the door and he watched her, intensely grateful for the change in their relationship. She stopped and looked back. "Michael ..."

"What?"

"Do you think I should cut my hair?"

He tugged at the knot in his necktie and pulled the tie slowly from under his collar. "Why would you do that?"

"I just wondered."

He eyed her cautiously. "Is there a right answer to this question?"

"Just tell me what you think."

"Okay. I like your hair the way it is."

"So, you like long hair?"

"Well, yeah." He hesitated, looking at her braids, then back to her gray eyes. "You'd probably look good with it any old way, but ... the way it is now ... " He took a step toward her. "Have I told you how beautiful you are?"

She held her hand palm outward, effectively holding him at bay. "Thank you. That's all I wanted to know."

The attraction that crackled between them was almost palpable. He wanted to touch her, to hold her in his arms. *This is right, Lord,* he thought. His gratitude was enormous. But the place wasn't right, no question about that. He made himself step back and say lightly, "Well, if you came to the Lions Club with me, we could take a survey and find out what they think."

She smiled. "It's only one opinion I wanted."

"Too bad. Those old Lions don't know what they're missing."

*****

His speech was excerpted in the newspaper Friday morning. Henry found it while eating breakfast, and read the article out loud to the family.

"Quite a young man you have there," Ellen said proudly.

"Thanks, Mom," Debra said. "He was very nervous about the speech. I'm glad he did well."

"He's funny *and* smart," said Henry. "Makes our cops look good."

"That's the idea," Debra replied. "He feels like he owes the city something."

"Do they pay him for things like that?"

"No, he just feels like he should take every opportunity he can to help the P.D.'s image."

It was raining, and she pulled a light jacket on over her navy blue suit and found an umbrella in the coat closet.

Her phone rang steadily from eight o'clock on, and Debra took calls from the presidents of several other civic groups who wanted the sergeant to address their members. Michael went out with Brian on an auto theft and was gone most of the morning.

"The Rotarians want you for a luncheon meeting Monday," she told him, filling his coffee mug as he perused her list of messages after the lunch hour. "They heard you were a dynamite speaker, and they'll feed you."

"Monday? That's a tough day for me."

"Well, the Rushton Kiwanis wanted you a week from Wednesday, but I told them you don't do Wednesday nights. Was that okay?"

"Yes, thank you."

"They said they'd take you for their banquet on July first instead. It's a Saturday night."

He laughed. "Persistent, aren't they?"

"Do you want to do it?"

"Sure, why not? It's good PR for the department."

"Wish I'd heard you last night. How can you just get up and talk to a room full of strangers like that?"

He shrugged. "I prayed a lot. I was nervous, but when the time came I just told a couple of funny stories from when I first became a detective, then played up our unit's work lately. We always get our man."

"You do, don't you?" There were still open cases, but she couldn't think of one they had given up on.

"Except for Mr. X," he conceded.

"Maybe he's quit pulling pranks."

Michael stood and went to the window. It was still raining, and the drops merged into blobs on the outside of the glass and ran down in streaks.

"If Bridget were helping Brian ..."

"Michael!" Debra's lips trembled at the thought of Brian being entangled with Bridget.

"Do you think Leon called her, then lied and said he hadn't?"

"I—no. Oh, I don't know what to think," she said in exasperation. "Someone else could have made the call. Bridget doesn't know Leon very well. She started work after I did, and hardly sees you guys, let alone knowing your voices over the phone."

He pushed the curtain back and stood with his hand on the window frame. "Still, it was something that didn't really hurt Brian, but it looked like someone was trying to mess with his routine."

"Someone was."

"Maybe. Brian could have made the call himself, if Bridget doesn't know him well. This really hurt Leon more than it hurt Brian."

"Because it looked like he was pulling a fast one on Brian?"

"How can we know?" He sighed and turned toward her.

"Isn't there a record of calls?"

"Not within the building."

"But if Leon called from his house, you should be able to prove that, shouldn't you?" Debra asked.

182

"I'm not sure. The 911 calls are logged electronically, with the origin. But regular calls to the non-emergency numbers—I don't think so."

"And there wouldn't be any way to trace calls from one extension within the building to another."

"Afraid not."

Debra shrugged. "So, do the Rushton Rotarians get you for lunch Monday?"

"Oh, I guess so. I'll have to come up with something different from what I told the Lions, though."

"Do you get overtime for doing this during your lunch hour?"

"I doubt it. I almost forgot. Leon and Calla want us to eat supper with them tomorrow night."

"Us, as in you and me?"

"Yes, he asked me in the parking lot this morning, but it slipped my mind."

"What do you think?" Debra asked.

"It's fine with me, if you're up for it."

"I guess I could. I mean—"

"You're so much more confident lately." He hesitated. "I know there's been a lot of talk this week, but, Debra, it doesn't matter to me."

"The men are all talking about us, aren't they?" She bowed her head in dejection.

"It's okay. I've taken a little teasing, but everything anyone's said to me has been positive." He took a step closer and reached toward her.

She looked up at him through damp lashes. "What kind of things?"

"I don't know if I should tell you." He smiled. "You might get a big head."

"People saying things about us ..." her voice trailed off.

"It's not malicious. Pete thinks it great, and he told me Gretchen was ecstatic when he told her we went out."

"Every time I go outside this area, the patrolmen stare at me."

Michael pushed her hair back and tipped her face up. "It's because you're beautiful, not because they're thinking horrible things. By the way, this is a great hairstyle, too." Her hair was hanging loose, from a silver barrette at the back.

She smiled.

"That's better," he said. "When I was over in the duty room the other day, one of the patrolmen said, 'Hey Sarge, I heard you're dating that gorgeous secretary. Lucky you.' And Johnny said he knew he should have moved faster."

"Oh, come on. Johnny likes Wendy." The familiar blush was beginning.

"Johnny likes women, period. He flirts with Wendy, but I'm not sure he's seeing her outside the office. Speaking of which … " He reached for her hand. "I feel like I've hardly laid eyes on you all week, we've been so busy. I was hoping we could go out tonight, but I need to work with Jared on his drug case. Some criminals only come out after dark."

"You'll be careful."

"Of course."

"Well, we can go to Leon's tomorrow night. Do you want me to tell him?"

"Sure." He squeezed her hand. "I've been thinking about a trip to Ellsworth. Would you go with me next weekend?"

She peered up cautiously into his eyes. "That would involve meeting parents and such?"

"Well, yes, but it's not hard. I know; I've been through it."

"No fair. You knew my parents before you met me."

He smiled. "I promise they don't bite. Please?"

"Next Saturday?"

"Maybe stay over for Sunday?" he suggested.

"Oh, Michael, I don't think—no, that is definitely too—I don't think I could live through two days with you like that."

"All right, just Saturday. We'll leave early, though, and drive back that night."

"I—okay, but you'll have to—" She looked up at him, her eyes pleading.

"I will."

She nodded. "All right. Let me out of here. I need some nice, mundane work right now."

She went to her desk and plunged into her routine. Michael was out of the office most of the afternoon, but came in at five o'clock as she was locking the desk drawers.

"You're leaving?" he asked.

"Yes. I'm glad I got to see you again."

"Come into my office for a second."

She picked up her purse and followed him. He closed the door behind her and took her purse from her, laying it on his desk, then drew her into his arms.

"Michael, you can't do this here," she whispered.

"You're not on city time. It's a minute after five."

Her hand went up to his shirt front, and she froze. "You're wearing your bulletproof vest."

"Yes, the chief thinks we need to anytime we're on field work. It was hot today, though." He released her and pulled off his suit jacket, throwing it over the back of his desk chair. He held out his arms to her.

She went slowly into them, her pulse hammering, and stood with her ear over his heart.

"Debra, I love you."

She sighed. "I thought so."

That made him laugh. He stroked her hair and laid a soft kiss on the top of her head. She knew suddenly that she didn't want their first kiss to be in the police station, with him wearing his shoulder holster and the Kevlar vest. She pulled away reluctantly.

"You take care tonight."

"I will. Jared's nerves are steady."

"I don't like you having to trust your life to men you're not sure are trustworthy."

"We'll be all right. I've got eight patrolmen lined up to go with us. But it's very hush-hush."

"You shouldn't tell me, then."

"I know my secrets are safe with you."

She nodded slowly. "You should have had a nap this afternoon. You never sleep anymore."

"I'll be fine."

"Could you—"

"What, sweetheart?" He tried to pull her to him again, but she kept her left hand firmly against his necktie, holding herself apart from him.

"Would you call me, so I'll know you're okay?"

"What if it's late? I don't want to wake your folks up."

"Call my cell phone. Please, Michael?"

"All right. But you can't spend the whole time worrying. Pray for us, but don't stew about it."

"I promise." She let him fold her in his arms then, and soaked up courage from him. Then she pushed away from him, retrieved her purse, and opened the door. "I'm going home now. I'll talk to you later."

"You want it this way?" The tenderness was still in his eyes.

"Yes, for now. This place has too many associations." She stood looking at him for a long moment wondering what it would be like to kiss him, wanting to know. "When will you be leaving?"

"I'm going to do some paperwork and get supper. Jared's coming back at 7:30."

"You ought to come to our house to eat, or go home and sleep for a couple of hours."

"I'll be fine."

"I know, you said that." She saw ahead of her many lonely nights of prayer, of pushing away fear and worry. "Michael, how does your mother deal with this?"

"With my work? I don't know. She never says anything negative about it."

Debra nodded. She almost flew back into his strong, protective arms. "I'm proud of you, too. Of what you do, and the way you do it."

"Trust God for me," he said softly. "Nothing will happen to me unless it's part of His plan."

*****

"Going to bed, Debbie?" Henry Griffin asked at eleven that evening. He put a bookmark in Dickens's *The Old Curiosity Shop* and set the book on the end table. It was still raining, and the family had spent a quiet evening at home. Grant had gone to bed an hour earlier, but Debra had lounged on the sofa, listening to her father reading aloud.

"I might just stay down here," she said.

"What is it, dear?" Ellen asked, putting her knitting away. "You've been fretful all night."

"I'm sorry. I've tried not to be." She looked at both her parents. "It's Michael."

"Something wrong?" Henry asked with concern.

"He's out on a case tonight. It's—it's a big drug raid."

"Oh, no," Ellen said.

"Oh, yes. I'm trying to trust God to take care of him, but I can't seem to stop worrying."

Henry reached for the Bible on the coffee table. "Let's read a bit more." He opened to Psalm 37 and read the ancient words. "Fret not thyself because of evil doers..."

"That's what I need," Debra acknowledged. She settled back in the corner of the couch and closed her eyes.

Henry went down through the chapter, his fine voice making the words sparkle, to the final verses. "But the salvation of the righteous is of the Lord; he is their strength in the time of trouble. And the Lord shall help them, and deliver them; he shall deliver them from the wicked, and save them, because they trust in him."

"You can be thankful Michael trusts in Him," Ellen said quietly.

"Would you like to pray for the men now?" Henry asked.

"Thank you, Daddy."

187

Ten minutes later her parents headed up the stairs, and Debra prepared to settle on the couch with a pillow and an afghan, her heart calm.

She was praying once more, silently, when she heard a car roll quietly into the driveway.

She stood up to go to the window, and a soft knock came at the door. She tiptoed into the entry to open it. Michael stood in the shelter of the porch, out of the rain.

"Debra!"

She threw her arms around his neck and sobbed, clinging to him. The rain was streaming off the roof beyond him, and the smell of wet earth and mint came up from her mother's perennial beds that flanked the porch.

"Baby, it's okay," he murmured, holding her close.

"I'm sorry."

"No, it's okay."

"Come in," she choked.

"Is that all right?"

"My folks went upstairs just a few minutes ago."

"I saw lights on up there." He stepped into the entry and shut the door.

"You're all wet," she said, her hand on the sleeve of his jacket.

"Well, we were outside a lot." He peeled off the damp jacket, and Debra dropped it on the bench beside the stairs. He unbuckled the holster and laid it carefully beside his jacket.

"Debbie," Henry called from the top of the stairs, "is it Mike?"

"Yes, sir, it's me," Michael replied. "I won't stay long. Is it all right?"

"Certainly. Just lock up after him, Debbie."

"I will, Daddy." She turned to Michael. "So everything went all right?"

"Yes, like clockwork. We made seven arrests."

"Wonderful! Thank you so much for coming here. I couldn't have slept without knowing."

188

He put his arms around her, and she snuggled in, burrowing her face into his shoulder on the dry cotton shirt. It smelled faintly of leather where his holster had been.

"I took my vest off at the office when we were done with booking," he whispered.

"Thank you. I'm glad you have it, but it's—" She dashed tears from her lashes with the back of her hand.

"Yes. I thought so."

His voice, by telephone, would have been enough. Debra felt doubly blessed to have the warmth and comfort of his embrace.

"Do you want to sit down?" she asked.

"I don't think I'd better stay that long. I just wanted you to see that I was in one piece. No, that's not true. I wanted to see you. I love you."

She closed her eyes and said softly, but distinctly, "I love you, Michael."

He squeezed her and whispered, close to her ear, "I knew it, but I really wanted to hear it."

He tipped her chin up and slowly, deliberately kissed her. Debra exulted in the joy that shot through her.

"I've never, ever been so happy," she whispered.

"Me either." He held her a moment longer, then kissed her temple and stood back, his hands on her shoulders. "Can you sleep now?"

"I sincerely doubt it."

Chapter 21

Calla Beaulieu was very nervous, Debra could tell. It stripped away her own edginess, and she set herself the task of making sure her hostess was comfortable with her husband's boss and the boss's girlfriend. She followed Calla into the kitchen of the little house and persuaded her to let her help put the food on the table.

Calla wore a print cotton dress, white with green and yellow lilies strewn over it. Debra was glad she had chosen a skirt for the occasion. Her blue skirt and cream blouse, with an embroidered vest, seemed to fit Calla's dress code. Michael had worn brown slacks and a cotton shirt, with no necktie, and Leon was casual in black jeans and a navy polo shirt.

Calla took aprons for herself and Debra from a drawer. Hers was green calico, with a red patch pocket and ties. Debra's was gray with a pink crocheted edging and a heart-shaped pocket.

"These aprons are wonderful!" Debra cried. "They remind me of my grandmother's house."

Calla smiled. "My mother made that one, and I think her mother made this one. I inherited about a dozen."

"My mom does a lot of needlework," Debra said, tying the strings behind her. "I was never much good at sewing."

"I like it," Calla said, "but I don't do much now. Maybe if we'd had a girl, I'd have sewn frilly little dresses and things, but I don't sew for the boys."

She stooped to open the oven door and drew out a flaky pastry.

"That looks delicious," Debra said.

Calla smiled shyly. "It's tortière. It's Leon's favorite. His mother gave me the recipe when we got married. It took me five years to get it right."

Debra smiled. "That's dedication."

"Well, it seemed important. It's hard marrying into a family that's different from yours."

"You're not French," Debra said.

"Oh, no, I'm as Anglo Saxon as they come. My maiden name is Williamson." She was pretty, with hair a shade darker than Debra's and blue eyes. She wasn't startlingly beautiful, but Debra thought she could see the loveliness that had drawn Leon to her fifteen years earlier.

"Your older boys look like Leon."

"Yes, Leon Junior and Matthieu both have the look. Eddie favors my side."

"They're all handsome boys."

"I think so. But then, I'm partial."

"Michael's family is Dutch, but they've been in this country a long time."

"Leon's the third generation in America. But he has cousins and aunts and uncles all around."

"I guess that makes a difference," said Debra. "Do the boys speak French?"

"A little, not much. Leon Junior is going to take it next year in school. His father wants him to." Calla stood back and looked at the kitchen table, accounting for all the dishes. "I think we're ready, Miss Griffin."

"Please call me Debra. The men all call me that at work. We're very informal."

"Leon says you keep the office running, and without you they'd be in chaos."

Debra laughed. "I'm not that important. I do the drudge work for them."

"Leon was very pleased when—" Calla broke off, and tried to backpedal. "I mean—he likes the sergeant a lot."

Debra smiled gently. "I'm glad. It makes it easier if the men respect each other. I know Michael thinks highly of Leon."

Calla nodded. "The last sergeant was kind of picky. Of course, Leon was training under him. But he says Sergeant Van Sant gives him a lot more freedom and lets him make all the decisions on his cases. He treats him the same as he does the other detectives, even though he doesn't have as much experience."

"I know he feels Leon is competent."

Calla smiled. "Well, I'll call them." She went to the door of the living room, where Leon was showing Michael the reloading press he kept in a cupboard in one corner. The three boys hovered near their father.

"Dinner is ready, Leon," Calla said quietly.

"All right, good." He put away the dies and a box of shells they had been examining, and padlocked the cupboard. "Have to keep the boys out of this stuff," he said to Michael.

They moved into the kitchen, and Calla directed them to their seats.

"So, boys, school out for the summer?" Michael asked as they began to pass the serving dishes.

"No, sir," said Leon Junior. "Not until next week."

"Then you'll be a freshman," Leon said with a smile.

"Going into high school in the fall?" Michael asked.

"Yes, sir," said the boy.

"Rushton High?"

"Yes, sir." He kept his eyes on his plate.

"What do you want to study?" Michael asked.

Leon Junior looked at him blankly.

"He doesn't want to study," said Leon. They all laughed.

"Do you have any thoughts about a career?" Michael asked.

"I want to be a pilot," Leon Junior said.

Michael nodded.

"He's thinking about the Air Force," Leon said gruffly.

"We'll see," said Calla.

"I want to be a game warden," said Matthieu, the middle boy, holding out a bowl of salad to Debra.

"I'm going to be an astronaut," little Eddie declared.

"Fine ambitions for all of you," said Michael.

Calla sighed. "They can't pick anything safe."

"Well, they have their father's daring," Mike said.

Leon laughed. "I tell her the truth: being a detective is a boring job. Paperwork and court, that's about it." He winked at Michael.

"I know better," Calla said.

"How long have you been a detective, Leon?" Debra asked.

"About a year and a half."

"You like it," she said with certainty.

"He *loves* it," Calla said fiercely.

Debra nodded, knowing that Michael loved it, too. It was an occupation that suited his temperament and intellect, and she thought Leon had some of the same propensities.

"You like it, too, sweetheart," Leon said. "No more uniforms to iron."

"I don't miss that," Calla agreed. She smiled at Debra. "Leon has three suits now. He only had one before this, the one he got married in."

"I never had so many neckties," Leon laughed. "Calla goes wild in Penney's when I get the clothing allowance."

Mike smiled. "I know what you mean. Wearing a coat and tie every day was a bit of a shock at first for me, too."

"What do you do outside the office, Debra?" Leon asked.

"Well, I just finished college a month or two ago. I'm enjoying being at home with my folks and my brother again. I like to cook and read."

"Calla reads all the time," he said. "She's worn out three library cards."

"So, Leon, you haven't put in for the deputy's job," Michael said.

"No, no, I don't fancy myself deputy chief."

"No?"

"Aw, I'm still learning to be a detective. I wouldn't want to give up the field work, but I don't suppose they'd pick me, anyway."

"Why not?" Debra asked.

"There are lots of guys with more seniority than me. Jared, for instance, or Zack Brown. They'll have a lot apply from outside, too."

"One or two résumés have come in," Michael acknowledged. "It's early yet."

"Well, I'm happy where I am." Leon helped himself to more of the savory meat pie. "You get into management and you get headaches, right?"

Michael smiled. "Maybe a few."

"Hey, I can't see myself ever outranking you, Mike."

"Coffee, Sergeant?" Calla asked.

"Oh, I—"

"Leon told me you're a decaf man."

He smiled. "All right, then. Thank you."

Debra helped Calla do the dishes, over the hostess's protests. The men lingered at the table over coffee, and the boys were allowed to go into the living room to watch a television program.

"They're good boys," Leon said. "We wanted to put them in the Catholic school, but we couldn't afford all three of them, so we kept them all in the public schools."

"We try to keep an eye on things at school," Calla said. "It's frightening the things they're exposed to nowadays." She washed the dishes at the sink, and Debra dried them and stacked them carefully on the counter. Mike and Leon talked easily about fishing and an upcoming procedural session the men would have at the police academy.

At eight o'clock Mike glanced at Debra and said, "I suppose we'd better shove off."

"You can sleep in tomorrow," Leon said.

"Well, Sunday school." Michael drained his cup.

"Where do you go?" Calla asked.

"Rushton Bible Church."

"We go to Saint Francis," said Calla. "We usually go to the eleven o'clock Mass."

Michael nodded.

"Calla, that was a fantastic meal," Debra said.

"Thank you. I'm glad you came."

"Me, too," said Leon. "This was nice."

When he dropped Debra off at her parents' house, Michael said thoughtfully, "Maybe I shouldn't socialize with the men after all."

"Why do you say that?"

"The better I know them, the harder it is to be objective."

"You don't still think of Leon as a suspect for Mr. X, do you?" Debra was shocked.

"See, you're not impartial, either."

"But he doesn't want the job."

"I think you're right, and I like him. I just keep telling myself it isn't over 'til it's over."

"I think he and Calla were surprised you came to their house."

"Come on, am I stuck up?"

"No, but Leon ... he's self-effacing. He wasn't sure you'd want to be part of his personal life."

"Like some other people I know, maybe." He smiled and took her hand.

"I'm glad we went," Debra said. "And I'm crossing him off my list."

*****

After church on Sunday, Jason Fuller approached Michael apologetically.

"Mr. Van Sant, I can't play Tuesday night. My folks are making me go with them to my sister's Class Night."

"Your sister is graduating?"

"Yeah."

"Don't worry about it, Jason," Michael said. "Family obligations come first."

"That's your big game with Clinton?" Debra asked as the boy walked away.

"Yes, and I think we're already down a man."

196

"Ask Mack to fill in."

"Does he play ball?"

"Are you kidding? He was the captain of our high school team. He's great. They won the tournament his senior year."

"Really? Did he play in college?"

"Mack didn't go to college, so don't ask him about it."

Mike grimaced. "Thanks. Anything else I should know?"

"He's a great guy, and I think he could use a night out with the boys." She looked toward the church doors. "They're headed out. You'll have to hurry if you want to catch him."

Mike left her side and went as quickly as he could through the crush in the aisle toward the exit. Mack Farnham turned in surprise when Mike called his name.

"Hey, Mack, I heard you used to play some B-ball. We need a player for the game Tuesday night. Are you interested?"

By the time Debra joined them on the sidewalk, Mack had agreed and the details had been settled. Mike was glad because he knew the boys would be relieved, but also because he knew Debra would be pleased that he was drawing Mack and Belinda back into the social side of the church family.

"It's been a while," Mack said diffidently. "I don't know how much help I'll be."

"You'll be fantastic," said Belinda. "Are you going Debbie?"

She looked at Mike, and he raised his eyebrows, smiling. "Will you, Debra?"

She took a deep breath, then chuckled. "Sure, this team is going to need all the cheerleaders they can round up."

*****

Debra sat on the bleachers between Belinda and her mother on Tuesday night, at the elementary school gymnasium where the men played regularly during the school's off seasons. The Rushton men wore gray T-shirts and mismatched shorts. The opposing team had uniforms consisting of numbered blue T-shirts and dark shorts.

"I can't believe Mack's father came," Debra said to Belinda. Bob Farnham sat on the other side of Belinda, shouting instructions at Mack as the teams warmed up.

"He never missed one of Mack's games in high school," Belinda said. "He loves this."

The pastor was the referee of the evening, and his wife and several other church members had turned out to watch the game. Ellen sat on a cushion she had brought along.

"Should have brought you a lawn chair," Henry fretted.

"I'm fine." Ellen had brought her knitting, and kept glancing up at the players as she stitched. "This should be an exciting game."

Debra couldn't stand up and scream the way Belinda did when Mack took a shot, but she found herself clapping and calling encouragement to the Rushton men. Her father's boisterousness surprised her.

"All right, Grant, take your time," Henry called as his son stood on the foul line.

Soon even Ellen was immersed in the action, her knitting relegated to her tote bag. The lead bounced back and forth, and the men were panting when half time came.

Belinda skipped down to the sidelines and threw her arms around her sweaty husband.

"You're doing great! Honey, I'm so proud of you!"

Mack kissed her and gave her a squeeze.

Debra smiled and wished she could be so demonstrative with Michael. He stood with Grant, drinking Gatorade and discussing strategy, and his eyes strayed to her often. Bob and Henry went over to talk to their sons, and Belinda came back to her place beside Debra, her eyes shining.

"They are having so much fun! Mack hasn't been this wound up since graduation."

"He ought to play all the time," Debra said.

"He's been too busy. But now that he's had a taste of it, he might make time, if they want him."

"Oh, I think they'll want him," Debra assured her.

"He's been out practicing for the last two days, afraid he'd let the guys down."

"No chance of that."

"Michael's really good," said Belinda.

"Yeah, he is, isn't he?" Debra smiled, watching him as he spoke earnestly to the other young men.

"You're looking at him like a Saint Bernard looks at Puppy Chow."

Debra sneered at her. "You are so crass."

"Ha!"

"Girls, girls," Ellen said gently. She had her knitting out again.

"We're not fighting, Mom," said Debra.

"I know. You two have always been oil and vinegar. I think that's why you've stayed friends so long. You temper Belinda's wild spirits, and she fans the embers of your emotions."

"Mom, you make it sound like I'm emotionally stunted!"

"Oh, no, dear. Your emotions are very strong, but you keep them inside."

Belinda squeezed Debra's hand, and Debra said to her mother, "I always wished I could be more like B'linda, just say what I felt without caring how it sounded."

Belinda laughed. "That's me. Just blurt it out now, and be embarrassed later."

The pastor blew his whistle. The players shuffled toward their positions, and Henry and Bob came back to their seats. Mack ran quickly up the bleachers and kissed Belinda, then jogged back down to the court.

"He's adorable," Debra said. "He never did that in high school, though. He's really cranked up."

Belinda smiled. "One of the fringe benefits of marriage. They can kiss you anytime, and no one gets upset."

Debra took off her sweater and folded it neatly on the bench behind them. "Well, I don't know if I'll ever be into kissing at public events, but I hope I have the kind of marriage where I'll want to."

Belinda leaned close and said in her ear, "We've made a decision, Mack and I—we're done waiting."

"For what?" Debra caught her breath as she suddenly understood. "Oh! Really?"

Belinda nodded, smiling. The pastor's whistle blew and the action began, with Michael passing the ball in for Grant to take it down to Mack.

"As of immediately?" Debra asked, clapping rhythmically with Belinda and the other Rushton fans.

"As of last night. We had a long talk, and Mack said he doesn't want to be old when his kids are growing up. He wants boys to play ball with and go camping with, while he's young."

"Wow. And you didn't disagree."

"Are you kidding? I was—Wooo!!" Belinda stomped her feet and pumped the air with her fists as Mack sank a three-pointer. "Way to go, baby!"

Mack's father was on his feet, too. "Yeah, Mack! That's the way!"

"We'd better give Mike and the other guys some equal cheering time," Belinda said.

Bob leaned forward and shouted past Belinda and Debra, to Henry, "Ice cream on me for the whole gang if the boys win this game, Henry!"

Belinda and Debra stared at each other, wide-eyed. Belinda pulled Debra to her feet.

"Go, Mike!" Belinda screamed. She glanced at Debra. Michael was dribbling methodically down the sideline, picking up speed as he approached his teammate, Tom Putnam. "Say it," she commanded.

"Go Mike!" Debra yelled.

Belinda slapped her on the back.

Chapter 22

Early Saturday morning the sun shone, promising a golden day, as Mike drove to the coast. His satisfaction was near complete with Debra beside him, eagerly watching the changing scenery.

"We're near the ocean, aren't we?" she asked, her nose wrinkling.

"Can you smell it?"

"Yes. When I was at college, everyone thought I must live right on the shore because I live in Maine. I haven't been close enough to smell salt water since last summer, when Dad took us to the museum at Owls Head."

"Do you want to drive out to Mount Desert?" he asked.

"Too many tourists. Isn't Acadia the most visited national park or something?"

"It's pretty popular."

"Let's postpone it, then. My folks took us a long time ago, and I'd like to go again, but not when it's bumper-to-bumper cars from New Jersey."

"All right. Ever been to Swans Island?"

"No."

"We can take the ferry from Bass Harbor. It's pretty out there, and not as mobbed."

"After Labor Day," she said.

"You got it. The Saturday after Labor Day. The lighthouse at Burnt Coat Harbor is worth seeing."

"I'd like that." She turned toward him with the smile he'd longed to see her wear. "Didn't Grant do a fantastic job at the science fair?"

"Yup, I'm proud of him."

"He should have gotten best of show." There was just a hint of poutiness in her voice, and Mike smiled.

"Well, that solar collector was pretty impressive." She was not mollified, he could see. "It's very subjective, you know. All it takes is one judge who wants gun control, and a ballistics project is out of the running."

"Why is everything so political?"

"I think it's part of our nature. The pride, the ambition."

"Speaking of ambition, how's the search for a deputy chief going?"

He turned the car onto a rural road with hardwoods growing thick on both sides. "Pete told me yesterday he has eleven applications so far. Four from the department, seven from outside."

"Brian, Jared, Johnny, and Zack?" Debra asked.

"Right. I think it was a relief to him when I told him I didn't want to put my name in."

"You're great where you are."

"Well, thanks. I don't want to move on until I've mastered this position." He slowed the car for a curve. "Almost there."

"What if I—"

"You won't."

"I might."

"You're over that." He squeezed her fingers, wishing he could infuse her with confidence.

"With you I'm okay, at least most of the time. But this is your *parents*."

"Parents aren't so bad."

"I don't know anything about them."

"It's okay."

"I guess they don't know anything about me, either," she reflected.

"I wouldn't say that."

She looked quickly at him, but he watched the road. "You wouldn't?"

He drew in his breath and admitted, "They know everything about you."

"Everything?"

"Just about." He put the turn signal on for a driveway ahead.

"Could we drive for another hour or two?" Her voice was small.

"Nervous?"

"Extremely."

He pulled the car into the drive and stopped it before the white-shingled Cape Cod. She was looking at him, breathing raggedly. He touched her cheek gently. "You're about to make my parents very happy."

She bit her trembling lip and looked down at her black slacks. "I should have worn a skirt."

"No. You're perfect."

The door opened, and his parents came onto the porch and down the steps. His fluffy Samoyed darted between them and circled the car, barking.

Michael opened his door and got out, saying firmly, "Down, Skipper. Down, you mangy idiot." He stooped to pat the dog. "Good boy. Heel." He and Skipper walked around to the passenger side as his parents approached.

"Debra!" His mother gathered Debra into her arms. "I'm so glad you came. I'm Margery." She was fifty, with only a touch of gray in her thick brunette hair, and she was still beautiful, Mike thought with a pang of pride. She wore white slacks and a screen printed green shirt with *Amsterdam* and pink and yellow tulips splashed across the front. Her smile was genuine and peaceful, and Debra seemed able to breathe.

His father waited patiently until the women had finished their greeting. He was tall, like Michael, but with fairer hair and skin.

Debra turned toward Mike expectantly, her eyes bright. "This is my dad, Pietr," Mike said.

"So pleased to meet you, Debra." She took his hand and smiled, searching his face intently. Mike hoped she didn't see the resemblance to the federal judge in the third district. Plenty of time to clue her in on his Uncle Neil later, when she was secure and comfortable with his parents.

Margery took them through the cheerful old cottage that smelled of wax, coffee and fresh bread. The living room floor was of wide pine boards, with braided rugs in bright colors of wool. Watercolors of the sea, ships, and lighthouses were tastefully arranged on white walls. The furnishings were sturdy, functional antiques.

They went on through the gleaming kitchen and sat on the deck behind the house, overlooking the tranquil lake, and talked for half an hour over coffee. Mike sipped his decaf and held Debra's hand as he told his parents about the cases he and his men had solved since his last visit home. He tried not to look at her too much, although he wanted to. He knew she was self-conscious enough with his parents practically staring at her. His mother liked what she saw, that was obvious. His father liked everyone, but even he seemed more gregarious than usual.

"What does your father do?" Pietr asked Debra.

"He's a millwright. And you, sir?"

"I teach."

Debra nodded. "You must find it rewarding."

"Yes, when the students are eager, it is worthwhile."

"Is the boat down there?" Mike leaned forward, balancing his mug on the railing, peering toward the waterfront.

"It's tied to the dock," Margery said. "Why don't you take Debra out for a while before lunch? It's very nice on the lake today."

He turned to Debra to see if the suggestion appealed to her. "Want to go?"

"Yes, that would be nice."

Pietr stood up and brought two life jackets from the far end of the porch.

"You'll need these."

Skipper trotted ahead of them down the sandy path. Michael tossed the life jackets in the bottom of the rowboat.

"Do you swim?"

"Passably. Where do you want me to sit?"

"In the stern."

He held the gunwale against the dock while Debra climbed in and took her seat, then untied the painter, dropped lightly into the dorey, and took the oars.

"I like your folks," she said as he settled into a rhythm that took them smoothly away from the dock, where Skipper sat watching them wistfully.

"Told you so."

"What's your father's discipline?"

"History."

"That can be fun with kids."

Mike hesitated. "Actually, he teaches doctoral level courses."

She swallowed hard. "Where?"

"University of Maine right now."

She nodded. "What does your mother do, besides keep a spotless house and pamper her family?"

"She's an artist."

"No. Those paintings—" She whipped her head around, staring back at the house, far behind them on the shore, the return of her inadequacy apparent in her anxious expression.

"All hers," Mike said softly. It was the first time he'd ever wished his parents were less creative. That was silly, though.

She stared at him, then back at the house. Pietr waved from the back deck, and Debra jerked her hand up and waved.

"I'm sure I should be able to divine all sorts of things about you now. You grew up with an artist and a doctor of philosophy."

"No, with my mom and dad. They're normal people."

"Not where I come from." She trailed her hand over the side in the clear water. "Your brother John ... ?"

"He's a surgeon."

She nodded. "I should have guessed. There were just two of you, right?"

"I had a sister. I'll tell you about it sometime."

She nodded thoughtfully. When he had rowed across the lake and turned back she said, "Michael, my estimation of you has been too—"

"Lofty?"

Her chuckle was almost a sob. "No, too limited. I thought we had some things in common, that you understood my life, but now—"

"Now?"

"I'm beginning to understand that you're from an entirely different universe."

"Don't do that, Debra. We're different, but we're the same, too. We have the same faith, the same values. I love everything about you. Your father's a millwright, and a good one. Do you know how solid and safe that is? You don't have to worry about what the whole world thinks you should do with your life. No one expects you to be brilliant or wonders why you didn't go on to graduate school. They just accept you."

"You live in an art gallery."

"Your mother makes quilts. She's as much of an artist as mine."

"No, it's different."

"Well, sure, but haven't you always thought of her as creative? Gifted, even?"

"No, she's just—Mom."

"Well, my mother is Mom to me."

He was beginning to feel uneasy. Debra had to get past this. If she couldn't love his parents, he wasn't sure he could bear it. Was this what she felt like when he'd come to her house on Memorial Day?

She watched the shoreline as the neat white cottage drew nearer.

"I like them," she said at last.

He closed his eyes for a second. "That's good. Really good."

It was warm, and he shipped the oars for a moment to take off his long-sleeved shirt. Debra took it and folded it, holding it on her lap as he rowed in his plain white T-shirt, past the house and on to a quiet cove in an angle of the lake shore.

"Dad and I go fishing here." He leaned on the ends of the oars, letting the boat drift, gazing at her. "Debra, I love your parents. They've made me feel like part of the family."

"I'm glad. Your folks are really nice. I guess I'm a little daunted. Your mother is famous, isn't she?"

"I suppose so. Her work sells. She goes to New York twice a year for shows, but mostly she stays here and paints, and dealers come to her."

"Don't you like her art?"

"I love it. But I'm used to it. How about you? Do you like the quilts?"

"Yes, I love being able to wrap something she made around me, and knowing it's beautiful."

He nodded.

"They're putting two of Mom's quilts in the big show at Colby College next month," Debra said, peering at him a bit anxiously.

"Does she ever sell them?"

"No, she gives them away, to people she loves."

"I like that." He started rowing again, steering the boat around toward the cottage and the weathered dock. Skipper had given up on them and left his post.

They ate lunch on the deck, with the breeze off the lake tempering the humid air. Salmon with a light sauce, a green salad, creamed potatoes, and flaky crescent rolls. Debra seemed relaxed. Everything was perfect.

"Debra's mother is having two quilts exhibited at Colby next month," Mike announced over ice cream and raspberries.

"Really? How exciting," Margery said.

"It's a big show the state quilters' guild has every year," Debra explained.

"I'd love to see it. Do you suppose if I drove up I might—" Margery glanced toward Michael.

"Meet Debra's mother?" he asked.

Margery nodded happily.

"She'd probably like that," said Debra, and he smiled at her, grateful and proud that she was facing down her fears.

"When is it?" Margery asked.

"July twenty-first and twenty-second."

"Does your mother make her own designs?"

"Sometimes she uses old patterns. She likes the simplicity, but she'll stitch over the seams with intricate embroidery. Lately she's been designing with her own ideas, though."

"Yes," Margery said with a faraway look. "I think it must be very satisfying."

"I'll take you to the quilt show and go over to see Michael," Pietr decided. "It's not far, is it?"

"No, I guess it's ten miles or so," he replied. "I'd like you to see my office, Dad."

"A policeman with a private office." Peitr winked at Debra. "Private secretary, too."

"Oh, no, I work for all the detectives," Debra hastened to correct him.

"But still—we *teachers* don't get secretaries," he said confidentially.

"Dad, the cat is out of the bag. I told her you're a professor."

"Ah, well, forgive my little ruse. People are intimidated when they think I am a scholar."

"You *are* a scholar," said Margery.

"Come on the Friday, then, Dad," said Mike. "Mom can eat lunch with Mrs. Griffin in Waterville, and Debra and I will show you the police station and take you out for a sandwich in Rushton."

They drove together in Michael's car to the shore of the estuary, and along the edge of Union River Bay. Margery pointed out one of her favorite painting spots.

"I've painted that view at least six times, but it's different every day," she said. "Whenever I see it, I think, *I didn't get it right last time. I need to do it again.*"

"You see, Mom has her compulsions, too," Michael said. "She can't let a wave get away without painting it. Sort of like you and ringing telephones."

Debra smiled, looking out over the rocks and the tide flats, to the water and Mount Desert Island beyond.

"I'm afraid I let the boys run a bit wild while chasing seascapes," Margery said ruefully.

As the sun set that evening they prepared to leave. Michael carried a box of books to the car.

"Take this." His mother placed a framed picture in his hand. He held it so Debra could see it, too. It was a nine-inch square watercolor of Skipper perched on a boulder beside the lake, his body bunched up and wriggly, his mouth open in a bark as he faced a seagull.

"Thanks, Mom. It's Skipper, all over." He kissed her and turned to put the painting carefully in the back seat of the car.

"Come back soon, Debra," said Pietr.

"Thank you. I'd like to."

"You've gotten over your awe of us, I hope."

She colored slightly. Pietr leaned toward her and kissed her cheek. "Mike doesn't bring women home, you know."

"Today was special," Margery agreed, embracing her. "We were very nervous this morning."

Michael closed Debra's car door. "Who's nervous?"

"No one now," said Margery.

Chapter 23

"They've narrowed it down to five candidates." Mike sat in his desk chair, and Debra, taking her morning break with him, sat near the open door to her office. Mike pulled his telephone close to her so she could answer it if the annoying ringing began.

"Five?"

"Yes, out of eighteen total. Jared, Brian, Zack and two from outside."

"They gave preference to our men."

"Yes. Those men have an advantage, since they know our people and our system. One of the outsiders is a woman from Lewiston, the other's a man from Bridgton. He's been in Massachusetts for a few years and wants to come back to Maine."

"Johnny's out of it, then?" She wrapped the end of her braid around her thumb.

"Yes. Pete had a man-to-man with him last night. Told him he's a good detective and has potential, but he's too young for this right now and needs to get some caution and precision."

"How did Johnny take it?"

"All right, I think. I saw him this morning. He said when I'm ready to retire, he'll go for my job."

Debra smiled. "He's nearly your age."

"He was kidding. If he takes it the right way, this will make him a better officer, and a few years from now some big city will snatch him away."

She nodded. "We can trust him, then?"

Michael sighed and picked up his blue mug. "If you mean he can't be the saboteur, I don't know. I wish I could say I have no doubts about any of my men."

"But the sabotage is over," she said uncertainly.

"It seems to be."

Two weeks had passed since their trip to Ellsworth.

"What's Brian doing today?" Mike asked.

"He's at the courthouse. So is Leon. Johnny went to Rankin Hill on that mini-mall burglary. Jared's in-house, I think, doing paperwork. He came to my office a little while ago to make some copies."

Mike nodded. "Well, they're going to interview the candidates next week."

"Who makes the final decision?"

"Pete and Chief Wagner will make the cut, then the city council will look at the final two or three. They asked me if I could live with any or all of these five as my new boss."

"What did you tell them?"

Mike smiled. They were close enough now that she could ask, and he liked that. "I hesitate on Brian. The others—well, I can't really say much on the outsiders. Don't know anything about them, except what's on the résumés."

"Did they ask Zack what he thinks?"

"Well, it's tricky with him being one of the candidates."

"Still, if they don't pick him, he'll have to work under Brian or Jared or whoever."

"Yes. I guess they should give him the same courtesy they gave me."

"Anybody home?" Pete Nye's voice came from the outer office.

"In here, Pete," Mike called.

Debra started to stand up, but Mike put his hand on her arm. "You still have five minutes. Don't let Pete make you nervous."

"Secret powwow?" Pete grinned at them from the doorway.

"Break time," Mike said. "Want some coffee?"

"No, I was just looking for Brian."

"He's in court," Debra said.

"Oh, well, I saw Jared just now and set up an interview with him for Monday, and I'd like to line one up with Brian. Get them and Zack out of the way, then schedule the other two."

"Want me to have Brian call you when he comes in?" Debra asked.

"Sure. Well, have you got those Post-its? I'll leave a note on his door."

Michael opened his desk drawer and found a pad and a pen.

Debra stood up. "I really think my break is over. Sit here, Chief."

He grinned at her. "You're a little hasty, but I like the sound of that."

Debra laughed. "How's Gretchen?"

"Counting the days. Only twenty-something left. I told her to come in and see everybody, but she says she's too fat."

"I'll go visit her tomorrow, if she's going to be home," Debra said.

"She'd love that."

Debra went out to her desk. Pete left a few minutes later, and Mike decided to go to the courthouse. Leon was testifying in a high-profile case, and it was part of the sergeant's duty to observe all of his men in action.

Before leaving, he stopped at Debra's desk and glanced toward the hallway. It was empty, and he bent down and kissed her cheek.

"Unprofessional," Debra murmured.

He smiled. "I'm taking you to lunch."

"I brought my lunch, as always."

"I know. I brought mine, too. I'm taking you to the park bench."

She smiled. "We're not cheating the city, are we?"

"How do you mean?"

"I spend so much time thinking about you, I wonder if I'm shirking my duties."

"You must be one of those amazing women who can think and work at the same time."

"Ouch. Get out of here."

*****

213

The office was quiet, and Debra caught up her archiving and typing. After half an hour, she locked the door and went down the hall toward the ladies' room. Johnny's door was closed and, she presumed, locked. Pete's yellow note fluttered against Brian's door as she passed, and diligent typing could be heard from Jared's office.

A few minutes later, as she returned to the hallway, she saw Zack Brown beyond Jared's office door, walking toward her. He broke his stride when he saw her.

"Oh, Debra, there you are. I guess Michael's out?"

She took her keys from her pocket and walked briskly toward him. "Yes, he went to the courthouse. Shall I page him?"

"No, that's all right. I'll catch him later. It was just something I'd mentioned to him earlier." He nodded and headed for the security door that led to the foyer.

As she unlocked the office door, Debra felt uneasy.

What's wrong with this picture? she wondered. By the time she had reached her desk, she knew.

The yellow memo was missing from Brian's door.

She went to the doorway and looked down the hall. Her eyes swept the carpeted floor, looking for a bit of yellow paper that wasn't there. She went back to her desk and punched in Michael's pager number.

It was a long three minutes before he called in. She sat staring at the white board, thinking, until the phone rang.

"Van Sant."

"Michael, I need to talk to you."

"What is it?"

"Is this line secure?"

There was a momentary silence. "I'll be right there."

She went into his office and started a fresh pot of decaf, then returned to her desk, but she couldn't concentrate on the details of her work.

214

The courthouse was just up the street, and it was only ten minutes before Michael entered. She heard him in the hallway, before he came into the office.

"Jared! How's it going? You're interviewing with Pete and Chief Wagner Monday?"

She stood up and went to stand in his doorway. When he came in, he went straight to her, followed her into the inner office, and closed the door.

"What happened?"

Her hand shook as she reached out and touched the sleeve of his gray suit. "The note. You remember Pete left a sticky note on Brian's door?"

"Yes."

"It's gone, and—Michael, I think Zack took it."

"Zack?"

"Yes. I went down the hall for a couple of minutes, and when I came back, he was up here, and the note was gone. He said he was looking for you. I had locked the office while I was gone, but he made an excuse, said there was something he had talked to you about earlier—"

"He did talk to me," Mike said. "When I was leaving for the courthouse, I met him in the foyer. He told me Johnny's missing vest showed up in the patrolmen's break room."

Debra's jaw dropped. "After all this time?"

"Well, he said it may have been there a while. People saw it and didn't think anything of it, but nobody claimed it, and it kept falling on the floor. He finally checked to see whose it was."

"Zack could have put it there himself."

"Yes, he could have," Mike said pensively.

"Can you get fingerprints from it?"

"No, afraid not."

"But, Michael, the note."

"Yes. You're sure it didn't just fall off?"

"I looked for it. And Brian isn't back yet."

"No, I saw him at the courthouse."

"So there is no way he or Leon could have done this."

215

"Jared?" Michael asked.

"He was in his office typing. I think he's still there."

"Hm. You didn't say anything to Zack about it?"

"No. What are we going to do?"

He took a deep breath. "Ever think about going to the Academy, sweetheart?"

"No, why should I?"

"You'd make a great detective."

She smiled but shook her head. "It would take too long. I'd have to put in years as a patrol officer first."

"You're right. I don't want that. I like having you right here in my unit." He lifted her hand to his lips and kissed her fingers.

"We're on city time, Michael," she said gently.

"Yes, and the problem of Mr. X. How can we set him up?"

"Set a trap for Zack?"

"Yes."

Her mind went back over the list of nuisance incidents. "Why did he bring the vest back?"

"Hard to get rid of. A pistol clip could be tossed off the bridge and be gone forever, but not a Kevlar vest. Besides, if he's the next deputy chief, he'll be the bean counter when it comes to expensive equipment. Why waste a perfectly good vest? Just hide it in plain sight for a while, then find it and save the city several hundred dollars."

"If he's that conscientious, how can he—"

"It's a paradox," Michael admitted. He sat down, and Debra took his mug to the coffee maker. "Let's see, now. If I told Zack I've got a high profile case and I need some officers to assist Brian and Jared, and implied that it's going to make my detectives shine when they go before the city council, what would he do?"

"You mean, if he is the saboteur?" Debra gave him his coffee. She didn't like the conclusion she was reaching, but it seemed only logical. "He'd try to throw a monkey wrench in it and make them look incompetent."

Mike nodded soberly. "Or try to grab the glory himself? Yes, that might be a nice touch for Zack. Take his men and rush in gangbusters before my detectives are ready to act."

"Wouldn't that backfire? I mean, if it was something detectives were supposed to handle..."

"He might find an excuse. It was so urgent, they couldn't wait for us. They do that on robberies and things. Whoever gets there first."

"So, give Zack the chance to get there first? Would that really prove anything?"

Mike rubbed his forehead. "I've got to think this out. We can't mess it up, or we won't have a hope of catching him."

"I'm sorry it's Zack," she said.

"Me, too."

When they ate lunch in the park later, Michael's plan was still nebulous.

"It's got to be foolproof," he said, unwrapping his sandwich. "I can't let them pick this guy for deputy chief and know he's been behind all this."

"We need evidence," Debra said. "Stand-up-in-court evidence. Zack was there when the note disappeared, but we have no proof he took it." She threw a bit of her bread crust to the pigeons that loitered near their feet.

"I have to get it," Michael said grimly.

*****

At five o'clock Debra began closing the office. Mike had gone to meet Johnny and advise him on his case, which had turned out to be more complex than anticipated. Several shops in the mini-mall had been burglarized during the night, and it was taking the owners hours to determine what had been stolen and gauge the extent of the damage.

Debra locked the file cabinets and desk drawers, turned off the coffee maker and the copier, and shut down her computer. As she turned the key in the lock, she saw that Johnny's door, across the hall, was still closed, but Leon's, farther down, was open for the first time all day.

She stepped down the hall. Leon was rummaging in his bottom desk drawer.

"Hi, Leon! Michael said court went well this morning."

"Yeah, not bad. I may have to go back Monday, but I hope not."

He crumpled a sheet of paper and tossed it toward the waste basket beside the desk. It bounced off the rim and landed at Debra's feet. She stooped to pick it up, and stepped to the waste basket. As she let it fall, she caught her breath, glanced at Leon, then back down into the trash can.

Slowly, she bent and retrieved a yellow square of paper.

Brian—Call me asap and we'll set up an interview. Pete Nye.

"Leon." Her voice quavered, and she swallowed hard.

He stopped rifling the desk drawer and looked up at her. "Something wrong?"

"Where did you find this?"

He reached for the memo and looked at it critically. "Never seen it before."

"Never?"

"I don't think so. Looks like it was meant for Brian."

"Yes."

He turned back to the desk and opened another drawer. "I can't find my—oh, there it is!" He held up an address book in triumph.

"Has Zack been in here today?" Debra asked.

"Zack? No. Nobody's been in here since I got back, except you. Well, Jared was here for a second." He picked up his telephone receiver and began jabbing at the keypad.

Debra went out quietly and stood in the hall, staring at the memo. She went back to her own office and unlocked it and went in, closing the door behind her.

She went to her desk and picked up the telephone receiver, quickly keying in Michael's cell phone. He didn't answer, and she left a brief message. What if he had his phone turned off and

218

didn't see the message for hours? She punched in his pager code. The pager system seemed antiquated and inefficient, but sometimes it served the purpose.

She got up and went into his private office and closed the door. She would wait there for his call. The painting of Skipper was mounted above the desk, and she smiled when she noticed it, remembering their day in Ellsworth. She touched the handle of his coffee mug, amazed at the deep feelings for Michael that had blossomed in her heart.

The phone rang in the other room, she quickly punched the line button.

"Hello."

"Debra?"

"Yes."

"What's happened?"

"Michael, I—I was wrong."

"You mean … about … how do you know?"

"I found—should I say it?"

"No. Are you at the office?"

"Yes. I'm sitting at your desk."

"Stay there. Johnny and I were about to wind things up here, anyway. I shouldn't be more than twenty minutes."

"I'll be here."

"Make yourself a cup of coffee."

She smiled and closed the connection, then dialed her home number.

"Mom? It's Debra. I'm going to be a little late tonight. No, don't wait supper."

She sat in the dim light, looking up at the painting. The dog was so lifelike, she could almost hear Skipper's short, excited bark. There had been a watercolor in the kitchen at the Van Sants' home of two boys on a raft with a ragged sail, and she had wondered if it was Michael and his brother on the lake. She decided to ask Margery Van Sant when she saw her again.

She knew that in her top desk drawer in the other room there was a folder of items she had planned to type on Monday morning. She might as well work on them while she waited.

She picked up Pete Nye's memo and opened the connecting door, but stopped on the threshold. A man was bending over her desk.

Chapter 24

The lower left drawer was open, and he had Michael's appointment book open on the desktop. He whirled and faced her.

"Debra," Jared said smoothly, "I thought you'd gone. I needed one more file tonight, and I thought you wouldn't mind if I helped myself."

Her heart raced. "That drawer was locked."

"Was it?" Surprise crossed his features as he straightened. "Are you sure?"

"Absolutely."

Their gaze held for several seconds, then Jared laughed and shook his head. "Not much of a lock, I guess."

Debra deliberated inwardly and decided she had better not tip her hand. "Want some coffee? Michael and Johnny are coming back soon, and I made a pot for them."

"No, thanks, I'll just—" he stopped, staring toward her left hand, and Debra was aware of the yellow paper she clutched. She tried to hold it lightly, casually.

"What case are you working on?" she asked.

His eyes met hers. "It's an auto theft ring."

"What file did you need? I can get it for you."

"Uh, Cochran. Alfred Cochran."

She pocketed the memo and took out her key ring, going to the open cases file. A moment later she turned around and said flatly. "There isn't one."

"Oh, well, someone else must have it." He edged toward the door.

Debra stepped toward her desk, watching him. When he had gone, leaving the door halfway open, she looked down at Michael's appointment book. A line was drawn through an entry for the following Tuesday: *Augusta Elks, 7 p.m.* She had scheduled the engagement herself. Michael was to speak to the men's club that evening. The Augusta Elks had heard from the Waterville Elks that the Rushton P.D. had a great speaker. He was funny and timely and upbeat. Would the sergeant consider …

Oh, that would be great, she thought. *The speaker doesn't show up for a civic club meeting. Lousy PR for Michael and the Rushton P.D.* She picked up the book and peered closely at the line, then flipped back a page to see if he had changed anything for Monday.

"Debra, I'm so sorry it's come to this." Jared was back in the doorway, watching her.

"Wh-what do you mean?"

He reached slowly inside his jacket, and his hand came out holding his pistol.

Fear flooded over her as she stared at the gun. "Jared!" It was a whisper.

"You're just a secretary. Did you have to do this?"

"Do what?"

"I saw the memo. You figured it out. And you know what I did in here. Now what am I going to do with you?"

"If you're smart," she said slowly, "you won't do anything with me. Playing pranks on your co-workers is one thing, but you're digging yourself into a hole now."

"I was all done. I figured I had a pretty good chance. But then Mike started sniffing around."

"You should have just stopped." She shook her head, unable to believe he would really take it this far.

"I couldn't, once I'd started. I had to keep evening things up so no one person looked a lot better or worse than the others."

"But Michael and Leon don't even want the job," she protested.

"I didn't know that at first. And Mike—well, he was the golden boy, wasn't he? They brought this shining young man in from outside. He was in diapers when I became a policeman. I've been here twenty-seven years! I deserved to make sergeant. But, no, they brought in the great Van Sant."

Debra couldn't speak.

Come on," he said with decision. "We've got to get out of here. If Van Sant comes back, that's it." He took off his suit jacket and laid it over his arm, concealing the weapon.

"It's over anyway, Jared," Her throat tightened.

"Move!" He motioned toward the door with the gun.

"Where are we going?"

"Not far. Now get going, and don't make any noise."

She walked slowly to the door, and felt him close behind her. In the hallway, she looked quickly around, but all the office doors were closed. They went down the hall and turned the corner, but Bernice was gone, and Pete's office was closed. The entire wing seemed to be deserted.

"Punch in the code."

Debra prayed frantically as she pushed the number for the security door. In the foyer they would pass the dispatcher's window, and someone would see them.

"Now the basement," Jared said, low, as she stepped through the doorway.

She turned her head toward him in surprise.

"Keep going. Don't stop here."

She took a few steps to the basement door, realizing that they wouldn't pass the window, and the dispatchers would not see them after all, unless they were watching the monitor for the camera that panned the foyer.

"Quick," he hissed.

She punched in the code.

"Open it!"

She hesitated. The records department would be closed, and there would be no one working down there. She didn't want to go farther from other people and away from the route Michael would take any minute.

"Come on!" Jared prodded her with the gun muzzle.

She didn't believe he would shoot her in the foyer of the police station. He wouldn't stand a chance at getting away with it. But if he took her someplace else . . .

"I said move!"

223

"Jared, this doesn't make sense. If you—"

He reached past her and jerked the door open, shoving the gun hard against her spine. "Walk, or I'll push you."

Trembling, she stepped through the doorway and flipped the light switch. She went shakily down, one hand on the railing, the other holding up her calf-length khaki skirt, searching frantically for a way to outsmart him. Could she reach back and overbalance him? She didn't dare try. At the bottom of the stairs, the door to Records was closed. She heard him fumbling with keys.

"Not here," he said. "Over there."

She looked at him, and he jerked his head toward the other side of the stairway. She went slowly around the foot of the stairs, curious. In the deep shadows at the back of the open space was another door. A closet?

He marched her toward it and put the key ring in her hand with one key extended.

"Open it."

She slipped the key in the lock. She had read that keys could be used as a defensive weapon, but still, when the adversary held a loaded gun ...

She turned the key and opened the door slowly. A damp, musty smell assailed her.

"Go in."

"Jared—"

"I'm not going to hurt you. I just need a place to keep you sequestered for a while. I need time."

She took two cautious steps into the darkness and stopped. He clicked a switch behind her, and the room was flooded with light from a bare bulb in a ceiling fixture. The walls were of unpainted concrete blocks, and the floor of cement. The ceiling was low, and the room was only ten feet wide and twenty feet long. The farthest quarter of it was sectioned off with bars.

"A-a cell?" Her adrenaline surged.

"The old cell block was down here. Come on."

"I thought they tore them out."

"They did, on the other side. If they decide they need more space, they'll probably remodel this side, too. Now move."

"Jared, please." She started to turn around to plead with him, but he leveled the pistol at her.

"Don't make me use force, Debra. I won't hurt you if you cooperate. I told you, I just need time. If I leave you upstairs, you'll have Van Sant on me in minutes."

"You're right about that." Her voice choked as she said it. "Jared, this is stupid."

He raised the gun, as if to strike her with it, and she cringed.

"Go inside, Debra."

"You could have explained things." She gasped for a breath. Her throat ached and felt as if it was closing. "Now you've gone too far. You're done as a detective now."

He glared at her. "You think I don't know that?" He shoved her inside the empty cell and closed the door, turning a key in the lock.

"Jared, you had a nice career," Debra rasped out. "You've done a lot of good. Why are you doing this?"

"I didn't plan for it to end this way."

He walked toward the door of the room.

"You wanted the deputy chief's job that much?"

He turned around and stared at her bleakly. "I knew I was taking a risk. And I lost."

"Was it worth it? You might have gotten the job without doing anything. You've been a good officer."

"I've been passed over so many times. They always have some excuse."

He stepped toward the door, and she was terrified. How long would it be before anyone came to release her? She was desperate for him not to leave her there alone. "Why not just give it up now? Let me go. I won't press charges." She grasped the cold bars and met his gaze, pleading silently.

He laughed. "Oh, right." He shook his head. "The only thing I can do now is to run."

"You know they'll find you."

He looked hard at her. "I've chased down a few myself. I know the mistakes they made. I won't make them."

He turned off the lights and went out the door.

"What about your family?" she screamed as the door closed.

She heard the key turn in the lock and stood holding the cell bars, shivering in the darkness.

For a long time she stood there.

She tried to map the police station in her mind. What was she under? She pictured the way the stairs came down and knew the records department must extend under the patrol officers' side, the duty room, the com room, their locker room, and Zack's desk in the alcove near the evidence lockers. This other room must be under the wing that held the chief's office and Pete's, and the detectives' area, where she had left her purse and cell phone locked in a desk drawer. The side where no one would be working that evening. No one would hear if she screamed, or if she somehow found a way to tap on the ceiling or beat on the bars.

She stood in the pitch blackness, not wanting to move. Finally, she fumbled for the button on the side of her watch. The face was very bright when she illuminated it. It was nearly six o'clock. Michael and Johnny must be back, looking for her in the office. She stood breathing raggedly, listening, hearing nothing.

At last she slipped slowly to the floor, praying.

Lord, please bring help, and please don't let Michael kill him.

The concrete was cold and gritty. She pulled one shoe off and experimentally banged the leather sole against the cell bars. The sound was pitifully small, and echoed back from concrete. Tears spilled down her cheeks.

I can't cry now. I don't have any Kleenex.

She pulled her knees up under her skirt and hugged them.

Chapter 25

Mike dashed into the office and stopped short. "Debra?"

The door to his private office was open, and the light was on. He strode to the doorway, but the room was empty.

When he turned around, Johnny was right behind him. "What's going on?"

"I don't know. Debra said it was urgent, but she's not here. I told her to always lock the door when she goes out."

Johnny frowned and looked toward Debra's desk. "Looks like she was working."

Fear stabbed at Mike's heart. "That's my appointment book, and the drawer's open."

"Not like Debra," Johnny said.

"Not at all. Take a quick look down the hallway and see if she's in the break room."

Before Johnny came back, Mike knew his errand was pointless. He picked up the phone and connected with the dispatcher.

"This is Sergeant Van Sant. Please put out an urgent page for all of my detectives except John Young. Tell them to call me here at my office immediately."

Johnny came in from the hall. "I checked the whole wing. The offices are locked up. She's not here."

Mike exhaled heavily. "Johnny, listen to me. Debra and I have been working together on this sabotage case."

"You mean here, within the unit?"

"That's right. I know I can trust you, and you've got to help me. I'm afraid Debra's in danger."

"What do we do?"

The phone rang and Mike pounced on it.

"This is Leon. What's up?"

"I need you," Mike said. "Get over here as quick as you can."

There was a click and Mike took a deep breath, grateful that he could depend on Leon and Johnny.

Johnny was watching him warily. "You think the person who's been plaguing us has done something to Debra?"

"She wouldn't leave here without letting me know. She had discovered something incriminating, and she was waiting for me here."

Johnny's blue eyes were troubled. "Do you know who's behind this, Mike?"

"I hate to say it, but I think it's Sergeant Brown."

"That's crazy."

"I know. But we narrowed it down—"

The phone rang again, and Johnny picked it up.

"Detective Young. Right, Brian. Get over here pronto. We've got an emergency."

He had barely hung up when the phone buzzed again, and Johnny picked it up impatiently. "Yeah? Thanks."

He looked at Mike. "Jared didn't answer his page."

"I'll call his house. We may need some patrolmen to help us."

"You think so?"

"If Debra caught him red-handed he may be desperate."

"Guess we can't call Zack to help us," Johnny said.

"I'll get Pete as soon as I touch base with Jared." Mike flipped through Debra's address file and punched in Jared's home phone number.

"Mrs. Dore? This is Sergeant Van Sant. Is Jared home this evening?"

The woman on the other end of the line began to sob.

"Ma'am? Are you all right?"

"He was here," she choked, "but he's gone now. Sergeant, what's going on? Jared was—he wasn't himself when he came here."

Mike's heart sank. "Do you know where he is now, Mrs. Dore?"

"No! He was acting wild and throwing things in a duffel bag."

"When did he leave?"

"Not five minutes ago."

"Mrs. Dore, I hate to ask you this, but was there a young woman with him when he was at the house?"

There was a sudden silence, then she asked softly, "A woman?"

"One of the civilian employees from the police station," Mike said quickly.

"No, no. He was alone."

"All right, stay calm, Mrs. Dore. I'm going to come over see and you." He hung up just as Leon burst through the door. "I was wrong," Mike said. "It's Jared. Call Zack and Pete. I'm going to Jared's house. Flak vests for everyone."

Leon stared at him. "What on earth?"

"Looks like Jared went berserk and kidnapped Debra." Johnny's tone was still a bit incredulous.

"From here?" Leon asked.

"Yes," Mike said, pulling his vest on. "I'm afraid he's behind all the sabotage in the unit. He's crossed the line and become dangerous. He could have Debra in his car."

Leon frowned for a moment. "Debra was asking me about a note to Brian. She pulled it out of my trash can."

"A yellow sticky note," Mike said.

"Yeah."

"Send my appointment book to the lab now. I don't care if you have to get a technician in special."

"I can lift the prints," Leon said.

"Do it. I'm heading for Dores'. He left there five minutes ago. Johnny, stick with me. Leon, get Brian to help you. Have the dispatcher call me when you know something."

Chapter 26

Two hours had passed. Debra fought back her panic. It was a matter of time, she knew. Sooner or later, Michael would find her. But still the frantic feeling was there.

Each breath seemed too shallow, without enough oxygen, and it hurt to grab for more air. Her heart drummed too fast and her head ached.

She stayed sitting with her back against the bars, afraid she would become disoriented if she left them in the utter darkness. It was terrifying not to be able to see a difference in the quality of the blackness. Her watch light seemed the only thing that anchored her to reality. She tried not to look at it too often.

If I have to stay here until Monday morning, I can yell when the records clerks come down the stairs. Lord, please don't make me stay here until then. She prayed earnestly for Michael and the others she knew were searching for her, and she prayed for Jared Dore.

She stretched her legs out in front of her, and drew them back in quickly when something skittered across the floor beyond her feet. She closed her eyes, then opened them, seeing no difference.

"Stone walls do not a prison make, nor iron bars a cage," she whispered. "Lord, don't let me give in to these feelings. I know you're here." She searched for a scripture verse that would give her more comfort than "The Prisoner of Chillon."

She thought of Psalm 37, which had comforted her the night of Michael's drug raid, but the last verse was all she could pull from the recesses of memory. "And the Lord shall help them, and deliver them; he shall deliver them from the wicked, and save them, because they trust in him."

The back of her head settled against two bars. Michael had said, "Nothing will happen to me unless it's part of His plan."

231

She tried to breathe slower. *This is part of the plan. I just need to wait. There's nothing here to hurt me. I'm safe in God's hand.*

She jumped at the feeling of something small falling onto her head, and slapped, gasping, at her hair. She jumped up and whirled, shaking her braid and brushing, panic stricken, at her aching head and shoulders. She stumbled, almost falling, and put out her hands to emptiness.

Very slowly, her heart racing, she stepped forward, her hands outstretched. Two steps, and her fingertips brushed the chilly concrete wall. She stood for a moment not moving, picturing the cell in her mind, then moved slowly to her left until she came to the place where the bars met the concrete and clutched the first two. She moved sideways, feeling the bars, and stopped where she judged she had been before, facing the door to the stairway, and sighed.

Lord, please not spiders. I can do mice, even rats, but not spiders.

She stood, her hands warming the cold metal rods. After ten minutes, she took a deep breath and lowered herself slowly to the floor again, her back against the bars. She repeated the verse, and prayed wordlessly.

She dozed off, then jerked awake. By her watch, it was 9:25. She reached into her pocket and came out with her key ring and the memo. If only she had managed to drop the paper along the way, where Michael would have found it. The keys were useless. Perhaps she ought to try them all in the cell door's lock, just for the knowledge that she had tried.

A noise came from behind her. She pressed against the bars and looked hard. There was a ray of light, down low, a line of light at the bottom of the door. She stood up, clinging to the bars, hope surging through her.

"Michael! Michael! In here!" Her voice echoed back.

More noise, thumps, and voices, then pounding on the door. "Miss Griffin! Are you in there?" A man's voice yelled.

"Yes!"

"Get Mike, quick!" she heard him shout. "Hold on, Miss Griffin. We've got to see if anyone has a key to this door."

She felt the tears flowing freely down her cheeks and stood clenching the bars, not taking her eyes from the slice of light. Murmuring and muffled shouting reached her, and what sounded like platoons of storm troopers running up and down the stairs double time.

"Debra!" At last his voice came, edged with fear.

"Michael!"

"Hold on! We'll get you out!"

"Thank you, Lord! Thank you!" She collapsed against the side of the cage, staying on her feet by sheer will power, the longing to see Michael overwhelming.

A few seconds later his voice came again, sheer comfort. "Debra, honey, Pete's coming with a key. Hang on. Do you hear me?"

"Yes. I'm okay, Michael."

There were sounds of a subdued melee beyond the door, then the slice of light lengthened, and the light in the room came on. Debra put one hand to her eyes and stood blinking.

"Michael?" She began to laugh, in spite of the tears. Thirty men had pushed inside the room, with Michael in the vanguard. He advanced quickly, eyeing her prison in wonder. She reached through the bars and he came close and clasped her hands.

"Debra, dearest Debra! How did you get in there?"

He spotted the door on the second side of the cell and rushed to it.

"Pete, have you got a key for this thing?" he yelled over his shoulder, and she saw Pete Nye and Zack Brown pushing their way through the crowd.

"We can't seem to locate it," Pete said, frowning. "I don't know what became of the cell keys. We haven't used it in ten years or more."

"We've got dispatch calling a locksmith," Zack said. "It will just be a few minutes."

"Jared had keys," said Debra.

Michael reached through the bars and put his hands on her shoulders.

233

"Are you all right, Debra?"

"Yes."

Pete shouted toward the doorway, "Johnny! Go up and get the key ring they took off Dore."

Zack said, "I locked it in Evidence. I'll have to go get it out for him." He followed Johnny out the door toward the stairway.

"You got Jared?" Debra's voice shook.

"Yes." Michael and Pete looked at each other. Michael pulled her in close to the bars and leaned his forehead against hers. "Baby, I was so scared," he whispered. "I thought he had you with him."

"Not for long."

"We put up road blocks all over the place, and I sent a team out to Jared's house. When we found out he was alone, we started combing this building. I was afraid he'd done something—"

"No, honey, I'm fine." She reached through the bars and laid her hand against his cheek. "He said he needed time to get away. He knew you would be after him."

"He had that right."

The officers had moved in closer, anxious to see that their search had been successful. Brian and Leon stood grinning at her.

"How did you find me?" she asked.

"Well, Leon pointed out that he couldn't take you out of the police station without going through either the foyer, the booking room, or a window. I started people looking at the security tapes for the last few hours, and I went around checking all the windows."

"We watched the tapes backwards, rewinding them," Brian said, crowding in close. "Finally, Zack spotted Jared on the tape, coming out of the basement door alone. We rewound a little more, and sure enough, he had you coming down here. A bunch of guys came down to search the records room, and I went to find Mike."

There was a shout near the doorway, and the men parted for Johnny Young. He came holding a bunch of keys over his head.

"You okay, Debra?" he asked with a grin.

"Yes. Thank you, Johnny!"

"No sweat." He bent over the lock and began inserting one key after another. At last one turned, and he swung the door open. Michael pushed past him into the cell, and pulled Debra into his arms. The men clapped and cheered.

*****

Camera flashes nearly blinded Debra as they came out of the stairway into the foyer.

"How did the press get here so fast?" she gasped, turning her face against Michael's jacket.

"Fast? They've been here three or four hours," Brian said. "They picked it up on the scanner as soon as we started looking for you."

"Debbie!"

She swiveled toward the far end of the long room and spotted her parents, waving at her. Her mother's eyes devoured her. Her father's expression melted from anxiety through relief to joy. Debra went as quickly as the crowd would allow, pulling Michael with her, and met them in front of the dispatchers' window. She threw her arms around them both.

"Debbie, honey, we were so worried," Ellen sobbed.

"I'm all right, Mom. Where's Grant?"

"At home, waiting for Rick."

"Rick's coming?"

"Yes, and Julie, too, if we give her the word," Henry said. "I told her to hold off until we got some kind of news. We'll call her as soon as we get home."

"Can you take her home right now?" Michael asked. Reporters were crowding around, shouting questions.

"Miss Griffin! Are you all right?"

"Where were you, Miss Griffin?"

"Come with me," she pleaded, holding tight to Michael's hand.

He turned around, searching for someone he could delegate his duties to. "Zack, can you and Pete handle the press?"

Zack nodded, and Michael pushed with the Griffins out the door into the parking lot, past more reporters.

"Sergeant, where did you find Miss Griffin?"

"Miss Griffin, can you describe your ordeal?"

"Sergeant, is it true the kidnapper was a police detective?"

"Get in the car," Michael told her. He stopped and turned around, holding up his hands. "You'll have to get your information from Sergeant Brown or Deputy Chief Nye tonight. They'll handle the questions."

"Detective Van Sant," a local reporter jumped in, "was the kidnapper dead when you found him?"

"Who fired the fatal shot?" asked another.

"See Sergeant Brown," Michael insisted.

Debra felt sick. She climbed into the back seat of her father's car and fastened the seat belt with trembling hands. Michael dove in beside her and closed the door and locked it.

"Drive, Henry."

He put his arms around Debra and held her without speaking. She closed her eyes and breathed raggedly, her head against his shoulder. His body was rigid at first, his muscles taut. When they were out of the parking lot and headed out of town, she felt him relax and sigh. He pushed back the tendrils of soft hair escaping from her braid, and laid his cheek on her forehead.

Chapter 27

At the house, Rick's white car was in the driveway. He and Grant tore down the steps and opened the car doors. Rick swept Debra into his arms.

"Debbie, Debbie. What have you been up to?"

"I didn't do anything, really."

Grant stood by, looking from Debra to Michael and back. "Everything okay?" he asked doubtfully.

Mike clapped him on the shoulder. "Going to be fine."

"Just give her some time to unwind," Henry recommended.

Ellen hurried inside. By the time they reached the kitchen, she had started coffee and had Julie on the phone. She held the receiver out to Debra. "She wants to speak to you."

Michael stood close, his arm around her. "Hi, Julie," Debra said. She wanted to sound strong and buoyant, but failed miserably. "How you doing?"

"Me? How are *you* doing?"

"I'm fine."

"Mom said some maniac had you locked in a dungeon."

"Sort of."

"So, what happened to the guy?"

"I—I don't know." She looked helplessly at Michael.

"Are you really okay? Should I come home?"

"No, I'm fine. He didn't hurt me." She leaned into Michael's arm, and he tightened his grip.

"So, tell me about it."

Debra looked around at her family. They all stood silent, listening and waiting for her to be done talking to Julie. Debra felt suddenly lightheaded. "Can you talk to Daddy?"

She passed off the receiver and stumbled toward the living room. Michael followed her, and she turned wildly, throwing herself into his arms.

"Michael, Jared is dead, isn't he?"

He held her firmly and stroked her hair and her shoulders. "Come on, sit down." He drew her to the couch, and they sat, holding each other.

"You didn't—did you?"

"No. No, they got him at a road block in Augusta. He was headed for I-95." Michael sighed and kissed her hair. "He wouldn't get out of the car."

She raised her eyes to his. "I told him he couldn't get away. He should have just quit doing those nuisance pranks. It was so senseless."

"Something was eating at him," Mike said. "It had to be more than the job."

She remembered Jared's bitterness and despair. "He said he'd been passed over too many times. When they hired you, I think that was the last straw for him. He was determined to do anything this time for the promotion. He wanted the job, and he wanted to outrank you."

Michael sat still, subdued by what she had told him. "I had no idea. Are you sure?"

"Yes. He was adamant about it. He—he hated you." She shivered.

"How did you know it was Jared?" he asked. "When you called me, you were sure it wasn't Zack, weren't you?"

"I found the memo Pete left on Brian's door in Leon's trash. Leon said the only person who had been in there was Jared." She pulled the crumpled yellow sheet from her pocket.

Michael took it from her and smoothed it out on his knee. "My appointment book was on your desk. What was that about?"

"When I was in your office, Jared came in and took it out of the drawer. I didn't know he was there until I opened the door. I saw him with it, and he saw me. I tried to just talk naturally to him, but he came back and saw me looking at your schedule. He'd crossed out an appointment. He'd seen that I had the memo, too, and he pulled his gun on me."

"I'm so sorry. I should have been there for you."

238

"No, I was so sure it was Zack. I owe him an apology. I wanted to leave you a clue, but I was too scared to think straight. How did you know it was Jared?"

"I didn't at first. I knew it wasn't Johnny; he was with me. You'd said you'd wait for me, and I knew you wouldn't stand me up without a good reason, but you weren't there. I knew you wouldn't have left the office unlocked. Zack was still on duty, but I was still wary of him at the start. I called the other men and told them to come back. Leon and Brian responded right away, but Jared didn't answer his page. I called Jared's house, and his wife said he'd been home and left again. She was hysterical. When Leon came in, he told me about you pulling the memo out of his trash. I had the guys take fingerprints from the appointment book and started organizing a manhunt, with Zack's help."

"Were his prints on the book?"

"Yes. Yours, mine, and Jared's."

Debra shook her head. "Even though you weren't up for Pete's job, he had to do some mean thing to you. He couldn't leave things the way they were."

"If I'd known how he felt..." Mike began, and his voice trailed off. There was no repairing the relationship now.

She sat up, needing to hear the truth from him while she was in the shelter of her home, not from a callous reporter or a friend who assumed she knew all the details. "Please tell me what happened, Michael. Did he kill himself?"

Mike's expression was sorrowful, but unyielding. "He sat in the car a long time. They were giving him some space and trying to talk him out. Brian and Johnny and I were on the way down there, and keeping in touch with the state police on the radio. They had him surrounded, and I thought when I got there he'd surrender to me."

"No," she whispered with certainty. "Jared would never surrender to you. That would have been too humiliating."

Distress clouded his brown eyes. "At that point, I thought maybe he had you with him in the car, even though the S.P. kept telling me they couldn't see you. I thought maybe you were … in the trunk, even."

He clung to her, and Debra held him close, drawing comfort from his warmth, and hoping he was comforted, too.

"We got there a couple of minutes too late." His voice was low and flat. "They said he just came out blazing. I thought in the end he couldn't face going through the system, but he didn't want to do it himself."

"It's awful." Her tears welled up and spilled over. Michael took out a clean white handkerchief and placed it in her hand. "Did anyone else get hurt?"

"A state trooper took a bullet on his vest. Knocked the wind out of him."

She nodded, wiping the tears away, but more replaced them. "What about Jared's family?"

"He went to his house first and tried to get his wife to go with him. He didn't tell her everything, just that he needed to leave fast, and if she wanted to go with him she had to hurry."

"She didn't go?"

"No. She was scared, and she tried to talk him out of it. He told her he'd contact her later and took off. She was in shock when we got there. Couldn't make sense of his behavior. We've called her daughter, and I think she's gone to the hospital. I feel bad for Mrs. Dore, but we had to go there and question her."

Henry Griffin came to the living room doorway and looked in anxiously.

"How are we doing, kids?"

Debra turned and managed a watery smile. "I'll be all right, Daddy."

"Your mother wants to know if you're hungry."

"Starved."

"All right, I'll tell her. She's got plenty of spaghetti left over. You come to the kitchen when you're ready." He left the doorway.

"My parents are almost painfully tactful," she said.

"Debra, I don't ever want to go through something like this again."

"That makes two of us."

Michael stood up, and she let him pull her to her feet. He put his arms around her again, and she slipped her hands around his waist, under his suit jacket. He kissed her tenderly.

"I love you, Debra."

"I know." She rested her head against his chest. "Michael, I'm so glad you didn't get there in time. Unless he would have listened to you, but I don't think he would have."

She wiped her eyes again, and they went into the kitchen. Ellen fixed plates for both of them, and Rick joined them. Grant perched backward on a maple chair, eating cookies one after another.

As they ate, Michael told the Griffins about the sabotage the detectives' unit had experienced over the past few months, and how it had doomed Jared Dore.

"He could have had the job if he'd just done nothing?" Rick asked incredulously.

"He had a good chance," Mike said. "Out of the batch of candidates they've got, I think Zack Brown would be my first pick, but then Debra and I thought we couldn't trust Zack. Jared would have been my next choice."

"What happens now?" Henry asked.

"I'm not sure. I hope they wait a while to make a decision on this. At least a couple of weeks, to let the dust settle. They may want to re-advertise."

"He must have really hated you," Grant said.

"I didn't realize how bitter he was. Maybe Mrs. Dore can tell us more when she feels better."

Debra took a bite of spaghetti and chewed without tasting it.

The telephone rang, and Henry answered it.

"Debra, do you feel like talking to Belinda? She just saw it on the TV news."

Debra put her fork down. "Not really, Daddy. Just tell her I'm okay, and I'll call her tomorrow."

241

He nodded and turned toward the wall. "Can she call you tomorrow, Belinda? She's bushed tonight, but she'll be all right."

"So, Jared was doing all these weird things to the other men, and you couldn't figure out who was doing it?" Rick asked, trying to piece together what they had been through.

"Right. Debra and I were trying to identify him. We called him Mr. X." Michael shook grated cheese over his spaghetti. "We had pretty much ruled out Johnny and Leon, but we still had at least three suspects."

"What kind of things did he do?" Rick asked.

"Well, he took things, a pager and a bulletproof vest, made phony telephone calls, and messed up one guy's report," Michael said. "He intercepted a message so that one man missed responding to a call. Generally tried to make the other men look bad. And he broke the headlight on his official car, to make it look like Mr. X was plaguing him, too."

"He made a piece of evidence disappear." Debra turned to Michael. "How did he do that? We'd about decided it could only have been Zack or Johnny."

"On the way back from Augusta, when we were racking our brains, trying to think where he could have left you, Johnny all of a sudden snapped his fingers and said, 'Of course, it was Jared.' I said, 'What was Jared,' and he said, 'The ammo clip.' When he realized Jared was behind it all, it just clicked for him. He said Jared came into the duty room the day he filed the gun and the ammo clip. He just popped in for a minute, and was kind of watching over Johnny's shoulder as he logged the evidence. Johnny said he put the gun and the clip in the locker, but he guessed he'd turned back to the computer to enter the locker number. Then he went back and shut the locker."

"And Jared was just hanging out?" Debra asked.

"Yes, just shooting the breeze, curious about the kids they'd brought in from the high school. Johnny didn't think anything about it, just forgot he was even there."

"So Jared copped the ammo clip while Johnny was looking at the computer," Grant said.

"I think so." Michael took a sip from his water glass. "Johnny thinks so now, too. It's the only way it could have happened. He just palmed it. If Johnny had noticed it was missing before he shut the locker, Jared could have bent down and pretended to pick it up off the floor. *Hey, Johnny, did you drop this?* But Johnny didn't notice."

The phone rang again, and Henry answered it. "Hello? Yes, she's my daughter."

Debra grimaced and shook her head frantically.

"No, she can't talk right now. She's resting. Could you call back tomorrow?" He hung up. "Reporter." He sat down, his determination to protect his daughter evident in his face.

"So, Mike, you didn't have to shoot him, did you?" Grant asked.

"Grant!" Ellen cried.

A vivid picture of Jared sprawled bleeding on the pavement flashed into Debra's mind, and she felt ill. She stood up and said faintly, "Excuse me."

Her knees buckled and she would have fallen, but Michael jumped up and braced her with his strong arms.

"Let me get her to bed," Ellen said. "Grant, that was entirely tasteless. Come on, Debbie, let's get you upstairs."

Debra took a shaky step toward the entry.

"Want me to carry you up?" Rick asked playfully, but Debra knew he would do it if she said yes.

"N-no. Michael—" She put her hand up to his shoulder.

"I'm here."

"Just stay with me a while."

"I will." He walked slowly with her, his left arm around her waist.

"Let me tell you something about women, brother," she heard Rick say to Grant as they left the kitchen.

They made it to the stairway, and Debra sank to sit on the second step. Michael sat beside her, holding her. She heard the telephone ringing sporadically. Her father firmly told all callers to try again the next day. Michael held her right hand with his, his left arm still encircling her. The image was still there in her brain.

"Did you see him?" she asked.

He hesitated. "Yes. Don't think about it, sweetheart."

"Could we pray?"

"Of course." He bowed his head, and prayed earnestly for God's peace in Debra's heart, for strength and healing. She felt calmer then, less nauseated, but still grieved. He sat with her, not speaking. Supportive. It was what she had asked for, not realizing how crucial that quality would become. The word was inadequate. He was solid and reliable, but unspeakably tender.

She turned away from him a little, and leaned her head back against his chest. He brought both arms around her and clasped his hands in front of her. *I could sit like this forever*, she thought. He was her fortress, and nothing, *nothing* could get to her unless he allowed it.

"I was scared, Michael, but I knew God was taking care of me."

His arms tightened around her.

"I knew it, too. No matter how it turned out, I knew God was in control. But I was terrified, Debra. I wanted to be there with you, wherever you were."

She rubbed her head against his sleeve. "I was okay, as long as I remembered God. When I got thinking too much about other things, it was pretty awful."

"I'm so thankful," he whispered.

After ten minutes, Michael's cell phone rang. He fished it from his pocket and looked at it.

"They need you at the station?" Debra asked.

"No, it's my dad."

"You'd better take it." She could picture Margery and Pietr watching the late news, seeing them pushing through the crowd at the police station, then trying unsuccessfully to call Michael at his apartment.

"I'll call when I get home."

"No, they'll be worried."

244

"All right. Will you be okay for a minute?"

"Yes."

"Hello?" He got up and walked into the entry as he talked. Debra hugged her stomach, shivering, noticing for the first time that her skirt and the sleeve and front of her blouse were smudged with grime.

Grant came in quietly and stood looking down at her. When she looked up at him, he said contritely, "I'm sorry, Deb."

"It's okay."

"I didn't think about how you knew him and worked with him every day. I was just thinking about Mike being a cop, and—" he shrugged. "I'm really sorry."

She nodded.

"Some TV people called. They wanted to know if you'd let them interview you. Dad told them to call tomorrow morning."

"I don't want to talk to reporters." Her stomach somersaulted, and she leaned against the balusters, but that felt too much like the cell bars, and she sat up again.

Ellen came timidly in from the kitchen. "Are you all right, dear?"

"No, Mom, I feel sick."

"Come on." Ellen helped her to her feet and walked slowly with her up the stairs to the bathroom.

Debra leaned on the sink shakily. "I just keep thinking about Jared, at the end."

"Don't."

"Oh, Mom!" She turned to Ellen and hugged her tight. "I was so happy to see you and Daddy again. I knew I would get out eventually, but it seemed like a long time, and I was afraid Jared would hurt someone, or that Michael would kill him."

She cried then, long, shaking sobs. Ellen patted her back.

At last Debra straightened and ran cold water in the sink. She reached for a washcloth and soaked it, and held it to her forehead.

"My head hurts," she said plaintively.

Her mother opened the medicine cabinet for pain reliever, and gave her two tablets. Debra swallowed them with a handful of water from the faucet.

"Do you want me to send Mike home?" Ellen asked.

"I feel selfish, keeping him here. He ought to be back at the station, wrapping things up."

"He'll stay here as long as you want him."

"He said that?"

"He didn't have to."

Debra looked into the mirror for the first time. "Oh, gross. He'll never want to come back after this." Her face was pale, but her eyes were swollen and bloodshot.

"No, honey, don't worry about that. He'll be here." Ellen brushed at a stain on Debra's skirt. "You'll feel better if you get a hot bath and some clean clothes."

"Yes. I think I'll do that. I shouldn't ask Michael to stay."

"Just go say good-bye to him, then. I'll run you a bath."

Debra went hesitantly down to the living room. Her father and Michael sat in chairs, while Grant lounged on the carpet and Rick leaned on the door frame.

"She needs time to absorb this," Henry was saying.

"Michael—"

He stood up quickly, and Rick stepped aside.

Debra looked up at him, into his loving, sorrowful brown eyes.

"How are your folks?"

"They're fine. Just had to know we were all right."

"I guess I should have a bath and go to bed. I'm sorry I'm so—"

"You're not. This is normal." He stepped close to her.

"*You're* not going to pieces," she observed.

"I'm holding it together with prayer and duct tape." He smiled and put his hands on her shoulders. "If you're sure you're okay…"

"Well, no, I'm not sure, but I can't keep you here all night."

"I don't mind. Go take your bath. I'll sit up with Rick. He looks like he's good for a couple more hours, at least."

"I had too much coffee while we were waiting for you," Rick said. "I probably won't sleep a wink."

"Do they need you?" Debra faltered.

"No," Mike said. "I called Pete, and he says everything is under control."

"Do you wish you were there?"

He considered for a moment. "No. There's no place I'd rather be than here. If you want to go to bed, I'll just camp out with Rick for a while. I—" he hesitated, shooting a glance toward her brother.

Rick walked lazily to the sofa and plopped down. "So, Dad—" he began cheerfully.

Michael leaned close to her. "I want to stay near you."

Debra nodded, a warm peace coursing through her again. "All right. I'll come back in a while."

Ellen met her halfway up the stairs and walked beside her. "I got out your baseball pajamas and bathrobe. The water's ready."

"Thanks, Mom, but I think I'll get dressed again afterward. Michael's staying."

Ellen followed her into the bathroom and gathered up the nightclothes.

"Then I guess you won't want these. Jeans?"

"Sure. Anything." Debra put her hand up to her head.

"Maybe you should see a doctor," Ellen said.

"No, it's just a headache. When the aspirin kicks in, I'll feel better."

Ellen left her reluctantly, and Debra undressed and eased into the warm water, pulling the glass door across in front of the tub. She soaked for several minutes, then took her braid out and stood up carefully, reaching for the shampoo.

When she was ready to dress five minutes later, she found black sweat pants and a soft pullover shirt on the hamper, with clean underwear and socks. Her moccasins were on the floor. She put them on and dried her clean hair. The blower fluffed it out in

247

a soft golden cloud. When it was thoroughly dry, she went down the stairs.

Grant had been sent to bed, and Ellen had followed. When Debra appeared in the living room doorway, her father rose and said, "Well, I'm beat. You all set, Rick?"

"Yeah, I think so."

He and Michael stood.

"Good night, Mike," said Henry. "Lock the door on your way out. Or, hey, if you want to sleep on the sofa—"

"No, I think I'll head out after a bit. Thanks, Mr. Griffin."

"Any time." Henry went off.

Rick said, "Well, it's going to be a pleasure to sleep in my old bed."

"You don't have to go yet," said Debra. "This family seems to think Michael and I have to be alone every minute."

"Not every minute," Rick said, "but there are some moments when privacy is indicated."

"He's an editor," Debra said to Michael, as though explaining something very profound. She turned to her brother. "I've hardly seen you."

"Well, okay, I'll sit for a minute."

Rick took his seat again in the rocking chair, and Michael hovered at Debra's elbow until she sat down on the couch. He grasped her hand lightly.

"Feeling better?"

She nodded, glad the headache had receded. "I always feel better when I'm sure there are no spiders in my hair."

"Spiders?" Michael was puzzled.

"Oh, no! Not spiders," said Rick. "She's deathly terrified of arachnids. Screams and cries. Totally helpless when facing a daddy longlegs, too."

"I see." Michael slipped his arm around her. "Were there ... those things ... in the cell?"

"There was something crawly in there."

"I'm sorry I wasn't there to smash it for you."

"You couldn't have in the dark, anyway. That was the worst part, I think. I've never had to be in complete darkness like that before. There's always a little light, somehow." She shivered, and Michael pulled her close.

"So, did you two get enough to eat?" Rick asked brightly. "I could check out the cookie jar."

"I'm fine, thanks," Mike said.

"Me, too," said Debra. Her eyes were locked on Michael's.

Rick stood up. "Well, as much as I know you love me, Debbie, I really think it's time for me to make my exit."

"Do you have to work in the morning?" Michael asked.

"No, I don't work Saturday, but I still think it's time I retired. Come back for breakfast, Mike. I enjoyed talking shop with you, but I think you have other things to talk about now."

Michael shook his hand. "All right, Rick. I'll see you."

Rick flipped the light switch on his way out, leaving them in the soft glow of the lamp on the end table.

"What did I tell you?" Debra asked.

"You have a family of romantics."

As Rick's footsteps faded up the stairs, Mike turned his full attention back to her. "Debra, let's talk about the future."

A thrill caught at her, but she pushed it down. Maybe he just thought she should quit working at the police station, to avoid risky situations. His eyes belied that. Their future together was the subject, she was sure. Her heart raced, and she felt as if she had stepped onto the elevator and Michael had pushed the button for the tenth floor.

She took a deep breath, then smiled at him and shook her head, pretending to misunderstand him. "I already told you, I'm not going to the Academy."

He looked at her quizzically. "Oh. You don't want to be a cop?"

"No. You know that."

He smiled. "Well, yeah. But you could maybe get a private investigator's license."

She eyed him thoughtfully. She hadn't considered that, and it interested her, diverting her from the harmless game she had been playing and his more serious purpose.

"Really?"

"Well, most of the licenses go to ex-cops, but the state gives a few to people who've worked with investigators for a while."

"Sort of an apprenticeship thing?"

"Yeah, I guess so." He lifted her hair with both hands and let it cascade over her shoulders, then pulled her gently toward him.

"Hold on." She rested her palm on the front of his shirt. "You mean I could get a p.i.'s license after I work for you for a while?"

"Well, I'm not sure being my secretary would count, but if I got a license and trained you in procedure on the side ..." He kissed her temple.

"You could do that?"

"I think so. Want me to check into it?" He didn't sound avidly interested at the moment. He ran his right hand through her hair, holding a soft clump out and letting it float gradually through his fingers.

"Yes. I think I'd like to be a detective, but I don't want to go through years as a patrol officer first."

"Well, if tonight's escapades haven't soured you on investigating, I think you'd be a fantastic detective. In the private sector, of course. We could start our own agency." His next kiss landed just forward of her ear.

Debra caught her breath and slid her arms up around his neck. "With the right partner, that would be great. Van Sant and Griffin," she said dreamily.

"I was thinking more of Van Sant and Van Sant," he said, just before their lips met.

Debra stopped thinking about the detective agency, the basement cell block, the spiders, and the bloody shoot-out.

"Is this why my brother left the room?" she whispered.

"He might have seen it coming."

She rested her head on his shoulder and sighed. "This is too—"

"Intense?"

"Maybe it's time for you to go, Michael."

"I'm not leaving until you say you will."

"Will what, be your apprentice?"

"Hm. You used to be afraid of me. Now you're torturing me." He bent his head and kissed her again. "Will you marry me?"

"Yes."

His sigh was deep contentment. "Can you sleep now?"

A sudden thought about what the next day would bring ambushed her. She sat up and looked at him, full of trepidation, her heartbeat accelerating again.

"What, Debra?"

"I forgot about the reporters. You're coming back for—"

"For breakfast."

"Will you—?" She stopped and looked at him a little wildly.

"Of course."

"And you'll tell them—"

"Everything. I'll take care of it."

She sighed. "Thank you, Michael. I think I can sleep now."

About the author: Susan Page Davis is the author of more than sixty published novels. She's a two-time winner of the Inspirational Readers' Choice Award and the Will Rogers Medallion, and also a winner of the Carol Award and a finalist in the WILLA Literary Awards. A Maine native, she now lives in Kentucky. Visit her website at: www.susanpagedavis.com , where you can see all her books, sign up for her occasional newsletter, and read a short story on her romance page. If you liked this book, please consider writing a review and posting it on Amazon, Goodreads, or the venue of your choice.

Find Susan at:
Website: www.susanpagedavis.com
Twitter: @SusanPageDavis
Facebook: https://www.facebook.com/susanpagedavisauthor

Discussion questions for The Saboteur

1. Do you think Debra should have gone to law school, despite her stress?

2. Have you or someone you know ever had an anxiety attack? What coping mechanisms have you used to help you with it?

3. Did Michael use faulty logic in ruling out Pete as the Saboteur? Should anyone else have been included on the list of possibilities?

4. Why can't Debra let the phone ring? Have you had other situations where you took on more work or went against your better judgment just to stop a repeated annoyance?

5. Why is Debra more nervous on her second meeting with Michael than on her first?

6. Do you think Mack and Belinda should close the store on Sundays? Why or why not? What steps can they take to give them more free time together?

7. Do you have a fear that makes you avoid certain situations?

8. Who do you think will get Pete's job, and why?

More of SUSAN PAGE DAVIS'S Mystery and Suspense books that you might enjoy:

The Maine Justice Series:
  The Priority Unit
  Fort Point
  Found Art
The Frasier Island Series:
  Frasier Island
  Finding Marie
  Inside Story
Just Cause
Witness
On a Killer's Trail
Hearts in the Crosshairs
What a Picture's Worth
The Mainely Mysteries Series (coauthored by Susan's daughter, Megan Elaine Davis)
  Homicide at Blue Heron Lake
  Treasure at Blue Heron Lake
  Impostors at Blue Heron Lake
Trail to Justice
Tearoom Mysteries (from Guideposts, books written by several authors)
  Tearoom for Two
  Trouble Brewing

A selection of Susan's Historical Novels:
River Rest (set in 1918)
The Crimson Cipher (set in 1915)
The Outlaw Takes a Bride (western)
Mrs. Mayberry Meets Her Match
The Seafaring Women of the Vera B. (Co-authored with Susan's son James S. Davis, set in the 1850s)

The Ladies' Shooting Club Series (westerns)
  The Sheriff's Surrender
    The Gunsmith's Gallantry
    The Blacksmith's Bravery
Captive Trail (western)
Cowgirl Trail (western)
Heart of a Cowboy (western collection)
The Prairie Dreams series (set in the 1850s)
    The Lady's Maid
    Lady Anne's Quest
    A Lady in the Making
Maine Brides (set in 1720, 1820, and 1895)
    The Prisoner's Wife
    The Castaway's Bride
    The Lumberjack's Lady
Mountain Christmas Brides
Seven Brides for Seven Texans
White Mountain Brides (set in the 1690's in New Hampshire)
Wyoming Brides (set in the 1850s)
Love Finds You in Prince Edward Island (set in the 1850s)

And many more
See all of her books at www.susanpagedavis.com.

Sign up for Susan's occasional newsletter at
https://madmimi.com/signups/118177/join

CPSIA information can be obtained
at www.ICGtesting.com
Printed in the USA
LVOW11s2317250417
532191LV00001B/171/P